THE DREAMING GODS

THE DREAMING GODS

A NOVEL

CHRISTOPHER R. NELSON

SNN Books

Contact the author: snnpublishing@yahoo.com

SNN Books

Seattle, Washington

ISBN: 978-1-7365536-6-4

Library of Congress Control Number: 2025913133

First Edition

To Frank DeMarco & Colin Wilson, for their friendship, encouragement, inspiration and work in the world.

1

THE RUMBLE OF TURBULENCE shook him awake. He stirred in his seat and the stack of conference papers slid off his lap, fanning out on the floor. As he bent to collect them, the woman in the window seat said,

"Can I help?" She had been asleep when he boarded the plane, her head turned away. She smiled at him now, blue eyes bright, black hair falling over her shoulders, traces of freckles dotting a small nose and round cheeks. She picked up the article that had landed at her feet.

Elliott said, "Thanks. I didn't realize I'd fallen asleep."

She scanned the cover page of the article before handing it back to him. "It's no wonder."

He read the title to himself – "Potassium-argon dating: a meta-analysis of significant studies" – and smiled. "Maybe you're right."

"I'm sure it's interesting if you know what it means."

"It's about as technical as I can get before my eyes glaze over."

"Are you a scientist?"

"An anthropologist. I'm going to a conference. This paper's by one of the speakers."

They sat back in their seats. Outside the snow-encrusted peak of Mt. Rainier jutted through clouds into the infinite blue. It was difficult to believe it was raining in Seattle.

"Are we landing soon?"

"Twenty minutes or so."

He extended his hand. "My name's Paul Elliott."

Her hand was warm. "Rachel. What do you study?"

He saw the glimmer of interest in her eyes and wondered if he would quell it by telling the truth. "Tiny little fragments of bone." She looked amused. "The origins of man, really, or when he diverged from apes but hadn't quite become human yet."

"That's fascinating."

He smiled, nodded, unable to tell if she was merely being polite.

"Have you been to all sorts of exotic places?"

"Mostly just fieldwork in Africa during grad school. Okay: only Africa. I'm hoping to get funding for a new program at my college in Ohio."

"I've always wanted to go to Africa."

"I spent my time in a twenty-foot-deep shaft drilled into the ground. Not quite as romantic as I was hoping for."

"You'll have to go back."

He nodded. "What about you?"

"I'm coming home from a European tour." She said it with a touch of self-mockery, affecting the flair of a posh world-traveler. "I'm broke now, but I just graduated with a degree in art history and I figured I'd better travel before I get a real job."

He tried to calculate how old she was. Definitely younger than his thirty-two years, but maybe not by much.

She said, "Have you been to Seattle before?"

"I went to school there. I graduated a little over a year ago and took a job in Ohio. This is my first time back."

"You must still have some friends in town."

"A few, yes."

"So, business and pleasure."

He nodded, smiling, but his buoyant feeling dipped a little as he remembered yesterday's call with Bill Mathiesson, former mentor turned friend. *I have good news and bad news, Paul.* No, he hadn't used the word "good"; he had said he had *fascinating* news. Good news would mean his cancer was in remission. Fascinating news meant, most likely, that he had made some kind of esoteric scientific discovery that he wanted to share with Elliott. Bad news was easy enough to guess at.

Rachel pointed past him into the aisle. "I think you missed one."

The yellow packet of papers – the conference agenda – lay just out of reach on the opposite side of the aisle, one row ahead of his own. He unbuckled his seatbelt and stood up, excusing himself to a heavyset, gray-haired man as he crouched down beside his seat and picked up the papers.

Elliott stood up again just as another burst of turbulence rocked the plane, sending him off balance. The back of his head slammed into an overhead compartment. His vision blurred and he fell forward, barely managing to grab hold of a seatback to avoid falling into the lap of an elderly woman. He stabilized himself, feeling stark embarrassment in the midst of dazzling pain. He resisted the urge to rub the tender spot and concentrated on getting back to his seat.

Rachel said, "Are you okay?"

He touched the back of his head, winced. "Yeah. It's going to be a nasty bruise."

Outside the blue sky succumbed to murky gray. Elliott buckled his seatbelt as the pilot predicted more turbulence. He thought: *A little late.*

Rachel put her hand on his arm. "That looked like it really hurt." Before he could reply the plane shuddered violently two, three times in quick succession, jagged tremors that brought to mind a roller coaster clattering over broken track. Overhead lights flickered, muffled cries erupted around him. He took a deep breath but failed to suppress the rush of fear.

Rachel's voice cracked as she said, "That does *not* feel like normal turbulence."

"No."

Another blast.

A bomb? Did we lose an engine?

The plane dropped abruptly. For an instant he was weightless, stomach rolling. Then he felt his body again, rigid and breathless, gripped by the seat, gravity reasserting itself as the plane struggled upwards. A crash sounded from somewhere behind him, followed by a cry of pain and an indecipherable flurry of words through the intercom. The old woman across the aisle from him bent forward, praying.

Rachel's grip on his arm was too tight. "How long—?"

He tried to say, "It never lasts long," but did not hear himself speak.

Weightlessness again, roaring engines like rushing wind, a metallic taste in his mouth. The lights dimmed, plastic ceiling panels clattered open and a yellow oxygen mask danced on its plastic tube before him. He peeled his fingers away from the armrests and fumbled with the mask, his swearing muffled beneath the constant rumbling and rattling of the craft as a giant hand shook it in the sky. He was desperate to reassure Rachel, himself, everyone, that all would be well. But in a flash of clarity it came:

This plane is my coffin.

He saw himself clinging to the seat, his body an iron rod of fear, thought of his mother, of Mathiesson dying, of Alex waiting at the airport, of Rachel next to him, of a career over before it started, of his perpetual confusion and feelings of inadequacy and how they had inevitably led to this moment, dropping out of the sky in a hulk of dead metal.

Then a warm glow suffused his body, fragments of thought fell away and the gray sky beyond the window acquired an unbearable, crystalline poignancy, blossoming, unfolding into him, absorbing and finally incorporating him—so that his own body ached with an internal pressure as something inside reached out, urging union with the sky.

He placed his arm around Rachel and drew her to him.

"It's alright," he said.

And he knew it would be.

The shuddering stopped. Overhead lights flickered on. Rachel stirred and he withdrew his arm from her shoulder. Her hair brushed his lips as she sat up.

"That's that," he said. A small laugh escaped him. "That scared the hell out of me."

He looked out the window at rolling masses of gray clouds, feeling a peace as intense as the panic had been, a lingering warmth, a sensual tickling in his gut. The clouds went on forever.

Flickers of light outside the window. Paralleling the plane.

They darted forward, then back, through drifting, translucent clouds.

Am I dreaming? They must be reflections on the glass.

He could not tear his eyes away until he felt a gentle tug on his arm.

Rachel's cheeks were damp, her blue eyes clear and bright. She had pulled her hair back, revealing skin shaded with the remnants of a tan. Youthful freckles. Her beauty struck him like a shock of cold water to his face.

"Thank you," she said.

He had a feeling of coming back to himself, like waking from a dream. "Not at all. I was scared too." He felt dull throbs of pain from the back of his head.

He glanced over his shoulder into the aisle to see if a light flickered there, causing a reflection, but there was nothing. He turned back to the window. The sky was empty, and as he watched, the plane dipped beneath the clouds and the lights of Seattle came into view.

2

"SO, TELL ME ABOUT THE GIRL."

Alex Deveraux sat across from him at a corner table in the hotel bar, his angular, handsome face split with a grin bordering on a leer. He leaned forward conspiratorially, hands encircling his pint glass as if it was something precious. "You could've offered her a ride back to Seattle. I wouldn't have minded."

"She offered *me* one. I would've accepted if I'd known you were bailing on me at the airport."

Deveraux gave him a pained expression. "I *am* sorry about that. I didn't know the interview would take so long. So, male or female?"

"What?"

"Her ride."

"I didn't find out.

Deveraux pushed himself back in his seat and gave a hapless smile. "Ahh, Paul… So close."

"We exchanged emails."

"You don't need a pen pal. We'll see if we can hook you up while you're here."

"No thanks. I've got a conference to go to. No time for a whirlwind romance."

"Priorities, Paul."

Elliott suspected he was more than half-serious. Deveraux's romantic accomplishments far outshone his own. But the reporter's good looks and charm had proven a mixed blessing. In the five years Elliott had known him,

Deveraux had dated a string of attractive, intelligent women. But his successes compelled him to keep trying for the next one, with the result that he cast aside relationships with women whom Elliott – who was far more cautious – would have snatched up on the spot.

"How's Ohio?"

Elliott shook his head with distaste – he had not grown used to the Midwestern winters. "Freezing. The first snow fell a few days ago. Now it's too cold to snow."

"And the job? Everything you expected?"

He nodded. "I'm still finding my way. I'm teaching two classes this semester."

"Any time for writing?"

Elliott sipped his beer and shrugged away the nagging guilt. "Still finding my groove. But I've got to get something else published in a journal to help my tenure prospects."

"How does that work again?"

"It's a probationary period lasting several years. The anthropology department decides if they want to keep me forever, so I have to be on my best behavior. I have to publish more papers in professional journals. My colleagues have to like me. My students need to write good evaluations."

"It sounds awful."

"It's all part of the process. A job in my field is hard to come by. Now I've got my foot in the door. If I play my cards right I'm basically set for life."

"They can't take tenure away?"

"It's hard to. Maybe if I commit some grievous scholarly sin, like plagiarism. Or start sleeping with my students."

Deveraux shrugged as if weighing the options. Elliott laughed, but the conversation had stirred his anxiety over the tenure process. He *did* have work to do. He had made good progress, but success was not assured. The thought of failing filled him with dread. He might be able to start over again somewhere else – probably at a lesser institution – but he did not want to be fifty years old before finding a bit of security. And who was to say it would happen even then?

Deveraux said, "What about the book you were planning to write?"

Elliott drained the last of his beer and said guiltily, "Ahh yes… *Evolutionary Origins of the Religious Impulse.*"

"I hope that's a tentative title."

He laughed. "It's on the back burner. It won't carry any weight for tenure, not like professional papers. I envision it as a popular book, the kind that inspired me to get into science in the first place. But the ideas are still floating around. In fact I'm co-teaching a class on the origins of religion right now. With a rabbi and a protestant minister."

"You being in the scientists' corner."

"Of course."

"I feel for your colleagues."

"We're all very civil. I think they even have some sympathy for my ideas about the biological and evolutionary origins of religion."

"Ah… but do you have any for theirs?"

"Of course. I studied all the major religions. I know what they're about."

"You know what I mean. You consider yourself a reformed Protestant, in the sense that now you know better."

Deveraux understood him well enough. "I respect them even if I don't agree with them."

"You grew up with it, though." Deveraux grinned. "Religion is in your blood."

"No. It was in my mom's blood. When my dad died she returned to the flock. I was only three. I couldn't defend myself." Guilt prompted him to add, "I don't mean it that way. It helped her and that's good. But high school biology was the beginning of the end of my religious upbringing."

"As I'm sure it is for many scientists."

"There's a reason for that, you know. It makes more sense."

"I've got nothing against science that I haven't got against religion. They both want all the answers to themselves."

Elliott leaned back, inadvertently pressing the back of his head against the chair. He immediately swore against the pain and sat up.

"What's the matter?"

Elliott touched his head gingerly. "I really banged my head up there in the turbulence. I'd bent over in the aisle to pick something up, and just as I stood up this tremendous blast hit the plane. And I, like an idiot, banged my head into the overhead compartment."

"So Rachel gave you her email out of sympathy."

Elliott gestured obscenely.

Deveraux smiled and sat back. "You want to get it checked out? I can probably find somebody to see you tomorrow."

Elliott shook his head. "No. It's just a bruise."

"Didn't lose consciousness?"

"No."

"No signs of concussion?"

"Not that I'd know what they'd be, but I don't think so."

Deveraux shrugged. "Think about seeing someone." At that moment a white-haired man, immaculately dressed in a gray three-piece suit entered the bar. Deveraux nodded in his direction and said, "Who's that?"

Elliott studied the man as he leaned over the bar, talking with the bartender. "Bob Knight, the conference organizer. A big name in paleoanthropology. We should introduce you since you're reporting on the conference. Although he's probably forgotten me. I met him years ago."

"I thought it might be your professor friend."

"Bill Mathiesson. I was hoping to see him tonight, but…" He glanced around the room then at his watch. "Dinner's probably on soon."

Deveraux drained his beer. "One more before we go. How's Bill?"

"Not sure. Probably not good."

"He means a lot to you."

"He and his wife practically adopted me. Not to mention how amazing a mentor he was. I don't know what he saw in me, but –"

"Latent genius. I saw it myself once."

The waitress returned, exchanged their empty glasses for full ones.

"Bill's a big name, like Knight. I read his popular books on paleoanthropology and archaeology before college. They inspired me to become a scientist."

"That's cool he was your graduate mentor, then."

"Yep. Though he was in the process of retiring towards the end of it. I think that might've hurt me a little."

"Why's that?"

Elliott shrugged. "Oh, he was wrapping things up. He didn't have any ongoing excavations at the time. Maybe he wasn't as cutting edge as he used to be."

"But you chose him anyway. Why?"

Elliott looked at Deveraux, feeling, perhaps unreasonably, that he already knew the answer to his question and shouldn't have to make Elliott answer it. "Hero worship, maybe. Romanticism. I'd read these great books of his and the thought of studying with him outweighed practical consideration of the consequences."

"It worked out, though, right? You landed a job."

Elliott nodded. "I did. And even that's probably because of Bill's connections. He knew the department Chair who hired me." He drank his beer and stretched out his legs beneath the table, feeling a warm glow inside, a deep satisfaction at being on the ground, and that curious, familiar thrill he felt when ideas were smoldering somewhere inside him, seeking expression. "Really, I'm damn lucky. There are very few academic positions out there for someone with my background. You get one of these and you hang onto it for forty-plus years. That's why they're so hard to get."

"No one wants to let go of them."

"On the other hand, without wanting to sound ungrateful, if I'd picked some up-and-coming faculty member to advise me I might've gotten a job somewhere other than a small private college in the Midwest. A public university, for example, where there tends to be more funding, more opportunity for advancement."

"Maybe more headaches, too."

"It doesn't matter. I wouldn't change a thing. I've got a job, and I plan to hang onto it for forty-plus years, if they let me." He grinned.

Deveraux raised his glass. "Here's to that." When they drank, Deveraux said, "Let's talk business a minute. Brief me on this conference? Let's start with Bill. What's he talking about tomorrow?"

Elliott slid his conference program across the table. "You'd better read that."

Deveraux smiled. "You're gonna have to spot me for this one. I only got assigned to the conference yesterday. And I bluffed my way into it in the first place."

Elliott could not help but admire Deveraux's cavalier approach, perhaps because it was the opposite of his own. They had befriended each other in a writing class despite distinct difference in personality. Deveraux was expressive, active, and decisive. He had been determined to be a writer and had leapt headfirst into the fray, reporting and writing articles about anything and everything to cut his teeth. Elliott recognized his own incompatibility with this approach. He could no more write an article about a subject he did not feel the master of than Deveraux could pen an exactingly detailed academic treatise.

Deveraux read aloud the title of Mathiesson's talk: "Wrestling with Pseudoscience: Light from the Darkness." He looked at Elliott.

"My guess is that it'll be a general talk, something about the challenges teachers face when their students bring up pseudoscientific ideas: UFOs, intelligent design, Atlantis, Bigfoot..."

Deveraux looked bemused. "What's that got to do with a conference on human origins?"

"I don't know. I imagine it's an ice-breaker. This is a pretty broad conference showcasing evolutionary theory in a bunch of disciplines: paleoanthropology, biology, history, linguistics, and so on. It's all tied together by this notion that things evolve. Not just biological organisms – you know, amoebas into jellyfish, apes into men – but nomadic groups into towns, into cities, into civilizations. The same ideas are being used in astronomy, linguistics, everything. So the audience for this conference is really broad, and consequently the talks will be more general, less technical."

"Which is why my editor thought I could handle it."

"Bill's talk will be common ground for everyone. He's a good pick for it because he's famous for both his popular and academic writing. But I'm just guessing. I didn't talk to him about it."

Deveraux returned his attention to the program. "Lots of talks about primitive man. *Neanderthal*, *Homo erectus*, *austral… australop –* "

"*Australopithecus*."

"Give me a quick synopsis so I can appear as intelligent as I am."

"Alright. Then let's go to dinner. *Australopithecus* is basically the first in line once you start thinking about 'man-apes.' They appeared four million years ago. They gave rise to *Homo habilis* – 'tool-user' – maybe two million years ago. Five hundred thousand years later you get *Homo erectus*, then *Neanderthal*, then *Homo sapiens sapiens* – us. The dates get murky around then, say between three and one hundred thousand years ago. Things seem to happen faster. Maybe you have two distinct species, *Neanderthal* and *Homo sapiens sapiens*, living side by side." He took a long drink. The beer was cold and bitter and thoroughly pleasant. "How did you say you got this job?"

"I've bluffed my way through worse than this, Paul." He leaned forward. "I've even covered technology fairs. Do you know how to network a bunch of computers between three or four buildings and make sure they all update regularly using minimum bandwidth?"

"How?"

He grinned as he sat back in his chair. "Well, I've forgotten. But I wrote it up for *PC Designs* six months ago and no one's complained yet."

***

They took their places at the far end of the buffet line. Elliott estimated there were seventy-five or a hundred people crowding the room, many of them in line, others sitting at or mingling around the large round tables set for dinner. Brass chandeliers cast yellow light over the group. The stained-oak walls were lined with framed photographs of the Pacific Northwest: Mount Rainier, the Space Needle, the Olympic range in the setting sun, the cratered remains of Mt. St. Helens.

Elliott scanned the crowd to see if he recognized anyone. No sign of Mathiesson. There were a few familiar faces, none familiar enough to call out to. His first conference as a full faculty member and he already felt out of place, self-conscious, as if he was at a party where he didn't know anyone. But this was absurd. If anything, this was the one place he truly belonged. He had earned the right to be here.

Deveraux was talking with a middle-aged woman behind them in line but when they reached the buffet table he broke off to say, "Ahh, the perks of freelancing."

Elliott surveyed the spread: salmon, soup, potato salad, cooked vegetables, breads, desserts, and just beyond that a cash bar for wine and beer. He filled his plate. At the wine table he took out his wallet, but Deveraux said,

"Allow me." To the woman next to him he said, "Would you like to join us?"

The three of them sat at the table furthest from the buffet, directly under a chandelier. A man and a woman were

15

already seated at the table, locked in discussion, not looking up when they sat down.

"Paul, this is Beth Ashmore. Beth, Paul Elliott."

Elliott shook her hand. She had a warm smile that accented the lines on her face. She was probably in her mid to late fifties. Her dark hair was streaked with gray. She was a full foot shorter than Elliott and comfortably plump.

"Pleased to meet you, Paul."

"Do you two know each other?"

"No, we just met in line."

"She's waiting for her husband."

"He was supposed to meet me for dinner but he probably fell asleep. We're three hours ahead of you. In New York it's ten o'clock and he tends to get up early to write."

Deveraux asked: "What does he write?"

"Science fiction. He has a popular series now, *The Sands of Time*."

"Of course! Anthony Ashmore! Rings a bell now." Deveraux gave an apologetic look. "I haven't read his stuff, but I've seen his name on the bestseller list. He writes kind of alternative history sci-fi?"

She looked flattered. "That's my Tony."

Elliott asked, "What kind of alternative history?"

"All sorts. The first one was Egyptian history. He mined me for ideas. Then when he was done soaking in the traditional history of the First Dynasty, he turned to some of the more fanciful stuff."

"Spacemen built the pyramids, and that sort of thing?" Elliott said, smiling.

She nodded. "Certainly not what we'll be talking about here. But it *is* entertaining – and it sells books!"

"You're an Egyptologist?"

She nodded.

Deveraux said, "Paul's writing a book, too."

Elliott was about to explain himself but the tapping of metal against glass cut through the noise, drawing their attention to the front of the room. Bob Knight stood waiting for the crowd to grow quiet. He reminded Elliott more of a businessman than a professor in his suit and neatly trimmed white beard, his bald pate shining beneath the yellow light. He wore fine, steel-rimmed glasses that suited the small features of his face.

"I want to welcome everyone to the third annual Conference on Human Origins. It's been my honor to pull it together this year, and I want to thank all the people who helped me do it."

Elizabeth raised her hand just over her head in a slight wave. Elliott followed her gaze to a short, bearded man in jeans and a sport coat lingering at the entrance to the room. He returned her wave but remained where he was as Knight read down a list of names. Elliott glanced around the room, scanning again for familiar faces, hoping to see Mathiesson. He looked at Deveraux, who winked at him then feigned dozing.

Knight wrapped up to polite applause. Elizabeth stood and waved again to the door, but her husband was already walking over. He kissed her lightly on the cheek.

"I'm sorry, dear. I just couldn't resist the temptation to lie down for a minute."

She gave Elliott and Deveraux a look that said, "I told you so!" Anthony Ashmore was the same height as his wife, and he seemed to share her cheerful disposition. His full beard made his round face look even rounder.

"Pleased to meet you both. Thanks for keeping Beth

company."

Elizabeth pointed to the buffet. "You'd better help yourself to what's left."

"Don't mind if I do."

Deveraux said, "And don't mind if I join you."

The dining room was full and bustling. Elliott sipped his wine and felt himself relaxing as he and Elizabeth exchanged comments about their respective jobs. She had begun her career in archaeology thirty years ago and now worked with a museum collection in New York.

"I spend my days archiving, sifting through uncatalogued finds. It's fascinating. I sometimes miss the actual fieldwork, but there's so much that's been found that's just wasting away in dusty basements. We could declare a moratorium on excavation for twenty years and still not catch up."

"Don't say that! I want to get funding to go back to Africa! I didn't do as much fieldwork as I should've before graduating. But for now I'm teaching and trying to get tenure."

"And writing a book?"

"Alex was being far too generous. I've gotten very little done on that."

"It's ambitious to be writing a book so early in your career."

"And irresponsible, perhaps. I still have papers to publish. But I was inspired to become an archaeologist by reading popular books – particularly Bill Mathiesson's. Do you know him?"

"By name only. I haven't read his books. What's yours about?"

"The ideas fit with this conference. I want to talk about the idea that religious thought provided a selective advantage to early man. Maybe even as far back as *Homo habilis*. It gave groups an intangible reason to stick together. Something beyond territory or possessions."

"Things that could be lost."

"That's right. I hypothesize that from the moment man became self-aware he would have recognized the impermanence of the physical world. The fragility of life. But religious ideas transcend that impermanence. And in prehistory religion gave groups a reason to stick together beyond their immediate needs, which, like you say, come and go quickly. And individuals in groups that stay together tend to survive. And the group grows bigger."

"Religion as glorified herd-instinct."

He laughed. "Yes. Well said. I'm trying to say there's no need to posit some kind of transcendent force in the universe."

"Only a need to believe in one."

"Does it sound simple-minded?"

"No. It's an interesting idea."

He could not read beyond her expression of polite interest. Her husband and Deveraux had returned and Ashmore was talking about the research he had done for the first book in his *Sands of Time* series. When he mentioned the word "Atlantis," the man sitting next to him interjected abruptly,

"That must be some kind of record. I thought we might at least get through the first night without hearing that word!"

Elliott decided the man had not intended to be rude; he was giving Ashmore a look of sympathy. The initial impression of abrasiveness may have owed more to his sharp New York City accent. He looked to be in his mid-thirties, with a full head of curly black hair and square face and jaw. He had turned in his chair, breaking off the conversation he'd been having with the woman next to him. "I just mean, you can't get away from it: students, television and new-age books. Everyone's got a theory about where Atlantis was."

Ashmore smiled politely. "I've dreamed up a few myself. I'm a writer, not a scientist, and this is my chaperone."

A round of introductions followed. The man was Bryan Messe, an archaeologist working at a school in Arizona. The young, sandy-haired woman sitting next to him was Sally Kessler, an archaeologist based in New Mexico. Both had worked on digs at first century Native American settlements in the southwest. They had been comparing notes.

Ashmore said, "So, Bryan, have you got a theory about Atlantis?"

"I do. I think Plato invented it to illustrate his philosophy, and that gullible readers took him literally and turned his metaphor into a modern fairy tale. It's an archaeological pseudo-mystery, like 'Who built the pyramids?' Sometimes people don't want to accept an answer even if it's right in front of their faces. So they create a sense of mystery that obscures the truth."

Deveraux had been leaning back in his chair. He said, "Sounds like you've encountered some true believers, Bryan." Elliott knew him, so perhaps he was the only one who picked up on the mild irritation in his voice. Deveraux disliked being preached to.

"You can count on at least one undergraduate in every course bringing up ancient astronauts and the Nazca lines. Or whatever. I joke that I'm teaching remedial archaeology."

Sally Kessler said, "I know what you mean. I think I sometimes spend the first half of an Intro to Archaeology course getting students to unlearn what they've picked up watching TV or reading the latest new-age book."

Elliott said, "I get that and religious questions. Intelligent design, God creating the Earth in seven days. It's difficult for some people to believe there's no need for that. I suppose it's the same with Atlantis and all the other mysteries. People have a deep-seated need to believe in something beyond themselves. A mystery like Atlantis keeps the door to the unexplained open."

Messe nodded, smiling broadly. "It's the curse of science. We've explained so much that we get accused of robbing the universe of its magic. We're spoilsports."

"It's true. Some students are really sensitive about that kind of thing."

Elizabeth touched his arm. "Not just students, Paul. Anyone made to question a dearly held belief gets... well, anxious."

"Defensive," said Messe.

"Okay: defensive. But scientists are the same way."

Messe shook his head. "Maybe a little. But there's no room in science for holding an idea on faith. Science is a process of continually testing ideas. If they pass, you keep them. If not, they're gone."

Deveraux laughed. "I've heard that so often it's beginning to sound like a party slogan."

"But it's true, Alex," said Elliott. "He's got a point."

Elliott saw his impatience. "Yes, it's true, Paul. But it's true of *science*, not necessarily scientists. You guys are human just like the rest of us. That's why you get so touchy when somebody starts talking about Atlantis. *They're* questioning *your* beliefs."

"Science deals with fact, not belief," said Messe.

"That's in the eye of the beholder, isn't it?" Elliott was impressed by how quickly Deveraux's tone shifted to reflect a sympathy with Messe that Elliott was sure he didn't feel. Perhaps he had realized the folly of arguing with someone he might want to interview later.

Elizabeth tapped her watch and smiled. "I'm sure this could go on all night, but I for one have had my fill. It's midnight by East-Coast time and I'm usually asleep by ten." She stood up. "I'm off to bed. Will you join me, dear? Or would you like another drink?"

Ashmore looked at Deveraux and shrugged his shoulders.

"If you wouldn't mind us stealing him for just one drink?"

"Of course not, Alex." She kissed her husband on the cheek. "Good night, dear. Good night, everyone."

Messe stood up. "That goes for me, too. I'll put some finishing touches on my talk."

Kessler excused herself. Elliott, Ashmore, and Deveraux found themselves standing around an empty table.

Deveraux said, "To the bar, gentlemen. I'll get the first round."

***

At 1:30 in the morning, Elliott lay his head on the pillow, turning on his side to avoid the painful swelling that had formed from the accident on the airplane. The turbulence, Rachel… Those odd lights. What had they been? An after-effect of emotional stress. Or had he banged his head so hard he'd seen stars, like a cartoon character? The thought amused him, but he was having trouble thinking deeply about any of it.

That's what alcohol will do to you.

He switched off the bedside lamp. The white noise of the room heater was too loud, but he could not bring himself to get out of bed to turn it off. Back home, with the time difference, it was 4:30 in the morning. He closed his eyes against the dim outside light filtering into the room, but this highlighted the spinning of his stomach, so instead he stared out the window. Flecks of rain dotted the glass, sidling down, merging into larger streams.

No sign of Bill tonight. What the hell is he up to?

Uncharacteristically coy on the phone. *Fascinating* news. What had he found? Why wouldn't he just say over the phone?

And when would he die?

The heater in the room abruptly stopped, leaving the sounds of distant traffic and late night revelers to drift up from the streets below. The sudden stab of anxiety was difficult to focus. He was too tired, too drunk, to analyze it, and he fell into a heavy sleep.

3

HE LEFT THE HOTEL EARLY the next morning and walked a few blocks to get coffee at a familiar café. Overnight the rain had stopped. The air was cold and clear and held the scent of damp earth. His americano was several notches above what he could find back home; he sipped the thin layer of smooth, bitter froth from the top with relish. On his way back to the hotel he peered inside the windows of closed shops. The sidewalks were empty of people but stained with the remnants of Friday-night revelry: torn flyers, a broken bottle, the acrid scent of stale beer.

If he didn't know better he would have assumed it was merely nostalgia and espresso that lifted him into a state of mild euphoria. Certainly they helped, but there was a difference now that transmuted nostalgia into renewal – a feeling that he had moved beyond these familiar streets and reached a new plateau in his life, his career, and there was no turning back. The initial challenges of proving himself worthy of an academic career were met when he received his doctorate and landed a job. At the moment, the anxiety associated with the tenure process felt distant and manageable.

As he entered the hotel he saw a stooped figure leaning on a wooden cane, hobbling across the lobby towards him.

"Bill!"

Mathiesson looked up and his taut, pained expression dissolved into a smile of relief.

"Thank God it's you, Paul. I was afraid I was going to

have to make small talk again."

Elliott hoped his surprise did not show on his face. The year had done Mathiesson no favors. His skin was pale, dotted with age marks, drawn tight over a thin face. Wisps of gray hair poked out from beneath a black wool cap, dusting a wrinkled forehead. His body was crooked, an old tweed suit hanging loosely from it. Even now Mathiesson did not stand up all the way as he offered a limp handshake that turned into a light embrace. The impression was of a grizzled, wizened sailor rather than the internationally renowned scholar who once stood taller than Elliott, who had made such an impressive first impression, both mentally and physically. Only the eyes, pale grey, sparkling, alive, reminded Elliott of the Mathiesson he knew.

"Let's go sit outside."

"Outside? Are you sure? It's a little cold."

"Just for a minute."

Elliott followed him, pacing himself to the clack-clack of the brass tip of Mathiesson's cane, first on the tiled floor, and then the cement as they stepped outside.

They found a bench in a small courtyard, shielded from the breeze but not the noise of intermittent traffic from the nearby road. A rusted fountain bubbled weakly in the pale morning light. Pigeons wandered the dull pavement.

Mathiesson sat and closed his eyes, sighing. Elliott studied his face in profile. Beneath the lines it was still well-cut, with high cheekbones, aquiline nose and a broad forehead projecting hints of power. The eyes remained closed as Mathiesson said, "That's better. I couldn't bear chatting with anyone else in there. I should've known not to show up early." He turned to face Elliott. "How are you?"

"I'd rather know how you're doing."

"Oh, we'll get to that." He waved his hand dismissively. "Don't worry about me. How's the job? Have you talked much with Niels?"

Niels Bjornson was the former Chair of Anthropology at Elliott's college, the individual most responsible for hiring Elliott.

"You know he retired recently?"

"Good for him. He was overdue."

"He's been helpful." As Elliott talked about Bjornson and the college, he watched Mathiesson struggle to stifle a recurring cough, his focus shifting intermittently from Elliott to somewhere inside himself. This gave the impression that Mathiesson had limited resources at his disposal. But the update seemed to satisfy the older man.

"He's a good man. I met him when I was a little older than you. I wonder – "

A delivery truck rumbled past, obscuring his words.

"What was that, Bill?"

Mathiesson shivered. "Oh, nothing. Just thinking about giving all this up."

"About retiring?"

Mathiesson lost his battle against the cough, and his whole body erupted in a paroxysm of motion. By the time it ceased his eyes were moist, his body draped against the back of the bench.

"Bill?"

Mathiesson forced a smile through his obvious frustration. "Let's hope that doesn't happen in there."

"Christ, Bill, you're not doing well at all."

But the light had returned to his eyes. He cocked an eyebrow and his smile grew looser, reflecting, it seemed to Elliott, a lack of concern. "No, Paul, I'm not. But it's good to sit in the sun for a minute. I didn't want to worry you over the phone. My prognosis is lousy. But you suspected that."

"I did. You could've told me."

Mathiesson shrugged. "It doesn't matter. You're here now. I'll fill you in tonight. You're still planning on dinner with us? Martha's looking forward to it."

"Of course."

"Good. Now listen, I have a favor to ask." He leaned in and there was a gleam in his eyes. "You and I have known each other a good while. I consider you a colleague and a good friend. So do me a favor in there, will you?"

"What?"

"Indulge me. Alright? And, while you're at it, *trust me.*"

"I don't understand."

Mathiesson gave a short laugh. "You will."

Elliott shrugged. He found Bill's look of mild amusement far preferable to the scene he had just witnessed, and it reminded him of their phone call the other day. Fascinating news. He opened his mouth to ask for details, but just then Mathiesson glanced at the watch hanging loosely on his wrist and said, "It's time to go back in."

***

The room resembled a university-style lecture hall, tiered rows of seats stretching back to the far wall; only those furthest from the front looked empty. Bob Knight, again dressed in a gray suit with a conference ID hanging from a lanyard around his neck, saw them as they came in and immediately approached.

"I wondered where you'd gotten off to, Bill." He nodded to Elliott and extended his hand, "Bob Knight."

"Paul Elliott."

Knight's grip was firm and brief. He turned and pressed his hand to Mathiesson's shoulder, directing him towards the podium and leaving Elliott to survey the packed room and despair of finding a seat. Then he saw Deveraux waving to him from the front row. The reporter removed his jacket from the seat next to him.

"Thanks, Alex."

"It's the least I can do for getting you drunk last night."

Knight and Mathiesson stood in discussion by the podium. Elliott could not help but note the differences between the two: Knight, short and compact, standing straight and powerful next to Mathiesson, who looked frail and old as he bent forward to hear what Knight was saying.

Deveraux said, "How's Bill?"

Before Elliott could answer, Knight tapped the microphone and the crowd grew quiet. "I know we're all excited about our first speaker, so I'll keep my opening remarks short. I'm glad to see we've got a full house. Welcome to the third annual Conference on Human Origins." Polite applause followed. "Bill Mathiesson has been in the business longer than anyone in this room, with the possible exception of myself. I think it's safe to say he's one of the grand old men, one of the intellectual giants, of paleoanthropology. What's more, he's kept himself current – researching, lecturing and publishing well into his emeritus status, no doubt trying to give me a run for my money." Mild laughter rippled through the crowd. "Bill's academic work is well-known for its far-ranging insight, accuracy, and paradigm-shaping ideas. His popular books cross numerous disciplines and have inspired colleagues and laypeople alike to explore the mysteries of the world around us. I can think of no finer person to give us the kind of broad perspective appropriate for this multidisciplinary conference. Please welcome Doctor William Mathiesson."

Applause erupted in the auditorium. Mathiesson rose to his feet and approached the podium, nodding at the audience and raising a hand in a gesture of humility. As the clapping faded, he cleared his voice, leaned into the microphone, and said,

"That's very kind of you all. You're easing my transition from professor to 'grand old man.'" He grimaced. "I'm not sure I appreciate the appellation, but I admit there's more than a grain of truth to it. I've been digging for buried treasure for a good sixty or so years. And I've occasionally found it."

The smile was there, the brightness in his eyes, but his voice was thin and weak.

"I wasn't part of those earlier generations of archaeologists and fossil hunters. People like Champollion, Layard, Evans, though. That was a time when no matter where you stuck your shovel you were likely to find something worth digging up. I was fortunate enough to come in on the tail end of that wave of discovery. In the forties I worked with Maurice Baker, a contemporary of Louis Leakey, near Lake Turkana in Africa. I felt then what many of you may have experienced yourselves: that feeling of perching on the edge of a mystery, as if your brain can somehow sense that beneath the soil lies a whole other world, a world far broader and richer than the surface one, stretching down through unimaginably vast spans of time. I'll bet early explorers about to set sail on uncharted oceans felt something quite similar.

"But things are a little different today. As with many fields – biology, chemistry, psychology – anthropology has reached a point where many of us feel we've got the basic picture sorted out and just need to fill in the details. That's the opinion you'll get if you talk to most biologists about evolution, psychologists about consciousness, and anthropologists about early man. Our age is ruled by the materialistic paradigm, and we generally operate under the assumption that ours is a purely physical universe. All processes, including mental ones, have physical causes. And when you look at how far we've come in the past hundred and fifty years – both technologically and in our ever-expanding base of scientific knowledge – it's difficult not to get swept up in the idea that we really are close to some sort of unified theory of existence. Something that goes beyond physics to encompass everything we know. The biologist E. O. Wilson wrote a book called *Consilience*, in which he argues just that.

"I don't know how each one of you individually feels about this. But I do know that in our work and our day-to-day interactions with one another, the assumption that we all basically agree on the big picture hovers unquestioned against the backdrop.

"Of course, there are plenty of people out there who don't agree with us, and I'm sure you've all had some of them as students." Mathiesson smiled with the ensuing laughter and took a drink of water. "That's what I wanted to talk about today.

"Back in 1967 a Swiss writer named Erich von Daniken published a book that even the non-archaeologists in the audience will likely be familiar with: *Chariots of the Gods?* In it, he argued that our barely-civilized ancestors did not have the technological know-how to build structures like the Pyramids at Giza or the statues on Easter Island. His explanation was an archeological *deus ex machina*: extraterrestrials, aliens from another planet, arrived on Earth and took matters in hand. They civilized savage *homo sapiens* and taught him the arts of construction and agriculture. His book has become the poster child for pseudoscience; it reads like a thriller and poses rampant questions in lieu of evidence. Does this rock carving illustrate an alien visitor in a spacesuit? Were the Nazca lines really landing strips for spacecraft? Of course the implication is always 'yes.' Scientists reference von Daniken whenever we feel the need to discredit this or that outlandish theory, and in that sense he's made our work easier for us.

"In point of fact von Daniken was not the first to suggest alien visitation in the ancient past, nor was he last. The idea is part of popular culture. It coexists alongside the paranormal, Atlantis, UFOs and the Loch Ness Monster. This doesn't surprise me. It illustrates a fundamental element of human nature, that we crave mystery as much as we crave certainty. If this weren't true none of us would be here in the room today. We became scientists because we were thrilled at the thought of the universe as a mystery to be solved, the one greatest, truest mystery of all."

Mathiesson took a long drink of water. He bowed his head as if studying his notes and Elliott wondered if he was staving off another fit of coughing.

"The trouble is, as I said, we need certainty. This is an essential paradox in our makeup: we want mystery, but not without a good dollop of understanding. We want problems, but not ones we think are unsolvable. I compare it to a rollercoaster ride: we want the thrill of danger, the rush of adrenaline, but only if we're absolutely certain we're not going to fly off the tracks. If there's anything I, as a scientist, ever felt truly uncomfortable with, it was the sense that some mysteries may never be solved."

The emphasis surprised Elliott. He was expecting a rousing, humorous and damning critique of pseudoscience, not an analysis of the scientist's psychology. From the sounds of shifting seats and murmuring around him he guessed the rest of the audience felt the same way.

"This, I think, is part of the reason why we share in the assumption that we've got the big picture worked out, and now only need to flesh out the details. This scenario gives us a mystery we can all feel comfortable with. And this, I think, is why we are so quick to tar the latest batch of so-called pseudoscientists with the same brush as von Daniken. The pseudoscientist represents the outsider who niggles us, who says we don't have the big picture solved. We may act as if we do. We may have the academic institutions of the world on our side, but we don't have all the answers. I always felt this type of behavior represents a sort of pathology: the individual who rebels against authority simply because it *is* authority, and not because there's anything inherently wrong with it.

"It is only now, from my perspective as a 'grand old man' of science, that I can see how foolish my own position has been."

Elliott shifted in his seat. He repeated Bill's words to himself but found it difficult to put them into context. And he was confused: the last thing he expected to feel today was irritation with Bill.

Over the rising murmur in the lecture hall Mathiesson said,

"Don't misunderstand me. I'm not lending my support to von Daniken and I'm not about to give you a new theory about Atlantis or ESP." He smiled, but atypically for Bill his look betrayed a certain impatience, perhaps even exasperation. "But what if I were? If there's evidence out there it should be considered with the same objectivity, the same neutrality as I would give to a jaw fragment of *homo erectus.*

"But my main point is that we're in a position to go the pseudoscientists one better. Let's face it, there are profound mysteries out there. For example: why precisely did agriculture appear in widely separated areas at close to the same time in prehistory? Why are there worldwide legends of floods and other catastrophes that share the common feature of a Noah-like figure escaping in an ark? What about the persistent question of advanced civilizations predating those of Egypt and Mesopotamia? Even the type of question many of us have grown to dread: how exactly was the Great Pyramid at Giza built?"

Mathiesson raised his hand again like a teacher trying to quiet a disruptive classroom. Elliott watched and listened in wonder; he had never experienced this type of a response to a lecturer. But Bill was bringing it on himself. He had an easy task, child's play for someone of his stature and experience: give a light talk on the differences between science and pseudoscience. Fill it with humorous examples of the crazy things people believe. This was what everyone had been expecting. A treat from one of the great names of science. Instead Bill appeared altogether serious and, even worse, vaguely accusatory. Furthermore it was clearly not easy going for him up there. His face lacked its usual composure. His voice sounded frail against the rumblings of the audience.

"These are mysteries. They may have perfectly

reasonable explanations, but you and I are unwilling to examine them honestly for fear we will end up guilty by association with von Daniken. But my point is this: in the end who's better equipped to deal with these mysteries than us? We have all the tools of our education and trade at our disposal. All I propose we do is examine these and other mysteries without our usual a priori assumptions."

The words did nothing to quiet the crowd. Elliott's sympathy was mixed. He felt a disturbing division inside. The thought of studying psychic phenomenon or the "Atlantis question" repulsed him. Was this what Bill was suggesting? Embrace the fringe ideas circulating through the popular mind, give them credibility? In academia, the only thing one learned about the wilder theories out there was to avoid them like the plague. Textbooks dismissed von Daniken-like speculations with one or two quick remarks, and this was just as well because it discouraged unwarranted speculation by students. It was hard enough keeping them focused on the facts. Let the popular literature feed the appetite for fantasy, but keep it out of academia.

And that, he realized suddenly, was exactly Mathiesson's point. Supposedly "unsolved" mysteries represented a vacuum. Because respectable scientists were unwilling to lend credence to them by serious study, the void was filled with the speculations of the pseudoscientists. Nature abhors a vacuum…

Robert Knight, irritation scrunching his face, took to the podium. Elliott wondered how surprised he was at the turn Mathiesson's lecture had taken. "I should not need to remind you that this is not an undergraduate classroom." His sharp tone abruptly dulled the clamor in the auditorium. "I think perhaps some questions are in order to help Bill clarify his position." Mathiesson nodded. "Good. I'll go first. I think the difficulty many of us have with your position, Bill, is that we don't share your view that what you've mentioned so far as unsolved mysteries are all that mysterious. You mention the Great Pyramid. I think that people who have studied this monument closely are in general agreement about how it was built; it is only those with a superficial understanding of the Pyramid who think there's any mystery involved."

Mathiesson cleared his throat but ended up launching into an extended coughing fit. Knight looked ready to intervene but Mathiesson waved him back to his seat. He emptied his water glass and said in a thin voice,

"Thank you for your point, Bob. It's true that the definition of what constitutes a mystery varies depending on perspective. But we have a habit of assuming that problems in prehistory have conventional answers – 'conventional' meaning ideas that already fit comfortably within the existing paradigm. The independent invention of agriculture, for example. As a rule we don't consider the possibility that agricultural techniques originated in a single 'mother' culture and diffused throughout the world. That smacks too much of Atlantis. Having taken that option off the table without any particularly compelling reason other than our own preferences, we assume the answer must have to do with a kind of natural law that dictates the circumstances under which agriculture will commence in a community. Now for all I know there *is* some set of preconditions that, once met, initiate agricultural development. My point is that we occasionally dismiss other possibilities, even if they resonate more with common sense, because we simply don't like them.

"Take the example of the Great Pyramid. The general

consensus among Egyptologists is that it was built using a combination of immense manpower, colossal mud ramparts leading up to the pyramid, and levers, ropes and pulleys to raise the stones. There's a time frame of twenty years allotted for its construction, the length of the pharaoh Khufu's reign, to whom this pyramid is attributed."

Elliott was sitting close enough to watch a strange mixture of expressions flicker across Bill's face. In place of the flash of impatience he had glimpsed earlier, Elliott now imagined he saw something like uncertainty – something he never expected to see. The antithesis of Bill's standard style of presentation: collected and assured, topped off with a casualness that somehow conveyed authority even more effectively than Knight's imposing demeanor. But for this lecture Bill seemed far from certain about anything. His hands gripped either side of the podium as if he needed the physical support. His face was taut with the effort at self-control, eyes narrowing in concentration when he looked down at his notes. And was it simply ill health that added the quaver to his voice? Or was this the first time he had faced open hostility from an audience that had revered him for most of his career?

But in the brief space between his comments on the Great Pyramid and the moment he spoke again, he visibly relaxed. His grimace collapsed into a familiar and warm smile. It was clear he had arrived at a decision.

"The truth of the matter is, most people who have studied the Great Pyramid closely do not have any idea how it was built."

A clamor arose from the crowd. Elliott gave an involuntary groan of surprise. Mathiesson may have reached some kind of decision just now, but it was clear that his audience would not accept it.

"Please, please," Mathiesson said, raising both hands. "Indulge me a moment. I only want to point out that the Giza pyramid represents a perfect opportunity for us to turn the tables on ourselves. We're always complaining that pseudoscientists plunge into a field without training, making speculations they have no right to make, finding mysteries where there aren't any mysteries. But who better to comment on the building of one of the largest monuments on Earth than engineers? Egyptologists aren't trained in construction techniques. They can read about them in their spare time and speculate on various methods the ancient Egyptians may have used to build, but then we're justified in calling them pseudo-engineers. When true construction experts are faced with questions like how exactly the technologically-primitive Egyptians lifted thirty ton blocks halfway up the Great Pyramid, most raise their hands in puzzlement. At such a juncture we stand as guilty of obscuring a mystery as we accuse pseudoscientists of creating one."

He cleared his throat and reached for water but a sudden spasm of coughing shook him. He mumbled an apology and stepped back from the microphone. Without the support of the podium he looked as if he might collapse. Elliott made to stand but Knight had already extended his arm in support. He was close enough to the microphone to lean forward and say,

"We'll hold off any more questions for the moment. Bill, is that okay with you?"

Mathiesson would have been unable to continue anyway; the level of conversation in the auditorium was too great. Elliott stood up, wondering if the hostility was at all tempered by concern. Even Knight wore an irritated look as he patted Mathiesson on the shoulder and whispered something in his ear. The coughing would not stop. As Elliott approached the podium he overheard Knight's comments: "Are you okay? Why didn't you tell me it was this bad?" And then, frustration breaking through: "Good Lord, Bill, you picked a hell of a time to switch sides."

4

ELLIOTT FOLLOWED MATHIESSON and Knight to the exit. As they were about to step outside Mathiesson said, "See you tonight, Paul?"

"Of course, Bill. I wouldn't miss it."

He already felt uncomfortable; Mathiesson seeking his reassurance made it worse. He watched the two professors walking away and tried to ignore a feeling of helplessness.

Deveraux tapped him on the shoulder. "Let's talk about it over breakfast."

Outside rainclouds rolled in from the west, accommodating his mood. He had lost interest in the conference and was grateful to Deveraux for providing an avenue of escape. The reporter lit a cigarette as they walked; Elliott refused one for himself.

Deveraux said, "I've almost given them up. It takes a while to get through a pack."

Elliott stuffed his hands into his pockets, pressing his arms to his sides, feeling cold and tense. "I don't get it. What the hell was he thinking? That wouldn't have been a good lecture to give even at the best of times."

"What do you mean?"

"He's dying, but he decides to give the most outlandish talk of his career as an introductory lecture."

Deveraux grinned. "I think it's kind of ballsy."

"It's crazy."

"Are you sure you're not talking about what he said?"

"I know you're thinking Bill didn't say anything

damning. Just 'keep an open mind'. But we both know it's more than that."

"Oh?"

"Keeping an open mind about UFOs and Atlantis is like… You know the saying: 'Keep an open mind, but not so open that your brains fall out.'"

Deveraux laughed. Elliott was irritated to think that the reporter was enjoying himself. They passed the café Elliott had stopped at that morning. In the past hour the streets had come to life: shops opening, cafés filling up, lines forming at sidewalk stands. The air smelled of curry and fried food. The sky was overcast, the air chilled. In another mood the scene would have made him feel exuberant. Now he could not help thinking: Why had Bill chosen this time to switch sides? Was Knight's question reasonable? Was it as drastic as that? Anxiety made it difficult for him to think clearly. For some reason he felt physically threatened.

"Almost there, Paul. Snap out of it."

Deveraux pushed open the door to a familiar Greek restaurant. Elliott recognized the middle-aged woman who waved them to a table by the window. A waitress brought coffee. After staring blankly at the menu for a minute Elliott remembered he liked the spinach and mushroom omelet. He closed his menu and looked up at Deveraux, who had already decided what to eat.

"Why is this hitting you so hard, Paul?"

He shook his head, not wanting to answer. But after a moment he asked again, "What was he thinking? Really? You know what? I'm pissed at him. He stood up there preaching to us like we were undergraduates. And whatever he said otherwise, it sounded like he wanted us to start searching for Atlantis."

Deveraux smiled. "I'm sorry, Paul. But you make it sound like he was insane."

Elliott regarded Deveraux with irritation. The reporter was amused. "For all practical purposes he might as well be."

"Oh, come on. Can it really be that bad?" Deveraux leaned forward and tapped the table with his knuckles. "Snap out of it, Paul. Ask yourself why you're taking this so hard."

Elliott felt embarrassment mixed with anger. He already had another explanation on the tip of his tongue: he needed his relationship with Mathiesson to boost his own sense of self-worth. If Bill Mathiesson of all people accepted him then he was okay. But if Bill Mathiesson was suddenly discredited then where did that leave Elliott?

Deveraux was saying, "You're worried about him. I understand that, but – "

Elliott cut him off in frustration. "It's not just him being sick. It's him making a fool of himself."

Deveraux leaned back. "Aren't you being a little harsh? He didn't endorse any of these pseudoscientists, these cranks you're so worried about. Everyone heard the word 'Atlantis' and overreacted like a bunch of old ladies. Probably no one really even heard what he said. Did you? Tell me what you really thought. Be objective."

He sipped his coffee and was surprised at the bitterness. He had forgotten to add his cream. "What's the point? Either you believe or you don't. Once you open the doors to these crazy ideas it's like opening Pandora's box. I can't think of a single scientist who started out respectable, entertained wild ideas, and then made it back into the mainstream. It's professional suicide. Actually it's more than that. It's intellectual suicide."

Deveraux looked surprised and was about to speak when

the waitress reappeared for their order. When she left, Elliott jumped in before Deveraux could speak: "In order to succeed as a scientist, I need to narrow my focus, to specialize to a degree that permits me to gain an understanding I would otherwise be incapable of. Something Bill said is true: there's a sort of unspoken agreement in the sciences. It's really about the parameters of investigation. We generally agree on the size and scope of the big picture so that we can work together to fill it in. There are variables and constants in the equation, but if we can't agree on them, we won't get anywhere. Deep down, we know this to be true –"

Deveraux interjected dryly, "You mean, deep down you need it to be true."

Elliott waved him aside. "Okay, okay, we need it to be true. But opening the doors to any crazy idea that comes along basically changes the rules. Maybe what was once a constant is actually a variable. Pretty soon the world doesn't make any sense. That's why I say it's intellectual suicide. You're bound to lose your footing if you don't clearly define the rules. Science needs firm ground to stand on or it can't make any progress."

Deveraux's laugh was mocking. "All you're saying, Paul, is that you tacitly agree on subjects you'll accept as worthy of investigation, and that you do this for peace of mind. You're not actually commenting on whether there's anything mysterious or paranormal behind UFO reports and pyramids. You'd just rather not think about it."

"I don't mean to give you that impression. If I thought we really didn't understand how the pyramids were built, or that people were seeing spaceships instead of the planet Venus, then I'd be all for investigation. But the truth is, I don't have any reason to believe that kind of crap."

"How on earth can you say that when you haven't even investigated it? You shut the door a priori with this 'tacit agreement' you just told me about. At best you let some other skeptic do your thinking for you and read his popular book about it." He softened his tone. "I'm sorry, Paul, I know I'm not being very helpful. It's just that you're a smart guy and it irritates me that you've got this blind spot."

Elliott said nothing. He sipped his coffee and tried to bring order to his thoughts. He was thinking emotionally, unproductively, and wanted something to cut through the internal clutter. But he could see the problem clearly enough: his emotional connection to Mathiesson on one side and intellectually abhorrent ideas on the other. At the moment they seemed pretty well-matched.

Deveraux thankfully recognized he had said enough. When the waitress returned with their food they ate for several minutes in silence. But Elliott found his mood interfering with his enjoyment of the meal, and to distract himself from his thoughts he said, "Tell me something that'll make me drop my skepticism."

"Really?" Deveraux transferred the slice of bacon dangling from his fork into his mouth. He nodded as he chewed, then reached into his jacket pocket and pulled out his wallet. "First let me show you something." He rifled through his wallet and pulled out a beige business card. He passed it to Elliott. "Recognize the name?"

"Adam Gaskell," Elliott read. "'*Strange Truths Magazine.*' No, I've never heard of him." Deveraux stretched out his hand across the table. "Allow me to introduce myself."

Elliott automatically shook his hand. The absurdity of the gesture distracted him, then he made the connection:

"*You're* Adam Gaskell?"

Deveraux scooped up a huge mouthful of egg and grinned broadly.

"You've been pulling double duty? *Strange Truths*. What is it, a paranormal magazine?" Deveraux nodded. "So tell me, Alex, what's brought about your open mind? Rigorous paranormal investigations or a careful review of your bank account?"

Deveraux washed his food down with a swig of coffee before replying, "Both. And the same goes for you."

"What do you mean?"

"You said it yourself. You're tenure-track, meaning you're being watched; even if you suddenly did an about-face and wanted to write about ancient astronauts you'd have to give up your chances for tenure. Hell, you might have to give up your career." He wiped his mouth and sat back. "Anyway, the rather ordinary truth about *Strange Truths* is that they don't pay much, but it's work. They keep me busy. They're actually the ones that asked me to cover the conference."

"Why?"

"We're not all crackpotsl. It's possible to be interested in modern science *and* the paranormal."

Elliott rolled his eyes. "I find that difficult to believe. They're polar opposites."

"A statement made in ignorance. Climb down from the ivory tower. There's a wide world out there of experience not covered by academic science."

"You were going to give me an example."

Deveraux nodded and thought for a moment. "Fine. By way of introduction, I'll remind you that I've interviewed plenty of people since I started writing, way back when for the campus paper and now for newspapers and magazines. I can't be picky about the stories I do and I meet people from all walks of life: scientists, lawyers, housewives, writers, construction workers, homeless people – you name it. Every once in a while something out of the ordinary comes up and piques my interest beyond the story. For example – do you remember about a year ago I might've told you about that little girl who disappeared on her way home from school?" Elliott did not. "She was eight years old and lived about five blocks from the school. One Wednesday in May she didn't show up at home. Her mother called the police.

"Sometimes I have to be a vulture in my line of work. So I was interviewing the mother within forty-five minutes of her contacting the police. There was a patrol car in front of her house and it must've drawn the attention of her neighbor, this seventy-year old woman who'd been a family friend for years." He had been holding his coffee mug halfway between the table and his mouth; now he drank, set it down and leaned forward. "This old woman looked perfectly normal. She came over and asked what was the matter. The mother started sobbing, so I explained the situation. The old woman just nodded and walked up onto the porch of the house, looking around for something – I had no idea what. For a second I even thought she was senile and looking for the little girl on the porch, but after a moment she picked up a doll, sat down in the porch swing, and closed her eyes. It was only at this moment that the mother seemed to pick up on this strange behavior, and she walked back up onto the porch. I followed her and I think both of us, as we stood there watching her, were afraid to interrupt whatever the hell she was doing. We both had a sense that something important was taking place. When the old woman opened her eyes a few minutes later and whispered something to the little girl's mom, I was close enough to hear it. It was like she was waking up from a dream, the way she talked, or I guess you'd say, from a trance, because it was obvious that was what she'd done. Gone into a trance. She said,

"'It's okay, dear. Sarah is okay. But she's a little hurt. She's –' and here she closed her eyes again, and I had the distinct sense she was visualizing a place. That is, she could see where this little girl was, and the way her eyes were shut tight in concentration it seemed like she was trying to figure out exactly where this place was. Then her eyes snapped open and she smiled and said, 'She's up the road, just off Forty-third and Winston, near the school. Near where the hill dips into that little patch of woods.' The mother and I stared at her in disbelief. She obviously had no doubt about what she was saying. Then she looked at me and said, 'Well, young man, what are you waiting for? Go get her!'" Deveraux laughed. "The way she ordered me like that was what actually convinced me she knew what she was talking about. I snapped into action. I knew the area, and I knew the spot she was talking about was very close. On the way to my car I told a cop what the woman had said, and we ended up taking his car to the spot she'd indicated." Deveraux spread his arms wide. "And there she was. She'd fallen down the hill, rolled until her head bumped a rotting log and got knocked out. She was lucky she didn't keep rolling. That little patch of forest drops over an embankment onto a busy street."

Their waitress stopped by to refill their coffee. When she was gone, Deveraux said, "Of course, this wouldn't be much of a story if it wasn't absolutely clear that the old woman had nothing to do with the girl's disappearance. But she'd been visiting her daughter in Queen Anne all day and hadn't arrived home until after the mother called the police. When

I asked the old woman how she knew, she said that she didn't really know how. She said – and I know this sounds corny – she said she'd had 'the gift' since she was a little girl, and when she needed to know something, she had to relax deeply and concentrate, and the answer would come to her in pictures. She held the girl's doll because, she said, it was connected to her and that made it easier to find her."

Elliott didn't know what to say. Deveraux was clearly sincere. But it sounded like a television docudrama, and he said as much.

"Yes, I know, Paul. It does sound like hundreds of other stories, but that's part of the reason why I told you that one. I've got others, believe me – UFOs over Bainbridge Island, a haunted pub downtown – even some that don't sound like they came straight out of a tabloid. But the point is, I was there for this one, and I knew in my bones that this lady was for real. I watched her the whole time. When I told her the news I saw the pain in her eyes. She knew the girl. When she was wandering the porch she looked completely in her own world, but focused, like she had a job to do. And then, as she sat in the porch swing I swear I saw the light of recognition come over her. It was like she was searching in her mind, and then suddenly she saw, and her whole body sagged with relief at what she was seeing. If I hadn't been there I wouldn't have realized how obviously truthful she was. How real the story was. I guess you'd say I wouldn't have believed it myself."

Elliott knew Deveraux was waiting for a response; he spoke before measuring one up. "I don't know what to tell you, Alex. You can't expect me to become a believer, even if it's my best friend trying to convince me. I mean, let's face it, there's always the possibility the old woman guessed lucky.

She probably knew where the girl went to school, maybe even how she came home." Even as he said this it felt unfair, a cheap reply to a story that obviously meant a lot to Deveraux. But he didn't know what else to say.

Disbelief flashed across Deveraux's face, quickly morphing into blandness. He shrugged and said, "Well, I don't know if I expected to convince you. But you asked. And, you know, the fact that this story sounds so familiar could be construed as evidence that there's something to all of these reports."

Again, Elliott spoke without thinking. "They're just anecdotes, Alex. I can't do anything with them. I can't test them. I can't replicate them. Scientifically, they mean next to nothing."

Deveraux shook his head. "You really are thick-headed, Paul."

"That's not fair."

"Oh yes it is. Look closely. You're not thinking about the content of what I said. You did the same thing with Mathiesson. All you're doing is reacting to the suggestion that the world is a hell of a lot stranger than you'd like to think it is. And you know what? You sound desperate, like you know the odds are stacked against you."

Elliott looked away. Outside a gray pallor hung over the street.

"More to the point, Paul, you're not asking the right question here."

"What?"

"No one undergoes a conversion like Bill's without good reason." Deveraux leaned forward with a gleam in his eye. "What made him change his mind?"

Now that it was asked the question seemed obvious to

Elliott. He suddenly remembered Mathiesson's "fascinating" news. "You think he discovered something?" He let this thought sink in until another one occurred: "Why didn't he talk about it today?"

"I'm just guessing. Maybe he was testing the waters. What happened when I told you my story just now? Compare it to what happened in the lecture hall. Bill couldn't even suggest keeping an open mind without getting booed off the stage. Maybe he thought that if he presented something specific it'd be even easier to dismiss out of hand. I don't know."

Elliott pushed himself up from his chair and pulled out his wallet. "I'll ask him at dinner tonight." He shook his head. "I can't believe I'm having this discussion with you. I can't believe that you and Bill sound like you're on the same page, that you both think the world's some kind of Pandora's box of unsolved mysteries." He smiled wryly. "To put it in terminology you can relate to, I feel like I've come back to a Seattle that looks the same, but where my closest friends have been replaced by aliens."

Deveraux grinned. "I can't speak for Bill, but I assure you I'm the same old Alex. You just aren't considering the most obvious possibility."

"Which is what?"

"That Bill and I are right."

5

Elliott attended two lectures after breakfast, one on the excavation of a newly discovered tomb in Egypt and another on fine-tuning radiometric dating techniques. He was too preoccupied to enjoy either one and skipped a third in the afternoon. He returned to his hotel, showered and lay down, intending to nap for twenty minutes but instead waking up two hours later feeling exhausted and disoriented.

He opened his blinds. The sky was the muted blue of twilight, the western horizon streaked with coppery-orange light from the setting sun. From seven floors up he could see the clump of skyscrapers downtown and the space needle lit up for the evening.

Shaking off sleep, he splashed cold water on his face and set coffee brewing using the pot in his room. He pulled his chair closer to the window and stared out at the silhouettes of the Olympic mountains. A thick band of mist hovered between them and the waters of Puget Sound. He exhaled deeply and conjured the image of a roiling mass of cloud suspended between sea and sky, solid-looking but intangible, almost not existing at all. The sun sank further and darkness embraced the entire scene, casting into shadow the water, the mist, the mountains and sky. A kind of peacefulness warmed him – not the complete peace of mind he craved, but a bodily calm that subtly influenced his mind; he was feeling it because his mind was still groggy from sleep. In this state he considered Mathiesson with detachment. Deveraux was right, of course, and Bill himself had hinted at it: he must have found something compelling. Elliott's emotional reaction had obscured what was only common sense.

His mind veered into speculation: What had swayed Mathiesson? But since he had nothing to work with he quickly gave up. As he sipped his coffee and let his mind wander he gradually became aware of his intellect regaining control, dismissing speculations and ordering his thoughts like a maid service cleaning a cluttered house.

The phone rang. Deveraux's voice rose over the background traffic noise. "Good evening, Dr. Elliott. Your limo will arrive in ten minutes."

He changed into a fresh shirt, brushed his teeth and inspected his face in the mirror. Dark circles, five-o'clock shadow. He ran an electric razor over his face and a hand through his hair then took the elevator to the lobby.

On the drive to Mercer Island Deveraux told him about the woman he was dating, a graduate student in English who waitressed at a bar Alex frequented.

"And the beauty of it is, she asked me out."

"Saving you the trouble of hitting on a waitress."

"I have too much class for that."

"I'll reserve judgment."

"I've been seeing Christine for six months. I'm all grown up."

They crossed Lake Washington on I-90. The sky was murky gray, the moon invisible. It was only six o'clock but it felt much later. Deveraux turned off the highway onto West Mercer Way and they drove along a tree-lined, winding road without talking, at one point braking suddenly to avoid an opossum waddling across the pavement. As they approached Mathiesson's street Deveraux said,

"Good luck tonight." They pulled up the drive to the

house. "Give me a call if you need a ride back tonight. Otherwise, I'll see you in the morning."

"I wouldn't dream of interrupting your date."

The porch light was on, the house lit up. As Deveraux drove off, the smell of exhaust gave way to the scent of pine trees. The house blended in with the forest encroaching upon it. The stone pathway leading to the front door was patchworked with clumps of moss and he had to sidestep a huge rhododendron bush hanging over the edge of the walk. He rang the bell and waited, watching the mist from his breath rise through a spider web in a corner of the awning.

Martha answered the door wearing a stained apron over a blue blouse and skirt. She welcomed Elliott with a formidable hug and drew him into the house.

"It's so good to see you, Paul. It seems so long." She swept aside a strand of gray and stood on tiptoe to peck Elliott on the cheek. She was slender and petit. Her face was well-lined but traces of her youth were visible through the wrinkles. Mathiesson had met her fifty years ago at a European conference. She had been an undergraduate student and he was presenting his first paper as a young Assistant Professor. She did not pursue an advanced degree after marrying Mathiesson and settling in the States. But she accompanied him on innumerable digs, receiving a field education that was certainly better than Elliott's, and one that probably rivaled the best university programs.

She stood back and assessed Elliott, shaking her head. "You need to gain ten pounds, my dear. Handsome as ever, but a little bookish." She smiled and looked at him as if remembering herself. "If you don't mind my saying, of course." She spoke with the trace of a Slavic accent; the first fifteen years of her life had been spent in Yugoslavia. "Have you got a girl in Ohio?"

Elliott felt his face redden as he fumbled for a response. "Uh, no. But I'm working on it all the time."

"Good."

"Yes, very good indeed," said Mathiesson as he emerged from his study. "I see Martha is making you feel right at home." He embraced Elliott. "Thanks for coming, Paul. I'm sure you haven't forgotten Martha's endearing directness."

She said, "Do you want some wine, Paul?"

When she had gone, Mathiesson directed them to his study and said softly, "She is my angel, Paul. When I was younger I didn't think I could love anyone for so long."

They sat in black leather armchairs by the bay window, the lights of Seattle visible across the water. The room was comfortably warm, walls snug with shelves of books and fossils and photographs. The ancient mahogany desk looked recently used, with a sheaf of papers resembling a handwritten manuscript and a pen resting on top of it. A striking painting hung over the desk, depicting a rocky shore battered by dark waves beneath a gray sky; it produced a pleasantly invigorating effect.

"I see you haven't taken retirement seriously."

Mathiesson glanced around the room. "No, I'm not very good at it."

Elliott pointed at the stack on the desk. "Is that a new book?"

"As a matter of fact it is. Curious?"

"Of course!"

"Good. You can take it with you tonight."

Behind Mathiesson's smile Elliott sensed a profound exhaustion. It made him wonder if his own presence was an imposition.

"Just how sick are you, Bill?"

"Martha is rubbing off on you."

"I'm serious."

Mathiesson raised a hand to pacify him. "Very sick. I'm not supposed to live much longer." He smiled faintly. "But then, I wasn't supposed to live this long."

It was a relief to hear him say it directly. "Is there anything more that can be done?"

"Medically? No, nothing. And I've had enough of that. All that's left is to put my affairs in order." Mathiesson's eyes drifted closed as if the strain of keeping them open was too much for him.

An image popped into Elliott's head: a funeral service in the green cemetery pasture across the street from where he had once lived, the Olympics stretching up into a clear blue sky in the distance. Without intending to he found himself imagining Mathiesson not here. The only corollary his mind produced seemed absurd. When he was sixteen his dog had died. For weeks afterwards he reflexively looked for her around the house, knowledge overruled by force of habit. Each time this happened his intellect jolted him: *She's gone*, and he had been struck with a sense of the finality of death.

"What are you thinking, Paul?"

"I'm trying to absorb what you've said."

"Well, don't try too hard. I'm the one who's dying, and I still can't believe it myself. I've been to plenty of funerals in my day, but I never got my mind around the idea that one day I'd be the guest of honor. Only now –"

With a gentle tap on the door Martha entered holding a tray with water for Mathiesson and red wine for Elliott.

"Anything we can help with, dear?"

"No. You two keep talking."

As the door closed behind her, Elliott prompted, "You said, 'only now'?"

"I'm getting used to the idea of dying. I'm grateful I've been given the chance to do so – get used to it, that is. It reminds me of the *Bardo Thodal*, the *Tibetan Book of the Dead*. That's the first place I came across the idea that you want to be ready for death, in a practical sense. Of course, in Tibetan Buddhism, you're dealing with an afterlife."

"And reincarnation and disembodied spirits and all that."

"Yes, that's right. But then you want to avoid being reincarnated. You want instead to attain enlightenment. And the disembodied spirits that haunt you in the bardo are projections from your own mind. You just have a hard time seeing them as such in the after-death state. That's one way of getting ready for death: learning the tricks of the mind and the afterlife."

Elliott said with surprise, "So that's what you've been doing? Reading the *Tibetan Book of the Dead*?"

Mathiesson chuckled and shook his head. "No, no. That's, I guess you could say, incidental. I reread the book. I could talk to you about it for hours. But I would still be talking to you one scholar to another. Part of me is intensely fascinated by it, wondering if it's true, wondering if I should have spent more of my life meditating in preparation for the moment of death. But I can't help feeling detached from it. From Buddhism, Christianity, anything presuming to help people find peace of mind or salvation or whatever. I've spent my life as a scientist. All my answers have to be empirical. I can't seem to let go of that even as I'm faced with the greatest mystery of all." He took a long drink, and when he set down his glass a smile played on his lips. "But now there's one essential difference. Now I feel that maybe there is something else out there."

"What do you mean?"

"What I mean is that despite my own difficulty opening up to the possibility of a more – for lack of a better word – *spiritual* universe, I finally see this as a limitation on *my* part and not the universe's."

Elliott tried to process this. "You're saying you still don't believe but now you think there's a chance you're wrong."

Mathiesson shook his head and a smile teased the corners of his mouth. "More than that, Paul. I *believe* I'm wrong. I can't help feeling that if I only had a little more time..." His voice cracked; he suddenly sounded almost desperate, talking half to himself as well as Elliott. "I could open that part of myself. It's just a trick of the mind. Over the years I've trained myself to see only what I want to see, but now I understand there's so much more out there. I just need time to break the habit. I need to teach myself to see everything anew."

Elliott listened in surprise. He had never seen Mathiesson like this. "Honestly, Bill, I'm not sure I understand. But let me ask you this: why now? I can't help thinking that..." Elliott paused. There was no delicate way to say what was on the tip of his tongue.

Mathiesson saved him the trouble. "You can't help thinking I'm getting soft in the face of death? That I'm embracing religion as best I can at death's door? You and everyone who attended my lecture today, no doubt. Well, I can't deny that knowing I'm going to die soon has put, shall we say, a different spin on things. But as I've just explained, I can't shake the trappings of a scientist." He leaned forward. "It's taken good old empirical evidence to make me open my mind."

Elliott opened his mouth to speak but Mathiesson kept talking: "And it's like Pandora's box, in a way. Once I was faced with something I really couldn't explain, something truly mysterious, well… One question led to another, each a little flame in the fabric of what I thought I knew. And pretty soon I had a conflagration on my hands. Everything I thought I knew was in danger of going up in smoke." He drained the water from his glass.

"If knowledge of my impending death contributed to this process, it did so by freeing me up to admit I couldn't explain the evidence in front of my eyes. I'd already had practice accepting that final mystery of human existence—" the tension in his face dissolved and he smiled at what he was about to say—"so acknowledging ignorance in the face of this new, rather earthly mystery was a piece of cake."

"Bill, what did you find?"

At that moment Martha's voice called them to dinner.

6

"GENE ATTENBAUM IS THE ONE WHO FOUND IT."

Mathiesson flicked a switch as they entered his basement workshop and a fluorescent light flickered on. A dropcloth stained with dried paint covered a large lump on a worktable in the center of the room. The air smelled of dust, rock, and wood from the two-by-fours supporting the unfinished walls. Mathiesson took hold of a corner of the cloth and twisted it between his fingers as he spoke.

"I don't know if you remember him. He was one of my oldest friends. A paleobotanist. We met at a conference in the 'fifties and hit it off. He came here a few years after me and we'd see each other for dinner every month. Trade stories about excavations in the good old days. It didn't matter that he was plants and I was hominids. We had a lot to talk about." Mathiesson pointed to the protuberance beneath the cloth. "But he never mentioned this to me."

He pulled the dropcloth away and let it fall to the cement floor. A brown slab of rock about a foot wide and deep, rested on the table. Tiny fossils dotted its surface; to an untrained eye they might have appeared to be merely scratches and pits on the surface. Elliott examined these. They were possibly some kind of plant material, portions of conifer needles, perhaps. He didn't know enough to date them just by looking at them. It would probably take an expert to definitively catalogue them. But they did not look like anything he hadn't seen before and he said so to Mathiesson, who showed no sign of disappointment as he responded,

"I know! I know! That's what I thought, too. Gene died a year and a half ago and, God rest his soul, he left this thing for me to deal with. It was part of his personal fossil collection, which he sort of willed to me. I had plans to get some grad students to help me archive it but, you know, other things came up. I halted the project before I'd barely started. All I really know from Gene's record is that it's around sixty-five million years old." He tapped the surface of the rock then traced his finger horizontally around its circumference, along a crack that Elliott had not noticed until that moment. "You see this? It's a perfect split, and anyone who's worked with rock knows that when it splits so evenly it means there's probably a different type of material on the inside, or an air pocket that causes the rock to be less dense than it appears. In our case, it's the former." He tapped the top of the rock and said, "Why don't you lift off this piece for me?"

Elliott pressed his palms flat on either side of the top portion of the rock and lifted it. It was not particularly heavy, but he concentrated on the task so as not to let it drop to the table. He set it down gently then focused his attention on the bottom piece.

A black, rectangular surface glistened beneath the fluorescent light. It appeared to be embedded in the sandstone because the brown rock rose over the edges, creating the impression that he was seeing a snapshot immortalizing the moment the object had sunken into the primordial mud – mud which was then compressed into stone as layer upon layer of sediment settled over it. The surface of the black plaque – for this was what it resembled – appeared to contain carvings of three simple symbols: an inverted "V" shape, a vertical line, and a circle. Each figure was no more than an inch high, but they might as well have been a hundred feet high for the effect they produced within Elliott.

"How old did you say this is?" Elliott looked up at him. "Is this some kind of joke?"

Mathiesson shook his head. "That's what I thought at first, of course. But if it is, I haven't figured it out yet."

Elliott hunched over the table, peering at the plaque. He stretched out an index finger and traced the outline of the triangular figure. A thrill of wonder rippled through him. He ran his finger along the border of the sandstone where the brownish rock covered the plaque. This looked convincing. The tan rock formed an irregular frame around the black one. The lower right hand corner of the interloper had sunken even further into the surrounding rock, which made sense if there had been no artist's hand to guide it. But as he stood up from the table he thought to himself, *In this day and age there must be some way to make this look real when it isn't.*

"What's its story?"

Mathiesson pulled a stool closer to the edge of the table and sat down before answering. Despite his enthusiasm, he looked worn out.

"First let me tell you that Gene Attenbaum wasn't one for a hoax. I loved him to death but he had very little sense of humor about anything. He took his business very seriously. I know to some people that might not mean anything, but I don't think Gene left this as a practical joke."

"Then why?"

"I have my ideas about that. But first, let me show you something." Mathiesson slid open a drawer on the workbench and removed a battered three-ring binder. "This is one of Gene's catalogues of finds for the period. Not as much detail as one would like but he probably has another notebook lying around somewhere." He leafed through it until he found the page he was looking for. "Here you go." He pointed at a date. "'August 14, 1953. Morrison Basin.'

"That's where Gene dug it out. I imagine he was drawn to the conifer impressions. He labeled his finds; this one was C63." Mathiesson pointed to a corresponding spot in the notebook. "He's written here that they're from a particular type of conifer, an index fossil. That is, this particular species of conifer went extinct during the late Cretaceous. Based on this and where he found it in the ground, Gene adduced that the rock is around sixty-five million years old." Mathiesson gave Elliott no time to react. Instead he pointed to a spot on the sandstone directly above the plaque, at the faint impression of what was perhaps a broken needle. "Would you mind lifting the top portion of the rock for me? Thanks." He pointed to this piece now, and drew his finger along another faint conifer needle impression. "This is a mirror-image of the one above that black thing. If we put the two halves of stone together again, they'll fit perfectly. And there are other indications that this rock hasn't been tampered with. There's a particularly nice impression – right there – that crosses over the split in the rock. This was one chunk of sandstone when Gene dug it out. He probably got it in a vice, trying to chisel it into smaller sections, and it split in the middle from the pressure. It's happened to me before. It doesn't take much pressure when a different type of material is encased in the rock."

Elliott looked again at the plaque. He felt a flash of irritation. The thing was so out of place that he simply did not believe it was real. He was not making a conscious decision not to believe. It was more that the two objects – a sixty-five million year-old lump of sandstone, a relic from the time of the dinosaurs, and the black rock of carvings bearing the hallmarks of human intelligence – did not belong together. Elliott's mind could not understand the two objects in conjunction with one another, only separately. He shook his head and involuntarily took a step back from the table.

"I don't know, Bill."

The professor gave him a sympathetic smile. "I don't blame you, Paul. I didn't know what to make of it either. Gene didn't know any better than you or me, so he buried it in a drawer for fifty years. He probably forgot he even had it sometimes. But I bet it nagged him. He knew as well as I do that one little rock like this isn't going to overturn the reigning paradigms of our day. It's more likely to destroy a career than a paradigm. This is the kind of find that if you don't want to believe it, you don't have to. It's completely out of context, and when my colleagues read about it in my last book most of them will dismiss it without even taking a look."

Throughout the evening Elliott had managed to suppress the anxiety he had felt earlier in the day. Now it came rushing back as if a dam had broken. "You can't write about this, Bill! It'll ruin you! There's got to be some kind of mistake."

Mathiesson's face collapsed in defeat and Elliott immediately regretted his remarks; the sight made him feel queasy. "I'm sorry, Bill – "

But Mathiesson had already composed himself: defeat was replaced with disappointment. He turned away saying, "Let's go talk for a few minutes in the TV room."

The rest of the lower level of the house was finished living space. There was an extra bedroom at the opposite end of the hall from the workroom. In between, at the base of the stairs, was a carpeted lounge with a loveseat and a reclining chair, both facing a small television set. Mathiesson dropped into the recliner and pushed himself back with a heavy sigh.

Elliott said guiltily, "Am I keeping you up too late?"

"No. I'm keeping myself up too late. But we have to talk."

"I'm sorry I overreacted."

Mathiesson waved a hand dismissively. "It's to be expected, Paul. That's how everyone will react." He suddenly smiled. "I just don't want to make it easy for you."

Elliott looked at him with surprise. "Why me?"

"You know the answer already, but I might as well say it since I haven't got much longer. Why you? Because you're my progeny, Paul. More than just the student I shepherded through college, more than just my friend and colleague… You know this." He sighed, looking at Elliott as if hoping he would not have to connect the dots for him. Finally he said, "You were the son I never had, Paul. The closest thing, anyway, without bordering on professional impropriety."

A thick swell of emotion rose up in Elliott; he resisted it. He was not going to cry in front of Mathiesson like a lost child. After a moment, irritation with his emotions helped him to subdue them. He said, "The feeling is mutual, Bill."

Mathiesson nodded. "So you see, I'm not being fair. I made a mistake, and in doing so I led you down the wrong path." He closed his eyes and shook his head. "No, not the wrong path, just too far down one path in particular." He again looked to Elliott to see if his meaning was clear.

Elliott said, "I'm not sure I understand, Bill. But listen. You don't owe me anything. You've given me more than I can say. Even before I knew you I would test my own ideas against your books. They were the benchmark. If William Mathiesson had reached a conclusion similar to my own, I'd consider myself brilliant. If not, back to the drawing board."

Mathiesson shook his head. "I was afraid of that. I often saw you using my work as a measure of your own, rather than as a springboard for you to jump off in new directions. The problem with your approach, Paul, is that it keeps you from going beyond me." He leaned in, and now there was warmth rather than weariness in his smile. "The truth is, Paul, you're brilliant. And you've got that same romantic leaning that I do. I think that's what got you into this business in the first place, and why I saw you as a kindred spirit. For people like you and me, science isn't just the technical details, it's the sweep of it all, the vision. It's a quest, not just a profession. Sure, it's an appreciation of techniques, of analysis, and all that. They ground the vision. But at its core there's an emotional need to understand. It's a quest for the ultimate meaning of things that's like the religious impulse, in the sense that it expresses a fundamental need to understand and participate in all creation.

"This is what drives you. And me. It's a profoundly powerful impulse. In Norse mythology it's what made Odin pluck out his right eye so that he could drink from the Well of Mimir to gain wisdom." He studied Elliott before speaking again, a cautious look on his face. "But you... for some reason..." His voice trailed off.

Elliott said, "Go ahead, Bill. Say whatever you need to say."

Mathiesson nodded. "You're too conservative, Paul. It's a strange mix but not an altogether incomprehensible one. Education by itself forces our minds into certain channels, makes others *verboten*. And of course life itself shapes us, circumstances making us more or less cautious, fearful, confident, loving… all that. And you're too cautious, too careful. Part of you wants to pluck out your eye and the other wants to drown yourself in a sea of other people's books, looking for answers the safe way." He looked apologetic, but Elliott did not find himself feeling offended. "I'm sorry to be so blunt, Paul. Really, I am. But you've got to take the leap yourself. You're smart enough, you've got the spark that I've seen so rarely in my academic life that tells me you should be blazing trails instead of following them. I took you on as a graduate student because of that, but in a way that was a mistake. Without false modesty I admit: I was no longer cutting edge. I was winding down, and in a way happy to be doing so. But I was selfish, too. I wanted one more prodigy, one more kindred spirit to share the joy of the game with me.

"So I nurtured you, sure, but in taking you on you could argue that I robbed you of other opportunities for professional growth, chances to take the leap you have *got* to make, Paul, not just as a professional academic but as a human being. I know I've got no right to say that, but there it is, anyway." He glanced away, shrugging at another thought. "Then again, that other path might've squashed that romantic side out of you. It has a way of doing that." He met Elliott's eyes. "There. I've had my say. Are you upset with me?"

Elliott felt a stir of elation. He struggled to understand it. The ideas racing through his mind were thin wisps of smoke, insights threatening to dissipate before he could capture them. It wasn't simply that Mathiesson's assessment was correct. Elliott had indulged in enough self-analysis to be painfully aware of his overly cautious nature. He had even learned to see it as a plus, convincing himself that – intellectually anyway – it resulted in a healthy skepticism that made him a better scientist. What came as a revelation now had more to do with the fact that Mathiesson was speaking these thoughts out loud. The professor's words took on the form of an incantation, transforming his inhibitions into secrets he no longer had to keep. And this induced a feeling of detachment and exhilaration. He had accepted his limitations as immutable boundaries, entrenched in his nature. Now he saw them – for the first time, it seemed – as nothing more than ideas that were holding him back.

"No, I'm not upset." He smiled broadly. "I'm grateful."

Mathiesson broke into a smile of relief mixed with surprise. "Well! Here I've been holding back these thoughts for fear of alienating you and –"

"I'm also shocked that we started talking about that rock in there and how you'd be crazy to go public with it, and that you somehow managed to make it all about me."

Mathiesson studied him briefly as if to make sure that Elliott was not actually angry; Elliott smiled again to cue him in. He shrugged and said, "In a way it *is* all about you, Paul." He sat up and pushed himself out of his chair. "Let's go back to the study. One more thing before I turn in."

Upstairs Mathiesson indicated an armchair for Elliott to sit in. He picked up the manuscript from the center of his desktop then dropped into his chair. "As I told you earlier, this," he tapped the pile of papers, "is a draft of what will be my last book. And when I say 'draft,' I mean *rough* draft. I've worked on it for the past six or seven months. Some of it's not much more than notes. Other parts are more polished. I don't have the energy to work my usual magic on it. So I've got one last favor to ask of you."

Elliott took the manuscript. Mathiesson sank back into his chair, expelling a sigh of relief or exhaustion or, most likely, both.

7

THE FLUORESCENT LIGHT FLICKERED on for the second time that night, illuminating the chunk of sandstone on the workbench and casting into dim shadow the rest of the basement. Elliott ignored his exhaustion as he bent over the table, peering again at the rock and the curious black artifact embedded in it.

Faced with one or the other piece his mind would have had no trouble processing Attenbaum's find. One was a brown lump of sedimentary rock containing remnants of conifer needles from about sixty-five-million years ago. The other was a peculiar black plaque showing raised, rudimentary geometrical symbols. This was possibly as old as a hundred thousand years, though likely very much younger. If one assumed it was actually writing, then it was likely *much* younger; accepted dates for the invention of writing by the Sumerians were in the area of 4000 BC.

By themselves, curious but not earth-shattering. Joined as they were, however, the pieces simply made no sense at all.

He studied the figures on the stone. They were clearly not natural formations. The partial triangle was perfectly cut. The hollowed-out circle was smooth and finely shaped. Taken in isolation the raised vertical line between them might just conceivably be interpreted as an accidental and random formation. But this would obviously be absurd to assume given its proximity to the other figures.

In fact, all three showed such care of design that he

caught his mind making the natural assumption that they were a kind of writing. But no, maybe merely aesthetic designs without specific meaning. Perhaps they represented inventory markings, although if this were true, why were they so finely carved? Either way, aesthetic or practical, this could push back the plaque's date as far as 45,000 years, around the end of the late Paleolithic period. Some of the most intriguing cave art dated from this period – those familiar scenes of spear-throwing hunters and bison and antelopes. Since these depictions were thought to have served magical purposes – ensuring a successful hunt – it was clear that at this stage man was already thinking symbolically.

And yet… The perfection of the carvings irritated him. In fact, they did not look carved. There were no tell-tale traces of chipped stone or other imperfections that would indicate the work of a rudimentary chisel. The characters were so smooth they looked like they were molded out of plastic. Perhaps there was a glaze over them that had smoothed out rough edges and filled in holes. Elliott ran his fingers over the figures.

For the second time that night he felt a rush of excitement. He could only explain it to himself by associating it with the thrill of discovery, the sense of first contact with a new world open for exploration. This was how he had felt as a student of Mathiesson's and, at first, on his only dig in Africa. Ironically, in the field the excitement had been less because the dig was already well underway when he arrived; he was less an explorer and more a hired hand. Now the feeling arose because of the rock his fingers ran across. The surface was indeed unnaturally smooth, although it did not feel glazed. That would have been extremely unusual in itself

– 45,000 year-old kilns. But the surface of the rock felt dry, like a piece of slate. The raised edges of the characters were finely honed.

Elliott stood up from the table, stretched his back and rubbed his eyes. He felt no closer to understanding how the two pieces of rock had come to be together. The sandstone was clearly genuine. He had seen similar fossil impressions before and the simple fact that there was nothing spectacular about them made him assume they were authentic. He examined both pieces of the outer rock again, tracing his fingers along the numerous impressions, noting the mirror-image impression Mathiesson had pointed out earlier.

He thought: *Sixty-five million years ago, end of the Cretaceous period, end of the dinosaurs by asteroid impact. Then the rise of mammals. When these fossils were formed man's closest ancestor was a diminutive tree shrew. Not likely to carve symbolic figures in rocks.*

In other words, there had to be another explanation.

But, for the sake of argument – and Elliott knew that what he meant was: for Mathiesson's sake – let's just try to see this differently. He stared at the rocks, letting his eyes glide over the rippled sandstone to where it overlapped the black rock. As he did this he told himself it was all of a piece, that the rocks belonged together. What if the knowledge he was so sure of was actually wrong? What if there was some sort of intelligence behind these carvings, and the plaque had been buried alongside the conifer impressions sixty-five million years ago?

Immediately his mind spat out the facts of the matter: nothing in existence at that time was capable of carving anything. The intelligence and tools simply did not exist. It was a world of animals.

But then, he wasn't looking for causes right now, merely trying to process the possibility that the artifact before him was genuine. He found the inner struggle ironic: part of him was willing to consider the possibility but another part of his mind would not let him do it. A computer analogy came to mind because he remembered how his old Macintosh would keep spitting out disks that it didn't like without bothering to explain itself. The only way to get the damn thing to work was to insert a disk that contained familiar instructions. And his mind was being similarly stubborn because he was trying to run a program on it that was designed to work on an entirely different operating system.

He concentrated on the piece of information that was most contrary: that there was nothing capable that long ago of creating the symbols on the plaque. His mind produced evidence to back up this assertion. He watched it rifle through mental textbooks written over years of studying archaeology, anthropology, paleoanthropology, biology, and other -ologies he had forgotten about. His mind tossed up fact after fact about the evolution of species, the development of writing and culture, and so on, until he became aware of an entire body of knowledge, a paradigm, in his mind. A discrete template, a reference book providing information and theories. And it was comfortingly consistent.

Drawing this template into clearer focus brought about a feeling of inner flexibility. It was a little like the sense of freedom and possibility that he had felt earlier in the evening when Mathiesson's analysis of his character had allowed him to objectify his perceived weaknesses. By isolating this inner paradigm, he was able to stand apart from it and ask, *What if?* And this is what he did.

He allowed the "What if?" to take form. What if the carvings are sixty-five million years old? Again he had the impression of having to dodge a barrage of facts that his mind shot out to counter the question. These he carefully sidestepped. The trick, it seemed, was not to forcefully resist his mind's attempt to control his thought process, but to treat it like a persistent child demanding candy: *That's okay, I'm busy now, but we'll get you some of that later.* There was an element of play to the exercise, as if he was engaged in a game of tag with his mind. The facts were "it," and they tried to end the game by tagging the question as too ridiculous to bother with.

It was a peculiar experience, because it made Elliott aware that he stood apart from his own mind. In a way, when it came to this inner array of knowledge his mind really was like a computer fed with information, ideas, perceptions, rules, feelings – and its job was to process everything and provide a response system for interacting with the outside world. The trouble arose when he forgot somewhere along the way that he had a measure of control over this process. He identified himself with his mind, and in doing so he was handing over control to a glorified internal database, losing sight of the fact that he was the programmer. At this point, certain opinions, ideas, theories, were transformed into unquestioned facts.

There had always been something comfortable about allowing this process to take place. Facts provided a sense of stability. Science, if not all human experience, was a schizophrenic endeavor, with a love of mystery on one hand and a quest for reassuring certainties on the other. This was exactly what Mathiesson had said during his lecture but it had not sunken in until now, until Elliott arrived at the same conclusion by himself.

He focused his attention again on the rocks. Even now as he allowed himself to consider the possibility that the carvings were sixty-five million years old, a voice in his head said, *probably not*. But that was better than a resounding no.

He yawned and leaned over, resting his elbows on the workbench. His fatigue was finally gaining the upper hand. Mental stress began to drain away and exhaustion blended with relief. His mind drifted. Mathiesson was at least *sane*, thank God. Physically sick, but mentally sharp.

He looked down at the rock. He was not convinced, but the problem at least seemed workable. He could read Bill's book and see what the old man had been up to. In fact, he would edit the book. He still felt a glow of satisfaction at having been asked to do so.

His eyes were drifting shut even as he stood over the table. He drew his index finger along the partial triangle and felt again that electrical shock of fascination, of other times and places, of distant shores and primitive oceans. In his mind's eye he saw a vast and empty sea, brilliant white beneath a raging sun. Expectancy hovered in the lifeless air; in response there arose a vision of virgin ocean floors slowly colored with slimy mats of primordial cells, then images of mushroom-like towers clogging the shores, of slowly spreading blue-green algae rippling along with the surface of the waters... Then an explosion of life: swarms of trilobites and other multi-limbed curiosities populating the oceans. Gossamer jellyfish drifting through streams of sea-grass, over pastures of varicolored sponges and algae-covered rocks, plump pink bodies contracting... an overpowering sense of life, swelling from the earth, squeezing between the cracks of matter, blending into the water, the air, the light. The vision rushed into him, a torrent of images that he quickly lost track of as they jumbled together… and suddenly ceased.

Elliott stood over the rock, no longer touching it, startled awake by the strength of his dream. He shook his head to clear it of stray images, looking at the rock reproachfully as if it were somehow responsible for the rush of pictures. His one desire now was for sleep.

Without further thought he turned off the light and felt his way through the darkened hall to his bedroom, quickly stripping down to his underclothes and climbing into bed. He pulled the covers over himself, shivering as warmth crept into him, and fell asleep dreaming of an ancient ocean.

***

His dreams raged through the night, and when he woke intermittently it was in a state of confusion. He sweat as he shivered beneath his blankets. He thought of Mathiesson upstairs, slowly dying, of Martha living on without him. Irrelevant facts from the two lectures of the day came into his head, mingling with Deveraux's tale of a lost girl and the psychic who found her. At one point he dreamed he was on the airplane again, shaking with fear as the plane shook with the storm, then watching peacefully as a group of white lights danced outside the window.

8

IN THE MORNING HE CREPT quietly upstairs. He smelled coffee brewing, and passing by the kitchen he saw Martha standing in front of the open refrigerator.

He whispered, "Good morning."

She took out a carton of milk and smiled at him. Her gray hair hung loosely over the shoulders of a pink robe. She returned his greeting in a whisper, "Good morning, Paul. Did you sleep well?"

He nodded. "I hope I didn't keep Bill up too late?"

"No, dear." She motioned to the table and they sat down. "Coffee will be ready in a few minutes. Would you like some?"

He glanced at the stove clock. "I'd better not. Alex will be here any minute."

"That's an early start to your day."

"I need to give the conference another chance." He shrugged. "Although my heart's not quite in it. It took me all of an hour after getting here to realize I was more interested in visiting old friends. Like you and Bill."

"And we were looking forward to seeing you." She leaned across the table and took his hands. "Thank you, Paul."

"For what?"

"I knew you would not disown him over that rock."

He opened his mouth to respond, but faltered. The thought struck him: *Could I disown him?*

"I will sound like a silly old woman, but I want to say it.

I knew you wouldn't let him down. Sometimes we think knowledge is everything. But there is something deeper in all of us. Without that, knowledge is" – she flipped her hand as if brushing away a fly – "worthless. Do you know, Paul, that the only person Bill was worried about was you?"

They heard the sound of a car pulling into the driveway. She released his hands and they stood up, walking to the front door together. As she hugged him she said, "You'll come again Monday before you leave?"

"Of course."

She pushed open the door. A blast of cool air rushed in and Martha pulled her robe tightly around her. Elliott kissed her cheek and stepped out into the morning.

***

"Slight change of plan." Deveraux craned his neck to back down the driveway. "Sleep well?"

Elliott tilted his seat back and shut his eyes. "Terribly. I woke up two hours ago and couldn't fall back asleep. Can we get some coffee on the way?"

"I don't see why not."

He rubbed his eyes and opened them. The pale blue sky suffered only traces of clouds. Even in October the road was lined with the deep green of pine trees, ferns, ivy. In Ohio all this would be buried under snow.

"What's the change of plan?"

"A call from my magazine to check out, of all things, a crop circle at Copper Ridge."

"What?"

Deveraux glanced at him sideways. "You heard me."

"Well isn't that rich." The dashboard clock read 8:00. "How far away is it?"

"A half hour. I'll have you at the conference by ten at the latest." Without taking his eyes from the road he reached into the backseat for his bag, which he handed to Elliott. "There's a conference program in there somewhere, in case you don't have one. You can see if you're missing anything important."

"I'd be missing something important if I let you do this alone."

"Yeah, well, I was hoping you'd see it that way."

They drove to the end of the island and headed east on I-90. The mountains towered into view, snow-capped, dark with pine trees. Elliott could have dozed off, lulled by the steady rumble of the car on the open road.

"So how's the old boy doing?"

"That depends. Physically, he doesn't look good."

"I'm sorry to hear that."

"Mentally he's still sharp." He caught Deveraux's eye and said, "Off the record?"

"Of course."

"You were right. He found something. I don't know what to make of it." He took a deep breath. Talking about the rock, even to a receptive audience like Deveraux, made him realize how absurd it sounded. He felt like he was jumping off a diving board as he said, "A sixty-five million year old rock with a plaque inside it that appears to have writing on it."

Deveraux looked to see if he was joking.

"No comment, Alex?"

Deveraux smiled, his eyes back on the road. "I'm speechless."

Elliott described the find in detail.

"What's your opinion?"

"If it was some other kind of fossil embedded inside the rock – let's say a tree shrew or lemur – I wouldn't question it for a second. It looks convincing, but…" He shrugged. "And of course I want to give Bill the benefit of the doubt."

"This is huge, Paul."

"Don't make a big deal of it yet. There's far too much work to be done before we can say anything definitive. Whatever you do, don't write anything about it."

"Don't worry. I said off the record, and I meant it."

★★★

They stopped at a gas station for coffee. Deveraux confirmed his directions and they started out again, following a winding road south through rows of trees. When they arrived at a small gravel parking lot and saw a sign reading "Copper Lake," Elliott remembered having been there before.

"I hate to say it, Alex, but I don't know of any crops around here that could have circles in them."

"I know what you mean. Maybe this'll be a short trip." He grabbed his camera bag and they climbed out of the car. "My editor had an anonymous tip on the office answering machine this morning. He gave it credence because there've been UFO sightings here in the past."

"UFOs and crop circles go together?"

Deveraux slammed the car door. "That's one theory."

They walked east along a gravel road through the edges of the forest, stepping around a metal gate that kept cars out. To their right the tree-lined mountain rose sharply towards a blue sky that grew darker as gray clouds rolled in from the west. The chill in the air made Elliott glad to have his sweater with him. When the road turned south the gravel gave way to mulch and grass. They passed an outhouse and a small dumpster. Just beyond this, on the left, was Copper Lake.

"Not enough rain this year," Deveraux said, explaining the barren look of the shrunken lake. Rotted tree trunks poked out of the pebble-strewn basin. A huge boulder, abandoned by a glacier, rested in the mud, and Deveraux made his way towards it. Elliott watched him crossing the basin. Twenty yards beyond the boulder the shallow waters rippled in the breeze. Adjacent to the massive rock, where the dry lake bottom stretched towards the parking lot, Elliott saw traces of some kind of pattern in the earth.

By the time he caught up to Deveraux the reporter had scaled the fifteen-foot high rock and was fumbling with his camera bag. Elliott scrambled to join him; the boulder was pockmarked with rough edges that made it easy to climb. When he reached the top, Deveraux said,

"Not exactly what I'd hoped for." He raised his camera and started snapping pictures.

Traced out in the sand was a huge smiley face, with two dots for eyes and an upturned line beneath them. It looked as if someone had shuffled along in the silt of the lake basin to draw the face. Tracks led from the shore to the edge of the face. The makers had tried to smooth over the footprints within the larger circle – necessary to draw the eyes and the smile – but even these faint trails were visible.

"I'm glad you didn't pay for this tip."

"Whoever did it must've made the call themselves." He lowered the camera, looking amused rather than disappointed, and gestured at the mountain behind them. "Listen, if you're not in too much of a rush, maybe we could hike a little way up and get some better pictures? I might as well let readers get a laugh out of it. And potentially get paid more."

The trail into the forest narrowed as it grew steeper, winding past moss-covered rocks and thick clumps of ferns. The breeze dropped but the air still felt cold and the gray sky threatened rain. In the stillness of the forest Elliott enjoyed listening to the thud of his shoes on the soft earth. His breathing grew labored, each exhalation forming clouds of condensed air, and the exertion had a pleasant side effect. It took him a moment to realize he had stopped thinking. Only for an instant. But in that instant he was a participant rather than a detached observer, his mind rolling over the surrounding environment like an amoeba, absorbing instead of analyzing.

They paused at a spot where the trail doubled back as it ascended. Deveraux handed Elliott a bottle of water. He had a few beads of sweat on his brow but he was clearly better prepared for the hike than Elliott. They peered through the trees towards the lake.

"Can't see much from here."

"I think the trail opens up a little further on. Do you mind if we keep going?"

"I'm enjoying myself."

But when they passed the quarter mile marker he allowed himself the vanity of thinking that the trail must be particularly steep. Sweat trickled down his forehead, beneath his clothes, sliding under his arms and pasting his shirt to his skin. Slowly each step began to remind him of his physical discomfort, of the growing ache in his legs and feet, of his inability to suck in enough air without slowing down. For the sake of his pride he refrained from asking how much further they had to walk.

Finally the trail leveled out, only dipping and rising

gently as they followed it along the side of the mountain. At the bottom of one of these gradual slopes the path grew lighter and they stepped out from under the trees onto a ridge overlooking the lake. Elliott breathed a sigh of relief and broke into a smile.

Deveraux said, "Ah, much better," and began snapping pictures. From this height the smiling face in the sand looked unspoiled. The tracks inside the circle and those leading to it from the shore were invisible.

Elliott took a long drink of water. His shirt clung to his skin and he thought of how nice it would be take a warm shower. At this exposed spot the wind carried a bitter chill through his sweaty clothes. Far to the east the last patches of blue were disappearing. A light rain began to fall. He sat down on a log bordering the trail.

"I really appreciate this, Paul," Deveraux said, putting his camera away and pulling out a handheld recorder. Just a couple quick notes to myself and I'll have you back down the mountain before the rain really gets going."

It felt good to be off his feet. Behind him, Deveraux mumbled notes to himself, his voice indistinct in the rustle of the breeze and the soft patter of rain. The mountains on the other side of the lake blurred as strands of fog formed in the air. The rainfall took on a steady, rhythmic patter on the leaves. Elliott drew in deep, regular breaths and relaxed into the pleasant heaviness of his muscles. His eyes drifted over the muddy earth and he amused himself trying to remember the names of the plants he saw: lupines, foxglove, rhododendrons. It was more difficult without their flowers.

As he watched his imagination supplied color to the scene. Hints of purple and white appeared on the tips of the surrounding green. He sensed movement around him, a rustling of foliage, and with it an image of stunted green bodies raising themselves above the forest floor. He felt a tightening in his stomach, an almost sensual squeezing, and heard a rushing noise like wind in his ears. He raised his eyes to the swirling mists hovering over the lake and watched shimmering lights dart amidst the strands, shining like flashes of metal catching incidental sunlight. But the sky was gray and the rain lightly kissed his skin. He said,

"Something's happening to me."

From a tremendous distance he heard a single click, then Deveraux's muffled voice.

"Did you say something, Paul?"

The lights shifted from play into pattern, forming geometric outlines in the air: a triangle, a circle, a labyrinthine line starting as a singularity and swirling outwards in concentric circles.

"Paul? You still with me?" Deveraux's hand fell on his shoulder.

His first attempt to respond failed. His mouth felt like it was stuffed with cotton balls. He had to concentrate to get his jaw moving. Without turning his head, he said, "Do you see them?" The lights were still visible. Fainter now, as if the effort to speak dimmed the current running between him and them.

"See what? Are you dreaming, Paul?

This was a good point. Elliott considered it with amusement as he stared at the space between the mountains. If he was asleep, it was a strange kind of sleep. He felt divided, half of him absorbing the play of lights, the other half trying to home in on his conversation with Deveraux. Each shift required the conscious flip of a switch, a kind of mental gymnastic.

"I'm seeing lights, Alex." They were growing fainter. "Drifting in and out of the mist… Don't you see them?"

A series of clicks and whirs erupted behind him. The camera.

Deveraux said, "I don't see a damn thing."

Neither, anymore, did Elliott. The individual strands of fog coalesced into a heavy cloud. The mountains opposite were a single glob of dark gray. The raindrops broke against his forehead, inducing a giddy surge of excess energy, a strangely uncomfortable pleasure. The energy burst out of him in uncontrolled laughter.

Deveraux said with irritation, "I see. No lights, just a joke at my expense."

Elliott started to reassure him, but the irony of Deveraux not believing him caused another bout of violent laughter that forced tears from his eyes. He made an effort to control the rush of manic energy, drawing in deep breaths and focusing his attention on the forest around him.

Everything was suddenly, explosively real. The once muted greens came alive as an exuberance of shades. The breeze twisted a single fern leaf, exposing a yellow underbelly with hints of olive blurring into progressively deeper green. Trees pulsed with life as if breathing. Veins of soil ran in spectrum from deep black through sandy brown, crisscrossed with clutches of gray and white granite. He grasped a clump of cool earth in his hand and rolled it between his fingers, generating an intensely sensual feeling of connection with the physical world. The pleasure rolled over him in waves, gently ebbing; it could not have lasted more than a minute.

He struggled to overcome an immense reluctance to speak, then explained to Deveraux what he had seen.

9

THEY DROVE WEST ON I-90, black clouds dumping heavy rain as they approached Seattle. Deveraux proved a patient, fascinated listener, only once commenting ruefully, "What I don't understand is why *I* never get to see anything." In Elliott's mind the experience held the peculiar quality of a particularly vivid dream, the kind that seems more real than reality upon awakening.

"When I tapped you on the shoulder, it seemed like you were in a trance. You weren't all there."

The observation struck Elliott as ironic. "In a way I felt more 'there' than usual. It's hard to describe. I was seeing everything so intensely… Especially after the lights faded." Language was failing him. What was worse, the more he thought about the experience, the more his mind muddled it. He had the sense again that some kind of internal computer was trying to make sense of something it didn't understand and in the process distorted beyond recognition the data it had received. "But it was probably just a side effect of being so tired. Half-awake, half-dreaming."

"Don't be so quick to dismiss it."

"Why not?" He gave a short laugh. "What do *you* think it was? UFOs?"

Deveraux shrugged. "If you want to talk about UFOs, I'll start off easy. No alien abductions, not even spaceships. Some might say you saw 'earth lights' – the result of friction caused by shifting layers of rock. The friction creates an electrical charge that's released – like sparks – into the atmosphere. This is earthquake country, of course, so it's possible."

"Why didn't you see anything?"

"It's possible you're more sensitive to the electromagnetic disturbances that kind of seismic upset could cause. The brain depends on electrochemical processes to function. That's why they use electroconvulsive therapy to treat depression – it's based on the notion that a jolt of electricity somehow 'reorganizes' the brain. In your case, we could string together a set of assumptions: a seismic disturbance created an electromagnetic disturbance that affected the electrochemical processes in your brain. It might have affected mine, too, but I was too dense to pay any attention to it."

"That has a satisfyingly scientific ring to it."

Deveraux smiled. "It does, doesn't it? I said I'd start easy. No point in mentioning little green men just yet."

They drove on in silence. Elliott stared out at the rain, physically relaxing in the warmth of the car. But his mind remained agitated. He pictured the lights again. Some kind of "electrical storm" in his brain? The phrase sounded uncomfortably close to a description of an epileptic seizure. He suddenly remembered the incident on the plane: slamming his head into the overhead compartment with that random burst of turbulence. And seeing lights in the sky afterwards. It was absurd that he was only remembering that now. What was the chance that he'd gotten a minor concussion? Could that account for seeing lights? Should he take up Deveraux's offer to find him a doctor?

Maybe. But think for a minute of other possibilities.

Concussion was one possibility, but were there others?

Consider it rationally.

When watching the lights he had been in a trance-like state, a kind of waking-dream, only distantly aware of his physical surroundings. Preceding this was physical strain – the hike – and mental strain: lack of sleep, his interactions with Mathiesson, the rock. The list could go on. But when he had sat down to rest on the ridge he felt a profound relaxation. The physical exertion had dampened his thoughts, quieted his body. On the plane he had seen the lights immediately following a period of intense stress, just as he dropped into a state of profound relaxation.

Quiet mind, quiet body. He had never tried meditating, but he nevertheless understood from his academic studies that something like this was one of its main goals, whether practiced by a Buddhist monk or a Christian mystic or anyone else. For some reason meditation led to altered states of consciousness. In the East it might be called enlightenment, in the West, among Christians, the rapture, the feeling of being one with God. In shamanic traditions, the discipline produced visions of other worlds.

Had he experienced an altered state of awareness on Copper Ridge?

He shook his head then glanced at Deveraux to see if he had noticed.

He had never given much thought to whether there was anything substantive – that is to say, *real* – in the various beliefs of the cultures and religions he had studied. The modern scientific mind, with its penchant for objectivity, does not give much consideration to altered states of consciousness beyond trying to cure dysfunctional ones with medication. But there was no point denying that something had happened in his own mind. Whether it was caused by an electrical storm from inside or outside of his brain, or by something else altogether, was only part of the question. The other part was: what, if anything, did it mean?

Because as he stared out at the passing scenery – jagged rocks and green forests now supplanted by business parks and malls as they approached Seattle – he recognized that his mind was telling him the experience *did* in fact mean something, and the thought unnerved him: how could a hallucination possibly mean anything? But then again, he knew enough about his own thought processes to realize that the feeling of meaning could be deceptive: the mind was always trying to impose meaning on things it did not understand. This was how people ended up seeing faces in clouds or, for that matter, on Mars. But he also knew that sometimes the brain picked out existing patterns and meanings without the conscious mind being immediately aware of them. And without being able to explain it to himself, he felt that the lights in the sky had been, of all things, some kind of *communication.*

Just how hard did you bang your head on the airplane?

He glanced at Deveraux in embarrassment, as if his thoughts had been suddenly, magically exposed, and resolved abruptly see a doctor.

10

THEY ARRIVED BACK AT THE HOTEL in time for Elliott to make a lecture on the origins of writing. His reluctance to do so yielded to guilty feelings for having missed so much of the conference already. It was Sunday; the conference ended tomorrow at noon and he could count the lectures he had attended on one hand. At the same time, he was interested in the subject matter and recognized the speaker, Leon Berringer, as the author of a book he had been required to read in graduate school.

To his surprise he found the talk engaging. For years the general assumption was that writing arose with the Sumerians in what is now Iraq. Recent finds in Egypt indicated a possible tie in the race to literacy between Egyptians and Sumerians. On the one hand this was not surprising given the frequent contact between the civilizations. On the other, the written languages that sprang from them were so different that it was difficult to see how they could have common origins. Further complicating the issue were even more recent finds in Palestine of another unique written language. Taken altogether, the evidence indicated that writing was invented independently several times, and at the same time in mankind's evolution, around four or five thousand years ago. Or – and this was considerably less likely given the time constraints – there had been a more universal language even earlier in man's history that evolved into three different but distantly related writing systems.

Berringer argued the former proposition. At a certain point in the growth of a civilization, written language becomes more or less indispensable to keep pace with increasing complexity, so it was not surprising to find it independently invented on several different occasions. Furthermore, there was no evidence of an earlier written language.

Elliott grew aware of the general air of conservatism marking Berringer's presentation. More clear than ever was a sense that certain rules were being followed. He knew enough of alternative theories to recognize that some people might argue that an earlier written language was far more likely than the three-times-over independent invention theory. But this proposition was dismissed with little fanfare, almost as if it had been brought up simply to provide a sense of contrast so that the answers wouldn't seem too easy.

All the same, there was something comforting about sitting in a lecture hall dealing with problems that had definite "yes" and "no" answers, or at least approximations of them. The underlying assumption was that even if all the puzzle pieces hadn't yet been found, when they were they would fit together comfortably. Examining the rock in Mathiesson's basement last night gave him the feeling that he was trying to join together two completely incompatible puzzle pieces. It suggested there was something fundamentally wrong with his knowledge base. If he accepted that the carvings in the rock dated from a pre-human time, he opened the door to wilder speculations: ancient astronauts, UFOs, Atlantis…

Another thought occurred to him: If Berringer considered all the fringe theories – not to mention all of the competing "legitimate" theories – with equal gravity he would never get anywhere. By limiting the field of inquiry he enabled a satisfying sense of comprehension. Setting parameters gave the impression that the seemingly infinite mysteries of the world were solvable. This, Elliott realized, was why people were so defensive about the boundaries of so-called legitimate inquiry. It was another expression of the "Pandora's box" metaphor. Too many quandaries thrown at the mind overwhelm it. If you dealt with the problems one or two at a time, the whole affair became much more manageable. This was not a methodology limited to scientists. It applied to all human beings. What is more, there was something fundamentally sound in it. It amounted to an acceptance of limitations – a focusing of the mind – that led almost paradoxically to an expansion of knowledge. The trick, as Bill pointed out, was not to confuse arbitrary parameters with objective facts.

Elliott smiled to himself, thinking: *How many times can these same ideas keep occurring to me until I catch on?*

The lights dimmed. As slides depicting fragments of cuneiform tablets flashed across the screen at the front of the room his mind drifted back to the events of Copper Ridge. The lights seemed unaccountably distant and dreamlike, and it was easy enough now to recognize them for what they were: waking dreams brought about by sleep deprivation and stress. Flashes of light in the gray mist. They could have been nothing more than those things – what were they called? – "floaters," except that his state of mind somehow enhanced his perception of them. In light of these thoughts, there was nothing particularly wrong with the theory that Deveraux had advanced, but it seemed unnecessary. Even the idea that Elliott had suffered a concussion on the airplane struck him now as unlikely at best. It had arisen in a moment of panic, but now that this had passed, he regarded it with detachment.

Berringer wrapped up and took questions. For the next twenty minutes Elliott lost himself in the ensuing discussion until a familiar female voice caught his attention and he turned in his seat to see Elizabeth Ashmore two rows back. She finished a technical question about Egyptian hieroglyphs, then noticed Elliott and smiled. When the session was over, Elliott followed the crowd to the door and found her waiting for him.

"How's your friend?"

"Bill?"

"Alex told me you two were close."

"He's not well. But you could probably see that yesterday."

"How do you know him?"

They entered the lobby together, still talking. As they stepped outside into the rain she looked at her watch.

"Do you want to join Tony and me for lunch?" He was about to decline but she said, "I think Alex will be there."

"Really?"

"He and Tony are bonding."

"Alex wants an interview with your famous husband."

She laughed. "Tony's already agreed to it."

He had forgotten an umbrella. Elizabeth offered hers and since he was taller he held it for both of them as they walked up the street to a deli. They squeezed past the line at the register and scanned the room. Elizabeth said, "There they are!" Neither her husband nor Deveraux had noticed them come in but at the sound of Elizabeth's voice they looked up.

At the table Deveraux said, "Glad to see you two found each other."

Tony clasped his hand. "I'm sorry to hear about your friend."

Deveraux looked embarrassed. "I'm sorry, Paul. It just came up in conversation."

"I'm sure Bill was the subject of many conversations yesterday."

"I'll order the sandwiches. What'll you all have?"

Alone with the Ashmores Elliott felt self-conscious. He said, "I'm honored to be sharing the table with a bestselling author."

The comment sounded banal the second it passed his lips but Ashmore smiled. "And I with a promising young scientist. Beth mentioned you were writing a book of your own?"

"Not a page-turner, that's for sure!"

"That depends on who's reading it. If people like you didn't write books, I'd have a hard time researching my novels."

"What are you working on now?"

Ashmore grimaced. "Ugh… I'm superstitious. I can't talk about a work in progress. But it's another in the *Sands of Time* series."

"Beth said they were about alternative history?"

"That's right. Not the kind that asks questions like, 'what if the Germans won World War II?' – although I've written one of those. More like historical fiction, only the history part's looser, more imaginative. I've always loved history – I majored in it in college. When I read about a period in time that needs some blanks filled in – you know, like why the Maya vanished – I step in and provide answers."

"Bestselling ones."

Ashmore rapped the wooden table twice with his

knuckles. "So far, so good."

Elizabeth said, "Tony's work gives me a good excuse to let my mind wander. What your friend Bill said in his lecture yesterday didn't sound unreasonable to me. I've been conditioned by reading the books Tony brings home."

"I'm happy to hear you say that. I'm ashamed to admit I was one of the many groaning in disbelief yesterday. It was an emotional reaction, not an intellectual one."

"That's exactly what you've got to overcome if you want to read some of the popular books on the pyramids, or theories about advanced civilizations like Atlantis. They're terribly speculative, sometimes, and they certainly don't read like textbooks."

Tony said, "More like thrillers."

Elizabeth nodded. "But it's not all raving. Bill's point about having prematurely made up our minds about all the mysteries of the past is well-made."

Elliott smiled. "But you don't feel like launching your own investigation?"

"I'll leave that to Tony."

On an impulse Elliott pulled a pen from his jacket pocket and sketched Mathiesson's artifact on a napkin, concentrating on reproducing the figures and not attempting to draw the chunk of sandstone. He turned the drawing to Elizabeth and asked, "Have you ever seen anything like this before?"

As she studied it, Deveraux reappeared. He looked at the napkin and opened his mouth to speak then glanced at Elliott, who motioned him to silence.

Elizabeth said, "I'd have to know more about the context. I mean, I've seen simple etchings like this, but…"

"Of course. It was just a long shot."

"Does it have something to do with Bill?"

He hesitated. "Can you keep it confidential?"

Both Ashmores said: "Of course."

He gave in to an instinctive trust. "Bill's found something rather strange."

He described the rock. Elizabeth pushed back in her seat and let out a short whistle. Other than that it was difficult to read her expression. "Sixty-five million years? That seems more up Tony's alley."

Elliott felt his face redden. He forced a smile. "I know." He was certain she was not convinced and he felt ridiculous for bringing it up. Guilt by association. "It does seem like something out of a science-fiction novel. I'm sure there's probably some reasonable explanation for it that Bill's overlooked."

"Perhaps if I could see it sometime? It might ring a bell."

This was her way of letting him off the hook. He agreed and changed the subject back to her husband's books. A few minutes later the sandwiches arrived. At the end of the meal Tony insisted on paying the bill. He took it to the register while Elizabeth excused herself to the restroom.

Deveraux said, "When do you have to be at your next lecture?"

Elliott looked at his watch. "An hour and a half."

"I'm taking Tony to a New Age bookstore. Want to join us?" He nodded at the napkin. "I'm sure you'll feel right at home."

11

ELLIOTT TOOK THE BACKSEAT, glad to indulge in nostalgia as they drove along familiar streets. He was filled with a sense of belonging that made it clear to him that he did yet feel at home in Ohio. He had a small house there, a promising job, a few budding friendships, but now, back in Seattle, it felt like a dormant part of him had come to life again.

"It's just up here." Deveraux turned left into a large parking lot. "Always hard to park."

"That's something I don't have a problem with anymore." Elliott sat up to join the conversation. The area had changed. Something that looked like a mall occupied several lots that had once been individual stores. "Why not park in that supermarket lot?"

"Just look really intent on buying groceries, then. I don't want another ticket."

They walked up a busy street beneath a gray sky. Inside the bookstore incense and subdued synthesizer music filled the air. The walls and carpets were beige, the ceiling pale blue. Elliott whispered to Deveraux, "This is my first time in one of these places."

"Well for God's sake don't let them know that. They'll eat you alive."

Ashmore said, "Where's the 'lost continents' section?"

"I'll show you the way. Paul, don't break anything."

They disappeared into the stacks. Elliott found the atmosphere relaxing. He followed the sound of trickling water to a small indoor fountain set up to look like a babbling brook. Water bubbled up from the center and cascaded down over smooth rocks into a ceramic basin. Beyond this he came upon a section of books about divination. As he glanced at the titles a female voice behind him said,

"My knight in shining armor!"

He turned out of curiosity, not imagining the remark was directed at him, and was shocked to see the woman from the airplane – Rachel. She hugged him warmly and this surprised him even more.

She stood back, smiling. "How's your head? Have you recovered?"

The incident on the plane came back to him and he tapped the back of his head lightly. Still a bruise. "I certainly have. And you?"

"I feel like I've got a new lease on life."

"Settling back in?"

"As if I never left."

His stomach contracted and he felt a flush of nervousness as he tried to decide what to say next to extend the moment. He opened his mouth without knowing what would come out, but she saved him the trouble.

"It's time I took a break. Care to join me?"

He couldn't believe his luck.

★★★

Cold rain drizzled down. They crossed the street and walked a half-block to a café. The whoosh of traffic on the wet pavement made it difficult to hear each other, so when he closed the café door behind them the relative quiet and warmth produced an instant feeling of relief.

She said, "What will you have? I'm buying."

"I can't let you do that!"

"I owe you for being so nice to me on the plane. I was terrified. I never knew I had a fear of flying until I thought we might crash."

"I was scared, too. I was lucky you were there."

They sat down beside a steam-covered window. "How's the conference?" She tapped his hand lightly and he wondered abruptly why fate had suddenly decided to shine on him. The thought made him intercept the nondescript answer he was about to give – "It's fine" – which was compelled by a familiar desire to move forward cautiously and not embarrass himself. But it suddenly seemed a travesty to be anything but open.

"Let's see: miserable, shocking, dull, fascinating…"

"I wouldn't have guessed it could be so dramatic!"

"Neither would I. Do you remember I told you about an old mentor of mine?" He recounted Mathiesson's lecture and its reception, surprised at how easily he opened up to her. "Everything else seems a little less interesting by contrast. Not to mention, being back in Seattle makes me realize how much I miss it."

"At least the conference got you out here."

"That's true. I'm grateful. So how about you? Have you readjusted or are you still dreaming of Europe?"

He enjoyed watching her talk. She had a touch of the dramatic to her. If she closed her eyes she did so for a split second longer than normal. She smiled without reservation, eyes widening to let out a glimpse of delight in some hidden surprise. He appreciated her habit of touching his hand for emphasis. And he was impressed with her spirit of adventure.

"Paris, Berlin, Prague, Greece – I hit up all the contacts I made in school and the rest of the time I found hostels or camped. I took a bunch of pictures, too, and kept a detailed journal thinking I could maybe make a book out of them."

"It's a shame I can't see them. Your pictures."

A look of uncertainty flickered over her face. It was the first time he had seen her hesitate. "Well, maybe you can. Do you want to have lunch tomorrow?"

He concluded with surprise that she was asking him out for a second date. "That would be great."

"Maybe around noon?"

He did not have a cell phone so he gave her Deveraux's number. Before they stood to go he gave in to an impulse.

"Can I ask you something strange?"

"Of course."

"Did you see anything odd outside the window of the airplane? Just after the turbulence ended?"

"No. I barely even remember looking out the window." She narrowed her eyes. "Why? What did you see?"

"Lights. Sort of darting around in the clouds."

Her cool fingers encircled his hand and squeezed it. "Gremlins on the wing?" Her expression turned mischievous. "Maybe you're psychic."

"How do you get that?"

"Well, first of all, do you believe in UFOs?"

He thought about this as reasonably as he could while distracted by the pressure of her hand in his.

He said, "I'm open to the possibility."

"Psychic people see more UFOs."

"I never knew that. But I guess that's not surprising. I mean, that I didn't know that."

"It has to do with something called the 'paraphysical hypothesis.'"

"What's that?"

She shook her head and released his hand. "I'll leave that

hanging in the air so you have another reason to have lunch with me tomorrow."

"I assure you I don't need another reason."

Outside the roar of the traffic precluded conversation. The drizzle had turned into a downpour. By the time they reached the bookstore they were soaked through, and both were laughing.

12

"YOU REALLY LIKE HER, DON'T YOU PAUL?"

"Leave him alone, Alex. Let's talk about the books I bought."

"Thank you, Tony. But it'll take more than mere ideas to distract Alex from women."

"Everything in its proper place." Deveraux ground the gears in his car and they missed their opportunity to pull out into the traffic.

Elliott said, "Concentrate on your driving, Alex."

"It'd be more helpful to concentrate on getting a new clutch."

Rain spattered heavily against the windshield. He was glad Deveraux was behind the wheel. This was the kind of day Elliott hated driving in: wet, traffic-filled streets and sullen sky. Deveraux said, "What did you two talk about?"

Elliott smiled. "Would you believe UFOs?"

"Hah!" To Ashmore he said, "I could give Paul all the evidence in the world for the paranormal but it would never compete with the power of a pretty face."

Five minutes later they pulled up to the front of the hotel.

Deveraux said, "Well, gentlemen, it's been a pleasure. I'm going to stop by my house and freshen up." He twisted around to face the backseat. "What's your plan, Paul?"

"The next talk is an hour long. After that I'm free."

"I'm doing an interview in an hour. Then I'll write and be done by six. Tony?"

"Time for a nap. I'll fall asleep reading one of these." He

tapped the plastic bag containing his new books.

Elliott and Ashmore parted ways in the crowded lobby. As they shook hands Elliott realized he had already grown fond of him. A glance down an adjacent hallway told him the conference rooms were filling up. Now more than ever he felt disconnected from all the activity. But the guilt that had compelled him to attend Berringer's lecture on writing this morning now prodded him in the direction of a discussion on – what was it? – stone-age religions.

The smell of coffee drew him to the bar. He stopped to order a cup but changed his mind and ordered herbal tea. More caffeine would only make him jittery and exhausted. He dropped into a plush chair near the bar and set his mug on the table, waiting for the tea to brew. *Erratic sleep, alcohol, caffeine, and a three-hour time difference. No wonder I just want to fall asleep right here.*

The soft lights and cloying warmth compounded his drowsiness even though he felt uncomfortable in his damp clothes. The sounds from the lobby were muted. The bar felt one step removed from all the bustle. But he resisted the temptation to close his eyes. He had just enough time to drink his tea then shower and change before the lecture.

To keep himself awake he concentrated on the people passing through the hallway by the bar, the one leading to the lobby. He recalled sitting here with Deveraux on Friday, only two days ago. Time seemed to have stretched to accommodate an inordinate range of experiences. Friday seemed far away. His entire life in Ohio seemed more memory than actuality.

So nice to talk with Rachel.

With their conversation in the café over and a second date lined up he felt like he had passed an exam. He smiled, conjuring an absurdly romantic vision of her wandering across Europe through ancient cities, over green fields in fading sunlight. His mind's eye drifted over the contours of her face, the curves of her body, before he recalled her question:

"Do you believe in UFOs?"

An image of the lights on Copper Ridge came to him. Resting now, eyes half-closed, the memory came into sharper focus. Gray, swirling mist and tiny lights like fireflies forming patterns in the void between mountains. The feeling he was witnessing something ordered.

No, not "ordered." That word implied that the patterns sketched by the lights were created arbitrarily, blindly, by some natural law, like crystals or snowflakes. The lights, on the other hand, gave the impression of intent, and accordingly the feeling that there was some kind of mind behind them. The difference between searching a database for information and asking a real person. He still held his earlier impression: the lights had been some kind of communication.

But communication with what? His thoughts ran up against a brick wall. In the back of his mind he sensed the line of absurdity running parallel to these thoughts: hadn't he decided only a few hours ago that the lights were merely a side effect of exhaustion? Why was he now reflecting on them as if they were an external phenomenon?

Did he believe in UFOs? On Friday he would certainly have said "no." This was one of the reasons Friday now seemed a world away. His new answer, "I'm open to the possibility," was punctuated by the thought: *Why the hell shouldn't I be? For all I know I saw some this morning.*

Is this how it all starts? Will I follow Bill off the deep end?

Lifting the lid of Pandora's box...

The thought of Mathiesson generated a tension in his gut that could not maintain itself. He felt too tired and too physically comfortable, and the feelings of affection that followed relaxed the tautness. He could work this out. Sooner or later it would all make sense: Mathiesson's change of heart, the artifact in his basement.

Recollections of Bill drifted through his mind. With a flush of embarrassment he recalled their first meeting: his awkwardness, eagerness to please, idealism... And yes, of course, romanticism. He had never considered that trait of his objectively, but Bill was right. Something in his temperament was fundamentally romantic, drawn first and foremost to the quest for knowledge that science represented. He preferred poetry to technique in his own vision of science. No doubt this could harm his career. But it was balanced by his caution, which compelled him to practice science the way it was supposed to be practiced: methodically, carefully – one step at a time.

Bill's books, with their dramatic tales of early discoveries, their skillful recreations of prehistory, had fed his romanticism, his yearning for understanding. They took a morass of chaotic data and transformed it into a grandiose vision. In their own way, they were thrillers as much as Ashmore's were supposed to be. And when he first met Bill he had seen – whether he had imagined it or not – that gleam of the intellectual adventurer in his eyes, in his bearing. He could not help but be drawn into it.

Then he was welcomed into the family. He met Martha. Frequent dinners at their house. Saw Bill as departmental politician, devoted husband, well-intentioned but occasionally irritable human being. That was a trick of Bill's, something Elliott saw had worked a kind of magic. *Bill, becoming by degree more human before my eyes. I realized I could succeed, I could do it, too. Bill wasn't perfect, so I didn't have to be either.* This was a more subtle debt he owed Mathiesson.

But he saw that he had played his own roles, too: disciple, colleague, son. They had been made for each other, coming together at a time when each could help the other most.

Memories coalesced, fragmented, took on new forms. He realized he was falling asleep. Even the discomfort of his wet clothes faded, supplanted by a dreamlike swell of impressions of Bill. He rode them, gentle waves, swept along, eyes half closed… until he felt himself in a spaceless, depthless abyss where he perceived the very presence of Mathiesson.

His eyes snapped open as the professor hobbled past in the corridor to the lobby.

"Bill!"

Elliott jumped up just as Mathiesson disappeared. He crossed the bar to the hallway. A sudden chill rifled through him. There was Bill, ten feet away, heading towards the elevators, hoisting his body as if each step required immense effort. He did not look well enough to be out of bed.

"Bill! What are you doing here?" Mathiesson did not respond. Hadn't he heard his name? A panicked thought occurred: *Was he delirious?* Elliott's ears buzzed with a sound like rushing water. Sweat trickled beneath his shirt even as another chill shivered through him. If he could just make eye-contact he could reason with Bill, get him to lie down while he called Martha.

But it was taking too long to catch up with him. No matter how fast Elliott moved he could not catch up.

Mathiesson reached the lobby elevator before him. The doors slid open and he stepped inside.

When Mathiesson turned around, Elliott barely recognized him. The face looked drawn and ancient, pale skin stretched tight over cavernous cheeks. The eyes were strangely indistinct, unfocused, unseeing. It was like staring at a fading ghost.

The elevator doors began to close. Elliott drove himself forward, feeling as if he were wading through waist-deep water. He called again, voice faltering, Mathiesson's skull staring emptily into space. A sudden, terrifying feeling of groundlessness rose up in him.

That's not Bill.

Then a strange sense of disconnection, mind slipping free of its leash, rising like a balloon into some unknown ether.

What is it?

He felt his "I" slipping away while something inside him scrambled to get hold of it, like a child grasping for the balloon string as it slips through his fingers.

Until, abruptly, like a dummy coming to life, Bill's eyes squeezed shut, upper lip curling into a snarl, teeth bared in pain. When his eyes snapped open again they immediately locked onto Elliott's, registering surprise and recognition. Elliott looked into Bill's eyes, and Bill looked into his.

The chime of the elevator sounded once, twice.

Bill's gaze flickered and broke away.

Elliott opened his eyes. His tea rested on the table by his chair. The hallway was empty. He shook his head to rid it of sleep and picked up his tea. Lukewarm. He would have been less surprised to find himself standing by the elevator.

He entered the lobby just as the elevator doors slid open. A group of people filed out. One was Sally Kessler, the archaeologist he had met Friday night. He was relieved when she simply smiled at him and continued with her group. The lobby bustled, filled with the sounds of disconnected voices from passing conversations, laughter, the shuffling of papers, the squeaking wheels of luggage carts.

When a voice behind him said, "Excuse me," he realized he was standing in the way, forcing people to walk around him.

He took the stairs. As he inserted his key card into the lock the telephone in his room began to ring. He was not surprised to hear Martha, her voice strained with sorrow. He knew what she was going to say, but he waited for her to speak.

13

THIS IS A STRANGE BOOK, one I never dreamed I would write. It comes at the end of a lifetime of exploration—but what I have learned in these past few years, and what I will try to convey in the following pages, has shown me that I have been an explorer who has missed his mark. I have been searching the dirt for trinkets when all along, a mere hundred yards away, the ruins of a lost city lie sprawled beneath the undergrowth.

I do not want to give the impression that my work has been wasted. But I have been misguided in my thinking. I have closed or kept closed doors that could lead to greater understanding of the world around us. I have molded man, history, and nature to fit my personal conceptions, so that when I wrote, spoke and even thought about them, I conveyed at best half-truths and incomplete pictures. At times, though unconsciously, I simply lied. I think this sort of misrepresentation of the universe is commonplace in science. As scientists, we excuse the practice as necessary to create "working hypotheses," or to distill complex information for the layperson, a sort of "artistic license" in the scientific world. The central thrust of the license we take is to present uncertainties as certainties, theories as facts.

The problem is that once successive generations are educated on so-called scientific certainties it can prove difficult to re-educate them in the concept of uncertainty.

Descartes began thinking with the proposition: Question everything. We begin thinking with certain absolutely fundamental assumptions about the universe already made. We accept the reality of matter, the existence of time and space, the fact of Darwinian evolution – all, for the most part, unquestioningly. From this allegedly stable foundation we practice our particular brand of science. And the results of our findings are published, popularized, and generally accepted into the mass consciousness of modern society. But we rarely, if ever, acknowledge those initial assumptions, either to the public or to ourselves.

As a result, at first glance all our assumptions seem perfectly reasonable. How could they not? We've grown up trained through education and experience to comprehend the world in a specific way. It strikes most of us as unnatural to consider the notion that time, perhaps, does not exist, or that solid matter is actually full of empty space. After all, these concepts serve us perfectly well in the world. We schedule our days by our watches, and we don't worry about falling through sidewalks on the way to work.

And yet something's missing. Consider the paradox of Apollo and the tortoise. Picture that the pantheon of gods, annoyed at the sun god's excessive pride, contrive to have some fun with him. They badger Apollo about how long it takes him to rise in the morning and set at night. Certainly he could move just a little faster? But no, he could not even win a race against a tortoise. Incensed, Apollo takes the bait and challenges the tortoise, even generously allowing him a head start.

But when he sets out to run, the sun god finds himself in a predicament. The distance between the animal and himself is trivial; let's say he can still see it crawling slowly past a grove of willows less than fifty meters away. We can draw an imaginary line between his position and the tortoise's. But here is where the problem comes in. Take that line and divide it in half. In order to reach the tortoise, Apollo must first cross the distance between his starting position, then reach the midway point, and finally engage the tortoise in a neck-and-neck race. But suppose we take the distance between the midway point and halve it again, and then again and again until... Well, there is no "until," because we all know we can divide a line infinitely into smaller and smaller sections. Following this logic, we can see that the distance between Apollo and the tortoise is infinite. There is simply no way that Apollo, even as the sun god, can cross this infinite distance.

We could say that the trick the other gods have played is allowing the mathematical concept of space to replace the perceptual, or experiential one. That is, in our experience we seem to move from one point to the next without difficulty. But the fact of the matter is, our intellectual understanding of a line is any distance between two points that can be infinitely divided. You might be inclined to say: then our understanding is wrong, and I would in turn be inclined to agree with you. But my point is that we don't understand how the fundamental process of crossing from one point to another takes place, irrespective of the fact that we seem to be crossing distances all the time. The same is true of time: if you take a moment of time, such as a second, you can divide this infinitely as well. First a half-second, then a quarter second, then an eighth, a sixteenth, and so on. By this reckoning, time should never pass. And yet it certainly appears to do so.

I elaborated this mystery to a colleague of mine and his response was to call it a philosophical problem, not a scientific one. This was his way of saying the paradox was *abstract and irrelevant. But the fact of the matter is that we exist in the space-time continuum. Experientially, we know nothing else. But the paradox of Apollo and the tortoise exposes a fundamental flaw in our perception. It seems to indicate that time and space are illusions. At the very least, upon close inspection they become utterly mysterious.*

I raise these points to demonstrate that while the assumptions we make can be useful, they are not necessarily true. Furthermore, it is particularly difficult to unlearn them, or to set them aside long enough to see what the universe looks like without them.

What is worse, we have grown so accustomed to our assumptions that we feel personally threatened when we question them. I believe that this is what happens to many scientists, myself included, when some of the more fundamental notions we hold about the mechanics of the universe come under scrutiny. This is certainly the case with the current neo-Darwinian theory of evolution. But it also appears, for example, that the case in favor of paranormal phenomenon is nowhere near as weak as modern science understands it and presents it to the public.

The fear, I think, is one of uncertainty. Humans have a tendency to seek stability. We breathe more easily when safe within our personal belief systems. I am reminded of a study done with infants, the results of which indicated that babies were pleasantly surprised by unexpected incidents only if they had had previous experience of such incidents. If nothing else, this example can be used as an analogy for how most human beings process experience. There is an inner template, a structure of belief, to which thoughts and experiences are compared. The initial reaction to an experience that does not fit into this template is a degree of unease, if not outright rejection.

This is the stage modern science is in. And our current template is commonly referred to as the materialistic paradigm, the collection of theories ranging from molecular biology to astrophysics, of which the primary assumption is that we exist in an entirely physical universe, that all processes, including mental ones, have physical causes. I have operated under this assumption for sixty years, and yet it now strikes me not only as bold, but foolhardy. As Thomas Kuhn demonstrated in The Structure of Scientific Revolutions, *paradigms come and paradigms go, but not without tremendous resistance. Before a "paradigm shift" can transpire, a significant number of observations running counter to the reigning belief system must be logged and noted.*

This process ushered out religion and replaced it with science in Western civilization around the middle of the nineteenth century. What happened was that, over time, observations of the natural world (as well as other factors, including the rise of capitalism) pointed out the dominance of material processes in the world and the apparent irrelevance of religious beliefs. More specifically, the geologist Charles Lyell demonstrated the tremendous age of the earth, and Darwin and Wallace the apparent likelihood that life was nothing more than an extension of material processes. Both of these "facts" ran counter to the Bible. Other observations seemed to justify similar conclusions. And ultimately the bubble burst, producing shock waves so great they still resonate today.

I am not suggesting a return to the dogmatic religion of past ages. In fact, I am not suggesting any specific course of action at all beyond an examination of what we know, or presume to know, about the universe. And, perhaps more importantly, to ask ourselves why we need to believe one thing versus another. Is scientific "truth" always and exclusively based on empirical observation and rational theory, or does what we want to believe play a greater part in how we perceive the universe than we're used to thinking?

My goal with this book is to provoke the critical examination of certain current "orthodoxies," particularly in the areas of paleoanthropology and archaeology, and to question the real reasons why many aberrant data haven't "made the cut."

I have spent my lifetime in the scientific field, and I have been honored to be a part of one of humanity's greatest endeavors. But as I approach the end of my life, I find it ironic that the only thing I can say with absolute certainty is that if the universe is an open book, we have only just cracked its cover. I wish I had a few more lifetimes to keep reading.

***

Alone in the quiet of the house it was difficult to believe Bill was dead. Elliott lay on the bed, staring at the ceiling. He thought of Martha upstairs and hoped she was not having the same trouble sleeping that he was. He turned onto his side, and in the faint light glimpsed the white pages of Mathiesson's manuscript on the nightstand. Reading the beginning pages made it seem for a moment that Bill was still alive.

Hours spent reminiscing with Martha gave him a hint of the bond she and Bill shared, and it was difficult to imagine exactly what she was feeling now. He felt an inadequate comfort for her. He was relieved to know that her sister would be in town the next day.

The thoughts tempered his own sense of loss. Beneath the confusion and shock he felt the loss like a real thing, a heavy, unmoving lump inside his gut. Somehow the unshakeable tightness there expressed the finality of Bill's death.

His mind drifted back to the dream in the hotel. Was that a premonition?

Yes. What exactly was it called? A death-bed vision.

That kind of thing was common in folklore, even in otherwise mundane historical narratives. A vision of a relative or loved-one at the moment of death. What surprised him now was the air of common sense that accompanied his thoughts, apart from his analysis of the event. He was not arriving at a conclusion by careful consideration, but was instead experiencing a certainty that expressed itself as such: *Of course that was Bill.* No further analysis necessary.

But at the same time, in the back of his mind, he was aware the sense of certainty would dissipate, and in no time he would be wondering just what had happened in the hotel. In fact, he could anticipate the arguments: Bill was on his mind, he was exhausted. It wasn't even a waking dream like the lights – the timing was mere coincidence. Such was the way of the intellect. Paradoxical, that it should destroy the sense of certainty he felt. For now, anyway, he knew.

Intellect – thinking, analysis, reasoning – could not touch the emotion he had experienced that evening, nor explain the profundity of Mathiesson's death, nor the heavy calm seeping into him as he stared at the ceiling, wide awake at three in the morning. But like any tool it had its uses. It took him a greater distance than he felt he could go without it. And even now, intellect rendered speechless as he stood on the edge of a precipice overlooking a vast, unknown ocean and a distant, unfamiliar shore, he still recognized its importance.

He could, after all, use it to build a boat.

14

ROBERT KNIGHT MODIFIED THE conference schedule the next morning to include a half-hour honoring Mathiesson. Elliott received an invitation to speak thanks to Martha, who had asked him to convey the news to Knight. Now he sat with a subdued crowd in a hotel conference room, listening to Knight's recollections about Bill and wondering what to say. There was something disconcerting in talking about Bill's death so soon after he had just seen him.

Knight kept his comments formal, collegial, respectful. Elliott listened expectantly, waiting for Knight to broach the subject of Bill's last talk, but nothing was said. A rather glaring omission, but to be expected. The main subject on the mind of everyone in the audience was demurely avoided.

He made his way to the podium during the soft applause for Knight, still formulating what to say. Knight shook his hand and whispered in his ear, "Try keeping it to ten minutes. I found another colleague of Bill's to go after you."

He began with the obvious, talking briefly about his idolization of Mathiesson and the welcome he had received as a student. The words came easily. Then, after a pause, he heard himself saying, "If the universe is an open book, we have only just cracked the cover," and felt a warmth rising in him. "That's something Bill wrote in his last book. It gets to the heart of the million-dollar question for anyone who saw his lecture on Saturday: What was he thinking?

"I suppose it would be easy to call that last lecture an aberration, to blame it on Bill being sick. And we have to ask:

wouldn't it be compassionate to see things this way, to leave his legacy untarnished?" He looked out at the audience feeling strangely disconnected. His thoughts concerned Bill. He could not decide what to make of Bill's final lecture, of his manuscript, of the artifact in his basement. But one thing seemed clear. "My answer to that question is 'no.'"

No reaction – although the heavy silence in the room was a kind of response. "I talked with Bill after his lecture. I've read some of his most recent manuscript. It's clear that Saturday's talk was no aberration. It was a continuation, another chapter to add to his tremendous body of work. He had simply reached the conclusion that he'd made some wrong turns and, typical for Bill, he was trying to find the right path again. We resisted because we didn't like the direction he was taking. But really, he wasn't telling us to abandon our training, to jettison critical thinking. Quite the opposite. He was suggesting we use all our smarts to look into questions that possess an aura of the forbidden, at least for scientists.

"It's a simple mandate, really, one that we supposedly adopted when we took the job. Question everything. Including our own preconceptions. Bill pointed out that we're part of the equation when it comes to deciding what's 'scientific' and what's not. The scientific method is our golden rule, but it's only a tool. The method doesn't define what subjects constitute legitimate scientific inquiry. That's up to us, and as Bill pointed out our answers are bound to be subjective.

"Understand that I'm speaking for Bill, here. I'm still sifting through these thoughts myself and, if you could allow me the presumption, I suggest you do the same. For Bill, at the very least, as a small 'thank you' for all he gave us during his lifetime. I know it would make him very happy."

To his mind, the ensuing applause carried a hint of relief.

★★★

As people filed out of the room he caught Deveraux's eye and waved. The reporter was about to interview someone. Elliott wished they could have left together. He felt at loose ends and was wondering how he would manage to sit through another lecture when he felt a firm slap on the shoulder and turned to face Robert Knight.

The professor gripped his hand. "Thanks for doing that, Paul." His small face wore a look of studied seriousness.

"I'm glad I could, Dr. Knight."

"Bob, please. I'll miss Bill very much." He looked at his watch and said, "Join me for a late breakfast? I'll pass off my commitments and we can reminisce. I'd like to hear more about Bill's last few days."

"Of course."

Outside it was gray and distinctly cold, the first true taste of October weather. Knight wore a tan overcoat and Elliott found himself wishing he had on something heavier than his blue sport coat. The sky threatened rain.

"I hear good things about the college you're at in Ohio."

"That's good to know. I didn't know much about it 'til I interviewed there."

"I know Nichelle Davies from way back. She was one of my earliest graduate students."

Elliott said with surprise, "She's the chair of my tenure committee!" But now that Knight had mentioned it he remembered her dropping his name.

"I figured you might know her. I'm happy she's done well for herself. She was always very bright."

Elliott held his tongue. After initially being impressed with her he had come to find her personality grating, always a little too eager to impress others with the depth and breadth of her knowledge. But Knight was correct: she was clearly very intelligent and accomplished. "It's a small world."

Knight nodded. "I didn't know you and Bill were so close. You must have been quite a promising student."

"I charmed him with my adulation. I was a pretty fervent admirer when I first met him."

Knight smiled. "Undergraduates are an impressionable bunch."

"He was the first author I'd met. His popular books made a huge impression on me – basically inspired me to go into science. That first meeting had a magical quality to it."

Knight laughed good-naturedly. They came to a crosswalk at a busy street, and both scanned the road until it was safe to cross. The first drops of rain spattered the pavement and the breeze picked up.

O'Doul's was an Irish pub that apparently served breakfast. Elliott had never been there. It sat on a corner next to a florist and the scent of fresh-cut flowers mixed incongruously with cigarette smoke from passersby. They took a booth away from the entrance, beneath a framed photograph of rolling green countryside. As they opened their menus Knight said, "The food is usually very good." A waiter brought coffee and they ordered sandwiches.

To overcome a feeling of awkwardness, Elliott spoke first. "Did you have any idea how sick Bill was?"

Knight shook his head. "Well, not from him. I hadn't seen him much this past year, but every time I did I couldn't help but notice. He looked weaker every time. But he was never one to talk about that sort of thing. And you've probably seen that his intellectual excitement could charm you into thinking he was fine."

"Wishful thinking, I guess."

"That's right. No one wants to think a good friend is dying. Besides, you get as old as Bill and I are and part of you expects this or that health problem will get you at one point, but you just can't bother much about it." Knight sat back, clasped his hands over his belly, and continued, "But of course it was obvious on Saturday. In a way that was a classic 'Bill' moment." He chuckled. "One day they'll prove it in a lab that a man can keep himself alive by force of will. Bill would have been the perfect test subject. I remember him telling me last year that the doctors gave him three months, tops." Knight leaned closer. "But clearly something sustained him all that time, something gave him the will to eke out as much life as he could for himself."

With sudden clarity Elliott realized Knight was on a fishing expedition. An image of the plaque popped into his mind and he tried buying himself a moment to think by saying simply, "I agree."

Knight nodded, but it was clear that the response would not suffice.

"But if you're hoping I can tell you what it was, I don't know." The lie came naturally, but Elliott was surprised with himself.

Knight's jaw dropped almost imperceptibly and he gave Elliott a curt nod as he sat back in his seat. Was it a gesture of disappointment or disbelief?

"Well, actually, he did leave behind an unfinished manuscript, which he asked me to edit and publish for him. I haven't had much time to look it over, but I think the gist of it was covered by what I talked about this morning."

Knight reached for his coffee. The waiter appeared and set their food in front of them. They were both silent as they began eating. Elliott had trouble concentrating on the meal. The awkwardness had suddenly become tangible. Knight's manner gave him the impression that he had failed an exam and was now dismissed.

Why had he lied? Fear of embarrassment? He still blushed thinking about what had happened when he sketched the artifact for Elizabeth Ashmore. Knight was one of the big names in paleoanthropology and it would be imprudent to appear foolish in front of him. But there was something else that must have occurred to him unconsciously before he replied to Knight. Bill could have discussed the artifact with Knight at any time during the last year but he had chosen not to. It made sense to understand why before going further with Knight. Whether it was foolish, egotistical, or both, at that moment Elliott saw himself as the designated guardian of Mathiesson's legacy. From now on he would have to think carefully about what he said and did concerning Bill and his research.

He stretched the silence further by taking a long sip of coffee, and a further realization came into his mind: he did not trust Knight. This seemed ridiculous – why should trust be an issue? But Knight had incurred irritation by so abruptly mining Elliott for information. His inability to warm Elliott up with a memory or two demonstrated a lack of interest in Elliott personally. He was only interested in what Elliott knew about Bill's work. Elliott did not take offence at this. What surprised him was the suspicion that Knight was also less interested in Mathiesson than in Mathiesson's work.

Elliott decided on a concession that he could delay

fulfilling if necessary. "I would be glad to copy the manuscript for you, if you'd like to take a look at it."

Knight was in the middle of chewing a large chunk of sandwich. He nodded faintly in what Elliott took as acceptance of his offer. Still looking at his plate, he reached for his coffee, blew the steam off it, then sipped slowly.

"Have you decided to accept the job?"

"Of editing the book?" Knight nodded. Elliott felt a sense of misgiving as he said, "I think so. I owe it to Bill."

Knight gave a tight-lipped smile and narrowed his eyes. "Would you accept some advice from someone who's been in the business a long time?"

"Of course."

"Don't." Knight sat back in his chair, the sternness of his features dissolving into a look of affability, eyes widening, smile relaxed. He chuckled and said, "I don't mean to scare you away, Paul. It's just that you've begun a promising career. You saw the reaction Bill got on Saturday. And his career was behind him. And a hell of a career it was! More papers than you can count, popular books, international respect... But what did it all count for when he started talking about the pyramids as if they were some great mystery?" His index finger tapped the table with his syllables as he finished: "Not a thing." He crossed his arms and stared at Elliott.

The display incited seemingly incompatible feelings of rebellion and confusion in Elliott. Up to this point he had not considered not editing the book. Actually, he had not given the matter much thought since Mathiesson had asked him. Too much else going on. But regardless of the subject matter, editing the book still seemed the obvious and honorable thing to do. Perhaps there was still an element of hero-worship involved, but it seemed preposterous to refuse.

Furthermore, it was Mathiesson's last request of him. Surely Knight could see that?

He said hesitantly, "I appreciate the advice, Bob, but I can't help feeling that would be unfair to Bill."

"I would ask yourself, Paul, if Bill was being entirely fair with you. Not to speak ill of the dead, but he's put you in a rather awkward position. It's noble of you to want to honor his request, but if you put your name on a book full of unsolved mysteries and wild speculations you won't get half the courtesy Bill's audience gave him on Saturday. You'll be tarred and feathered at a crucial moment in your career. You're up for tenure. How do you think your colleagues on your review board will react to you publishing a book giving credence to questions undergraduates ask in beginning archaeology classes? Ancient astronauts? Atlantis? How will that look?"

Elliott found it difficult to respond. Knight was right, of course. If the rest of Bill's manuscript read like his lecture, then irrespective of its merits it would be rejected by the bulk of his colleagues. And as Deveraux had pointed out when chastising him for dismissing the paranormal, many of those colleagues would never even read the book. They would base their opinions on negative reviews in the major journals. That, anyway, was what he would have done under different circumstances.

Knight took advantage of Elliott's hesitation to say, "Listen, Paul. Let me tell you what I really think. Bill was a friend of mine. We weren't *best* friends, but we had a healthy professional respect for each other's work and spent more than a few evenings talking shop over dinner. It's in this spirit that I want to suggest something to you." Knight cleared his throat and sipped his water before resuming with, "Bill was extremely sick. He knew over a year ago that he was dying. Now I may be old, but the truth is I see my death somewhere in the distant future. It's still pretty much an intellectual concept for me, as it undoubtedly is for you. My point is that neither of us knows what it's like to have your sentence handed down to you by the doctors: 'You have three months to live.' I don't know about you, but in my place that kind of knowledge would induce a level of desperation I don't think I've ever experienced before."

Elliott said without emotion, "The kind of desperation that makes a man find God on his deathbed."

Knight smiled. "Exactly! Only in Bill's case it wasn't God he was looking for, merely an idea that gave him some kind of hope for the future. He chose the most obvious one from his perspective, and it's summarized in that quote of his about the universe being an open book. Bill needed a sense of endless possibilities, so he set aside the foundation of knowledge that had supported him – and to which he had contributed – throughout his life." Knight chuckled as if a thought had just occurred to him. "It's kind of the scientist's way of finding God. Bill was trapped by how much he knew. The certainties science gave him became a psychic burden, and the only way to escape was to cast them aside. Bill was handed an immutable death sentence. In his desperation he reacted. He couldn't change the sentence, but he needed to rebel against it anyway. And in his mind the closest thing to the certainty of death was the certainty of science. So he rebelled against the scientist that he was. He convinced himself that he was onto something important, something that would transform certainties into uncertainties. Some idea that would throw a wrench into the machinery of the universe and allow him to escape the inescapable." Knight's voice grew quiet. "Do you see what I mean? You and I both know – and in fact, Bill knew – we are all going to die. And that fact stands alone. There is no 'what happens next,' no meaning to it all. We know that we're nothing more than atoms squeezed together first into molecules and then into bodies, in what is undoubtedly the most fantastic stroke of luck ever to grace the universe. Bill knew that intellectually as well as you and I do, but when it came down to brass tacks he couldn't accept it." Knight sat up and shrugged. "And I don't blame him."

Elliott found himself speechless. Knight had clearly thought this through extensively.

"So you can see why it's a mistake to publish this book. What you said this morning – that Bill would want to be remembered for these sentiments – is noble, and perhaps even true if you only take into account this last year of his life. But I for one don't think he was himself at the end. I think he was motivated by something other than science, and that if he had known at the prime of his career what he would be espousing at the end of it, he would have been ashamed of himself."

The words seemed unnecessarily brutal. More than anything they conveyed Knight's own sense of disappointment, one that seemed to go beyond Mathiesson's career to encompass something wider and deeper.

But he's right about me publishing this thing. It could ruin me. He felt drained, irritable and anxious.

"You've given me a lot to think about, Bob."

They finished eating and Knight thumbed through his wallet. "Allow me to get this, Paul."

"Thank you."

"It's the least I could do. I'm sorry we didn't reminisce

more. Maybe some other time?"

Elliott nodded, even as he sensed that both of them considered this unlikely.

15

HE SPENT THE REST of the day helping Martha finalize funeral arrangements and prepare for her sister's arrival from Chicago. When she did not need him he read in Bill's study. Mainly he kept her company with his presence. He was glad to do so, but knowing he would soon be off duty relieved him. Throughout the day he continued to glimpse hints of the intricacies of Bill and Martha's life together, seeing their relationship as something infinitely complex and, in a sense, beyond his comprehension. In the face of these impressions he felt poorly suited to see Martha through her grief.

In the late afternoon he left her to nap and went downstairs to collect his things. He resisted the temptation to lie down himself; he knew he would sleep for hours if he did. Travel bag in hand, he paused, looking out the window across the sloping lawn and down towards the lake. Twilight descended, a reddish purple sky over black water. The ache of beauty stirred in him. He thought of Rachel and smiled. Then of Mathiesson, of how a single conversation with him drew together the loose threads of his attention, gave him glimpses of his own abilities, of the grandeur and mystery of the past, of the hidden depth and complexity of the present, washed away insecurity, anxiety, inadequacy...

He would have loved to talk with him right now.

He returned to the workroom. The stone lay where he had left it, innocuous under the fluorescent light, the plaque a dull black in the center. He could not imagine how it was a hoax. The way the plaque had settled into the rock with several of its edges submerged seemed completely convincing.

When he reached out to touch it a voice behind him said,

"You should take it with you."

"Martha! You scared me! I thought you'd still be napping."

She smiled. "No, dear, I didn't feel like sleeping after all." She pointed at the rock again. "You might as well take it with you, and those books of Bill's you've been reading. I'm sure he would've wanted you to. You can keep the stone at your friend's house while you're in town and ship it home to yourself."

"Will you be alright when your sister's here?"

She took his hand. "You're sweet to ask. It will take some time, but I'll be alright."

He had the uncomfortable feeling she had said this more for him than herself. "I'd be happy to stay if you thought I'd be of some use."

"No, that's alright. I can't thank you enough for staying with me today. Bill would have been very happy to know that you were here to look after me." She pointed to the rock. "And I'd rather you took that with you when you go so I know it's in good hands."

A question suddenly formed and he was surprised it had not occurred to him before. He nodded in the direction of the rock and said,

"What do you think of that?"

"You mean, do I think it's real? Do I think Bill was fooled? You're hardly asking an objective source, Paul."

He smiled. "Alright, then. You don't have to declare a verdict. But when you take it in conjunction with his book... You're a scientist, too, right?"

"I *was* a scientist. At least in your sense of the word. I'm not anymore. Maybe I never really was. I've always felt that there are things that are real, things that the kind of science you and Bill practice can't decipher. There are mysteries that will remain mysteries, at least from our perspective."

She was, he realized, a perfect complement for Mathiesson. He smiled and pointed at the rock.

"I hope that's not one of them."

***

The sky was bright with stars. Elliott shivered beneath his jacket as they cut through an unpaved alley behind Deveraux's house, gravel crunching beneath their feet, breath forming small clouds of mist. When they stepped out onto the sidewalk a bus roared past them and up a steep hill. Deveraux pointed after it and said, "Thattaway."

A blast of warm air greeted them as they opened the door to the bar. They took a table by the front window.

Deveraux said, "This is where I met Christine. It's too bad she's not working tonight. I'd like you to meet her." He glanced at the bar then stood up. "I'll get the first round."

Elliott stared at his chapped hands pressed against the dark wood of the table. The contrast of cold and heat had turned the pale skin red. The table beneath them was carved with initials and mostly indecipherable phrases and letters scratched on top of one another. He could not decide if he was more mentally or physically tired.

"Wake up!" Deveraux put the pint glasses on the table, then sat down and raised his glass. "To Bill."

"To Bill." Elliott took a long drink. He felt a rush of affection for Deveraux. "I'm glad I was here when he died."

Deveraux nodded. "It would've been even harder

otherwise."

Elliott shook his head. "No, the sad truth is that if I'd heard about it in Ohio, I don't think I'd have felt it quite as much. I hadn't seen Bill in over a year. He felt distant. I felt distant." He drank again. He thought he recognized the melody coming through the speakers but could not place it. "It's insane that things that seem so important can almost be forgotten." He raised his glass. "That goes for you, too, Alex. I forgot how good a friend you are."

"Aw, shucks. That's just the beer talking"

The warmth of the alcohol sank into him. He felt heavy and relaxed. "I talked with Bob Knight this morning."

"I saw you as I was leaving."

"I gave him your number. He wanted to be able to contact me while I'm here, and I offered him a copy of Bill's manuscript." He thought about this as he took another drink, and said, "Sight unseen he advised me not to publish it."

Deveraux looked sufficiently surprised. "Let me guess. He thought it would destroy your career?"

"Yes. And having read half the manuscript I can see his point."

"I've read about that, about 'forbidden' ideas not being accepted by the 'establishment.' There was a professor at Harvard who studied alien abductions and almost lost his job because of it. But do you honestly think you could lose your job publishing a book written by someone else?"

Elliott shrugged. "It could depend on the ideological constitution of my tenure committee. And maybe by editing and publishing the book I'm tacitly approving of it. Certainly they'd ask me what I thought of it. If I gave it credence, which I'd clearly be doing by editing it, they'd likely say something like, 'You believe this? We can't have our students graduating with these ideas in their heads. They'll go into graduate school and suffer for it.'"

"Can't you just write an introduction sort of saying you're publishing it for posterity? You know, kind of disavow personal responsibility for it?"

This thought had already occurred to Elliott. "I don't want to do that. That's not really the honorable thing to do, is it? For Bill?"

Deveraux shrugged. "What does Knight object to about it?"

"He thinks Mathiesson wasn't in his right mind when he wrote it."

"What do you think?"

"That's the thing. I've read half the book. I know that Knight's right in thinking it could damage my chances for tenure. But he hasn't even seen it yet." He felt like he was seeing the absurdity of Knight's position for the first time. "He's only got Bill's lecture to go on, and when it comes right down to it everything Bill said was reasonable enough."

Deveraux let the admission slide by without comment. "What did you tell him this morning?"

"Nothing I didn't say to everyone else. I mean, I hadn't read much of the book… I certainly didn't tell him about the stone."

"You felt on your guard."

He was surprised at Deveraux's perception. "I guess so."

"It reminds me of *Hamlet*. You know, the funeral meats weren't even cold yet. Or however it goes."

"You're right! That's what's been bothering me. He couldn't wait to find out what the hell was wrong with Bill. I might've told him more if he hadn't been so eager to hear it. I still don't know what to make of it all myself. Maybe I should've told him about the stone. I doubt it would have done any good, but you never know… I don't have any reason to actively distrust him."

Deveraux drained his glass and gave a conspiratorial smile, "I can help you out there."

A waitress appeared and leaned over the table for their glasses, drenching the air with the scent of patchouli. She said, "Another?"

When she left, Deveraux continued, "You know the conference ended today?"

"I almost forgot. Monday already." He thought of Elizabeth Ashmore and her husband and regretted not saying goodbye.

"Knight mentioned Bill in his closing remarks. He said he'd talked with another colleague this morning and confirmed his suspicion that Bill wasn't himself at the end. He didn't come right out and say it, but the implication was that Bill's sickness made him mentally unstable."

Elliott shook his head in disbelief. "He undercut my talk this morning."

"He seemed to take that into account when he said this was an emotional time for anyone who knew Bill, that it would be difficult for anyone in the situation to think clearly about it." Deveraux laughed. "Sorry, Paul. But you're right. He's an audacious son of a bitch."

Elliott felt only slight surprise. "He seemed in a hurry to wrap it all up neatly at breakfast." He summarized the discussion for Deveraux. "I got the feeling he was trying to come up with a rational explanation for why Bill said what he did. He couldn't accept that Bill would just throw away everything he'd believed in for so long."

"Unless he'd gone crazy."

"But why should he care? He and Bill were practically

competitors. Bill's transgressions might make him look better."

Deveraux shook his head. "I bet Knight's more interested in the philosophical issues. You scientists need to keep a united front. If one of you breaks rank – particularly someone as well known as Bill – it has the potential to reflect poorly on the rest of you. Or, I should say, on the field. The whole scientific endeavor." He leaned back from the table as their waitress put down two fresh pints, paying before Elliott had time to think about it.

"I don't understand."

"Remember how I got irritated at that guy at dinner the other night, when he talked about science being so objective and all that? 'Scientists test an idea and if it's wrong they move on to the next one.'"

"I remember. You said it sounded like a party slogan."

Deveraux nodded. "I think that there's a kind of elitism that can creep into your business, Paul. A sense that scientists somehow stand apart from common humanity in their relationship to truth, in their ability to understand the world. It's not often someone actually comes out and says it, but there's a feeling that scientists are like the gatekeepers of knowledge. They decide what's true and what's not. That's a very important, powerful position to hold."

"And when someone like Bill breaks rank it threatens that image."

"That's right."

"You make it sound like a conspiracy."

"If it's a conspiracy I don't think it's usually a conscious one. Sure, there are scientists who work overtime to discredit pseudoscientific ideas. People who think we'll enter a new dark age if too many people believe in astrology or the Loch

Ness monster."

Elliott grinned and raised his hand.

"To a certain extent it's your job. There *are* a couple of cases of alleged, active suppression I could share, where hardcore skeptics might have falsified evidence."

"I never knew."

"But you wouldn't, would you? You don't spend your time looking at the subject. I'm not trying to be an ass – you know what I mean, right? You've got your hands full with your own job. And you're trained to disregard pseudoscientific ideas as unworthy of investigation. That's the way it works." He smiled and pressed his hands flat on the edges of the table, pushing himself up. "If it's a conspiracy it's so insidious that even its perpetrators don't know they're perpetrating it. Excuse me a minute. Off to the gents."

Warm and relaxed, Elliott felt content to stare at the condensation on the window and sink into himself amidst the background noise of the crowded bar. But when he recalled the end of his discussion with Knight he felt a sudden pang of anxiety. There had been such an air of finality to his last words: Mankind was nothing more than an accident, death was inevitable, Bill knew this and in better times he would have been ashamed to see himself trying to escape that fact out of fear.

Was Knight correct?

He glanced around the room. The bar was filling up. Mixed clientele. He expected to see students but of course he was not in Ohio anymore, where his small college town had exactly four bars to accommodate everyone. He had stopped going out: a combination of getting old and not wanting to mix with inebriated students. Now he remembered the pleasant feeling of freedom of sitting in a bar with a drink, no computer to call him to write, just the warmth inside as rain sidled down the outer window, a relaxed, dull glow in his limbs from the alcohol.

Was Knight correct?

That depends.

If you believed that mankind was nothing more than an accident, a useless passion, then Knight was essentially correct. Bill might have questioned this message at the end of his life, but he had otherwise conveyed it throughout his career. It was really the only logical conclusion to draw from the materialistic paradigm. The universe is composed of matter. That's all there is. Cosmic accidents and natural laws create galaxies, solar systems, planets and – somehow – life, which is really just the *illusion* of life, because everything is ultimately composed of inert matter. It just so happened that – as Knight put it – the most fantastic piece of luck ever to grace the universe occurred, and mankind was born. The existence of conscious life did not reflect meaning any more than the pattern created by billiard balls broken up by a cue ball did; it was simply a consequence of natural laws acting blindly. In essence, life is an epiphenomenon of matter, just as consciousness is an epiphenomenon of organic brain functioning. To suggest anything else is to step outside the realm of matter, to cross into shady realms of divine intervention, intelligent design, or, at best, some kind of antiquated vitalism.

If Bill had chosen to forsake this picture of the facts because it scared him, just as he was about to die, then he had betrayed both science and himself. And Knight was correct. But if Bill honestly believed he had been mistaken in his assumptions, his biases – whether because of Attenbaum's artifact or his own independent research – then it did not matter so much *when* he changed his mind, only that he *did*. Bill explained himself by saying that death was the motivating factor, but not because of fear. Rather because it provided him with the sense of perspective he needed to step outside the intellectual barriers he had constructed throughout his life. He had suddenly seen these constraints as artificial constructs rather than objective facts, and so he had felt free to call them into question.

So Bill and Knight agreed on one thing: imminent death was the catalyst for the dramatic change in perspective. But was it the fear or the freedom of death?

"Look who I found!"

Deveraux's voice startled him. The reporter had his arm around an attractive blond-haired woman wearing jeans and a denim jacket over a tight black top. She was his equal in height, with straight hair that stopped just above her shoulders. Her large brown eyes and pale skin lent her a look of innocence.

Elliott stood up to shake hands. Deveraux said, "This is Christine. She just stopped by to pick up her paycheck."

"Very nice to meet you." Her smile was gracious and genuine, her hand warm and soft, and together these drew him gently back into the world of the bar so that he was pleased at the interruption to his thoughts. He realized that if he did not invite her to join them, she would probably not; Deveraux looked unsure as to whether Elliott wanted the additional company. Elliott nodded to the empty chairs and said, "Sit down."

Deveraux looked pleased. "Actually, Paul, are you hungry? Good. There's a Thai place a few blocks up the street. My treat."

The three of them stepped out into the cold night.

16

BEFORE THEY HAD WALKED half a block, Deveraux's cell phone rang. He said, "Dammit. Excuse me just a minute." Elliott and Christine exchanged a smile. Deveraux said, "Of course. I don't mind at all. Just a minute." He handed the phone to Elliott with a grin on his face. "For you."

Elliott wrinkled his face, perplexed, and took the phone.

"Hello?" It took him a moment to recognize the voice. "Rachel! No, I don't mind you calling me." He had left a message for her that morning, canceling their lunch.

Over the noise of the passing traffic he heard her say, "I just wanted to see how you were doing."

"I'm alright. Thank you." Deveraux and Christine walked a few feet away to look in the window of a furniture store. "I'm glad you called."

"Good. I was afraid to bother you."

"Where are you now? Can you meet us for dinner?" He called to Deveraux, "What's the name of the restaurant?"

★★★

She came in the door a few minutes after they sat down, wearing a paisley skirt and maroon top beneath a black wool jacket. When he stood to greet her she hugged him and pressed her cold cheek to his. Elliott made introductions and Rachel leaned across the table to shake hands. She made him smile; there was a brightness in her manner that he imagined Deveraux and Christine picked up on immediately, for they seemed as pleased as he was that she had joined them.

They sat down. When she took off her jacket Elliott pointed at the nametag pinned to her blouse and said, "I see you've just come from work."

She rolled her eyes. "I'm always forgetting that."

Christine said, "Where do you work?"

"At the bookstore up the street. That's one of my jobs. I also volunteer at an art museum and teach beginning guitar."

Deveraux said, "A woman of many talents."

"None of which by itself is enough to make ends meet." She directed her question to Christine: "What do you do?"

"Graduate student in English. Which means I might need to pick up a few extra skills myself to make ends meet when I'm done."

Deveraux said, "Don't talk that way! You're a genius. You'll have Harvard knocking down your door to get you to teach there."

Christine rolled her eyes and leaned into Deveraux as he put his arm around her. "And if that doesn't happen, you'll take care of me, right?"

"Of course." Deveraux flashed Elliott an exaggerated look of panic. Christine caught it and elbowed him in the ribs. "Oof! Just kidding. I'll be right there beside you. Really."

A waiter appeared with three bottles of beer. Rachel ordered a fourth and took the extra menu he offered her. They took this as their cue to figure out what to order. The restaurant was half-full, the lighting comfortably low. Elliott's feeling of relaxation mingled with the excitement of having Rachel next to him. His consciousness was split between the two and he felt pleasantly detached from himself, particularly from that part of himself that always second-guessed everything.

He could not decide what to order. When he tried calling

a ginger dish by its Thai name, mangling the pronunciation, he elicited giggles from the three of them. He took Rachel's hand in his, gently extended her index finger, and pointed at the correct spot on the menu. The gesture made him aware of how comfortable he felt with her. He realized this was not only due to the alcohol. It was because too much had happened over the past few days to allow for his usual reticence. Mathiesson's death weighed on him with an unusual combination of loss and heightened appreciation for the relationship. The intensity of these feelings bled over into these other relationships, generating a sweeping gratitude for his friends, for his experiences, for life itself.

He had a strange sense, then, of his own existence in a sea of existences, his consciousness rippling outwards from where he sat, embracing first all four of them at the table, expanding to drift across other minds in the streets, the city, encompassing even the deeper, slower minds of mountains, of oceans, stretching across time and grasping for things beyond his understanding. It was a sense of connection with the vastness of existence that his intellect could not keep up with. It slipped away as quickly as it had come.

Rachel said, "I'm sorry about your friend."

In response to their questions, Elliott told them about Bill, about their friendship, about Martha. He would not have gone on so long had the others not continually prompted him. There was a feeling of relief as he poured out details about the professor, skipping from one memory to the next, irrespective of chronology, like a painter throwing splotches of paint onto an empty canvas who only realizes halfway through the process that a comprehensible picture is taking shape. Their appetizers came and went, and he continued talking. By the time the waiter brought the main course – steaming plates of vegetables, rice, tofu, and chicken – his mind was sated. He sat back in his chair and drained his beer, watching as Deveraux, Christine, and Rachel began dishing the food onto their plates. He again felt an immense sense of gratitude, then relief as the conversation shifted away from his memories, and he joined them in eating.

★★★

Outside again in the cold air, Deveraux said, "What are we up for next?"

Christine answered first. "I'm teaching a class at seven-thirty tomorrow morning. I need to go home."

Deveraux said to Rachel, "Do you need a ride home?"

"No, thanks. I live about five blocks north of here."

"In that case, do you mind if I leave the two of you and escort my lady home?"

When they left, Rachel took Elliott's hand. "Walk me home?"

"I'm glad you're so forward."

She smiled and let her shoulder brush against his as they walked. "What exactly do you mean?"

"If you hadn't called I might not have followed up on meeting you at the bookstore. Not because I wasn't interested, mind you."

"Because you're shy?"

He laughed. "Yes. Usually. Not to mention everything else that's been going on."

They walked off the main street. The sounds of traffic grew distant; when a bus drove past, its fading roar accentuated the quiet of the side streets. A light rain began, soft enough to barely break through the trees lining the sidewalk. He said, "I forgot that the rain out here is actually pleasant sometimes."

"Have you had any more psychic experiences lately?"

He stopped and looked at her in surprise.

"What is it?"

He smiled and pulled her hand gently to continue walking. "Nothing. You're just a good guesser."

"More lights in the sky?"

"The same day I met you at the bookstore, in the morning. Alex and I had hiked up part of Copper Ridge. You know where that is? I vacillate between thinking I saw something inexplicably strange and thinking there's a reasonable explanation for it all. I don't know why I didn't talk to you about it earlier. Maybe for the same reason I'm hesitating now."

"Because you think I'll think you're crazy?"

He laughed. "I haven't decided myself yet."

"I won't think you're crazy. I've never seen any myself, but I've talked with people who have. They didn't seem crazy to me. Not anymore than the rest of us."

"What did their lights look like?"

"They usually did things that made it obvious they weren't airplanes. Like shoot straight up, then horizontally, then maybe get bigger or smaller too quickly. One of my friends said it almost seemed like the object wanted her to know it wasn't an airplane, like it was showing off for her."

"Where did she see it?"

"She was on the beach with her boyfriend. On the Olympic Peninsula."

"Did he see anything?"

"No. He was awake, sitting right next to her. He didn't see anything."

"Isn't that strange?" He experienced a pang of unease, but

at the same moment felt an undercurrent of excitement at the mystery. "It's like we see it in the mind rather than outside of us. You didn't see anything on the plane. With Alex yesterday, I... We'd walked halfway up and I sat down to rest..." His voice trailed off as he struggled to bring the details into sharper focus. It had been strange. "Alex didn't see anything. I saw the same kinds of lights I saw on the plane, but Alex didn't see them." He laughed. "He took pictures – I heard his camera. This sounds strange, but I think I was in some kind of trance. Alex wasn't. I was exhausted from the hike and from lack of sleep." A realization came to him suddenly. "I'm having trouble remembering because it's like trying to remember a dream. In this case, a waking dream. And when I think about what happened on the plane it's the same thing. I was so relieved to realize I wasn't going to die that I was flooded with… with a sense of well-being so intense that it opened me up completely." The phrase frustrated him. "That's not it, that's not quite right…"

She said, "I think I understand."

"I'm sorry I'm talking so much." He was aware they must be near her apartment and he was conscious of not wanting to end the evening.

She pointed to the shadow of a house about a half-block away. "That's where I live. Do you want to keep walking anyway?"

Leaves rustled in the steady breeze. The rain was intermittent, the cool air bracing.

He said, "You seem to know a lot about this kind of thing."

"I've always been interested in it."

"Why do you suppose?"

"I don't know. I've never seen any UFOs." She fell silent

and her hand found his. It was warm from having been in her pocket. "I guess for some reason the paranormal has never seemed totally strange to me. When I was younger I would sometimes dream things that would happen the next day. Nothing consequential. Once I dreamed that this annoying kid in my school had brought a radio to class and was playing it right behind me while I was trying to talk to someone. The next day I was in music class, talking to a friend – not the one from the dream – and I kept getting interrupted by someone banging loudly on the drums behind me. I turned around and it was the same kid from my dream, the one with the radio.

"I know it sounds stupid, but that's the kind of dream I had, enough times so that I could even kind of know when I woke up in the morning that it had been one of *those* dreams. On top of that, a lot of people I know and trust have had weird experiences. So I've thought about it, read about it. It's just kind of background material for my life, you know?"

"I understand." He was aware, too, of a difference in their approach to the subject. "I'm not like that. This is where my academic nature comes in. When people tell me strange things I dismiss them. It happened with Alex the other day and I regret it now. I tend to go more by what I think is possible rather than what people tell me they've experienced." He laughed. "Saying that makes me realize how absurd it is. It's backwards. It's not even good science."

"It's very intellectual."

"That's right. That's me."

As they approached the top of the hill the bright lights of a supermarket came into view. The sounds of traffic grew louder and the breeze picked up when they left the shelter of the trees on the side streets.

Elliott said, "This isn't quite as scenic."

"No. I guess we should turn around."

She took his hand again and they walked in silence until the brightness and sounds of the main street were behind them. When they were within sight of her street she said, "Maybe you're psychic."

"That's what you said the other day. You were going to tell me about something – what was it? The 'paranormal hypothesis'?"

"The 'paraphysical hypothesis.' I don't know if I can do it justice tonight. It has to do with the idea that UFOs aren't extraterrestrial objects, aren't piloted by spacemen. They exist in some kind of 'extradimensional' relationship with us. Like fairies, maybe even like ghosts or spirits. People who are called 'psychic' have brains that somehow interact more easily with this 'extradimensional realm.'" She gave a short laugh. "Now I'm the one worried about sounding crazy."

"Why? Does it make sense to you?"

"It's not that. I'm worried about sounding crazy to *you*."

They had reached her house, a small, faded-blue two-storey cottage. The porch light was on. He took her other hand and smiled.

"You don't sound crazy. It puts into perspective something else that happened." He told her about his vision of Mathiesson. "If it was a dream, it was the most vivid dream I've ever had. When I got to my hotel room a few minutes later I got a call from Martha telling me that Bill had died."

He was glad that she said nothing. Instead, she embraced him, pressing her head against his chest. His lips gently kissed her hair. "When I thought about it later that night, I knew I'd seen Bill. I have no good reason to say that other than a gut feeling. It didn't even seem that strange to me when I was thinking about it. It still doesn't. I have this feeling of certainty, of something so obvious I don't even have to question it. Not that I haven't questioned it, of course."

"You *are* psychic, you know. Whatever it means."

"You and Alex would get along well together."

She looked up at him. "Well, I want to hang out with *you*."

They kissed. The warmth of her mouth suffused his entire body. She rested her head against his chest. He wrapped his arms around her and watched the rain drizzle down through the light of the streetlamps. The night had grown perfectly still. He felt a tenuous confidence as he held her. The moment was like a dream – not because it was vague and distant, but because it was the opposite. The sounds of distant traffic, the patter of rain in the trees, the texture of her wool jacket against his bare hands, the scents of wet earth and the faint lavender of her hair, the mist against his face; all perceptions became intensely real, as solid and real as the pressure of her body against his. But beyond this there was something else, a hint again of something even more, something that was paradoxically denied him because he was so entranced by her physicality. There was no sense of loss, just the recognition of something more, something just beyond reach, if only he might let go of her and grasp for it.

But this he did not want to do. Not now. Because in this tenuous state, this feeling of being in between the familiar and the vastly mysterious, he felt complete. Neither letting go nor collapsing into the physicality of the moment would enhance this feeling.

After a while she stirred and said, "I really wish you didn't have to leave town so soon."

His hand drifted up her back. "I'm staying through

Friday. I changed my flight this morning."

It was pleasant to see the smile take shape on her face. It started with her eyes widening in surprise, then shifted to her upturned mouth and ended with the crinkling of her freckled nose. "That's wonderful," she said, and kissed him lightly. "Now I don't have to decide whether to invite you in tonight."

He laughed. "No, you don't. You're free to go."

"That's not what I meant."

"I know."

He kissed her goodnight.

17

I INTRODUCE IN THIS APPENDIX the object that instigated the line of inquiry resulting in this book. My primary reason for not basing any arguments on this peculiar artifact is that it has not been fully tested. It certainly appears to be a sixty-five-million-year-old plaque with rudimentary inscriptions. Nonetheless, Attenbaum's notebook could be more clear regarding the circumstances of its discovery, so until a more thorough investigation has been made we must reserve judgment. It's important to note, though, that the stone served as the springboard from which I plunged into the turbulent waters of alternative science. Had I not seen the rock with my own eyes, I would no doubt have gone to my grave clutching tightly to the beliefs I challenge in this book.

Yet I have an additional reason for leaving it out of the main body of the text. This is simply that should it prove to be false, I wanted it clearly separated from the mass of evidence presented in the book proper. Certainly some of that evidence may in time prove unreliable, or downright wrong. But this should not draw attention away from the fact that some, probably very much, of the anomalous evidence presented in this and numerous other works is impossible to disregard.

As the turn-of-the-century psychologist William James put it: If you to set out to disprove the notion that all crows are black, you needn't show that no crows are – you only need to find a single white one. If the stone in question proves to be genuine, then it is a white crow – that is, it proves one of the primary observations of this book, that our scientific understanding of the world is radically incomplete, even in areas where we suggest we have the basic picture worked out.

However, if Professor Attenbaum's find turns out to be a hoax it won't have any bearing on the other evidence presented in this book. Of course, in the minds of people predisposed to skepticism towards all things "pseudoscientific," the inauthenticity of the stone will "prove" to them what they already know. Any other evidence will be guilty by association. This is lazy and irresponsible thinking, but it's quite common, and I have been guilty of it myself.

So, to the stone...

I confess that most of the evidence cited in the book doesn't bring me any closer to understanding this strange find. I can speculate that it indicates the existence of a people possessed of at least a rudimentary symbolic language somewhere around the end of the Cretaceous period, some sixty-five million years ago. The actual carvings in the stone – unusually smooth, bearing no marks of the sort of chisel work one might expect – complicate the issue further. They appear to be poured from a mold rather than carved. Yet the temperature required to liquefy the rock they are carved in is likely to be absurdly high. At the very least, the technical know-how required to do so is relatively sophisticated. Certainly not the sort we would expect existed sixty-five millions years ago. But then again, we expect very little in the way of human-like intelligence so long ago.

The raised symbols strike one at first with their simplicity. It is difficult to imagine such rudimentary figures representing any sort of language of the type with which we are familiar, precisely because they are so simple. Early symbolic writing relies more on specific pictograms, and later ideograms, and less on this type of general geometric shape. The reason for this is simple, and in noting it we can also see the difficulty we have interpreting the stone: symbols this general convey very little meaning.

It is true that some of the earliest forms of "writing" we have discovered barely deserve the title: scratches on sticks to indicate the cycles of the moon or an inventory of livestock. To my mind this sort of marking qualifies as a rudimentary first step towards a more complex written language, but there is a difference between it and the molds on the stone. The mark on a stick represents a specific object or occurrence in the surrounding environment. No great care is placed in the process of carving. But the symbols on the stone have been set in place – via carving, or being poured from a mold – with great care for their representation. It is as if our attention is being called to the symbols for their own sake, and not as symbols of meaning like pictograms, ideograms, or phonetic representations.

I freely admit to the charge of speculation. There is little else one can do under the circumstances. The one thing that appears immediately certain to me – although I don't doubt this will be contested because it is too difficult to believe – is that the markings do not appear to be natural formations. It would require a potent imagination to explain how natural forces could sculpt such perfection in this fashion. So we can reasonably assume that the markings were shaped by an intelligence of some kind.

Beyond that, one can say little. The find remains an enigma, serving only to point out that our knowledge, though in many ways impressively full and detailed, is far from complete. I can only hope that further studies of this particular anomaly and others like it will encourage my colleagues to seek to fill in those gaps, rather than cover them over.

<h1 style="text-align:center">18</h1>

He awoke to the crackle of thunder. The windows rattled and the downpour followed within seconds. He fumbled for the lamp switch, knocking the pages of Mathiesson's manuscript to the floor. He sat on the edge of the bed, shaking off his sleep and collecting the pages before walking downstairs.

In the kitchen he turned on the light, then, blinded by its brightness, shut it off again. His eyes readjusted to the dark watching rivulets of rain sidle down the outer panes of the kitchen windows. Another blast of thunder shook the glass. Outside, the trees swayed to and fro in the wind, alternately letting more or less light into the kitchen from the streetlamps behind them.

He poured himself a glass of orange juice and sat down. Mathiesson's rock rested on the kitchen table, covered in a white towel, an innocuous lump in the dark. Seeing it like that made him think ironically: *What's all the fuss about?* He removed the towel and ran his fingers across the cool surface. Standing again, he lifted the top piece of sandstone and set it carefully aside. The plaque was little more than a black smudge in the dim light of the kitchen but he was reluctant to turn on the light again to examine it more closely. He sat and traced his fingers over the carvings, then rested his hand on the plaque.

The smoothness of the thing intrigued him, sending a ripple like an electric shock through his mind. He indulged his imagination as there slipped into his mind the image of a barren, lifeless plain of sand, a feeling of warmth from above, and a sensation of pressure that made him feel like he was underwater. He shifted his gaze upwards and saw through the surface of the water the sun, burning brilliant white, brighter than he had ever seen it. He suddenly found himself above the water, saw that it was an immense shallow sea stretching in all directions. The heat against his back felt unbearably uncomfortable, but as soon as this impression formed in his mind, the discomfort ceased.

He lifted his fingers from the plaque and looked around the kitchen. The shadows of trees swayed in the dim light. The patter of rain sounded from the roof.

What the hell just happened? Was I dreaming?

He closed his eyes and let his fingers rest on the surface of the plaque. Again the vision came: a seafloor, lifeless. Even the water was devoid of anything living, like microscopic plankton, though how he knew this he could not say. At the same time he was partially aware of the noise from the storm in Deveraux's kitchen, of the pressure of his fingers against the cool surface of the plaque. These "real" sensations seemed almost to alternate with the visions of the "other" world.

He experimented, rising up then slipping under the water again. There was the sensation of pressure, even a hint of moisture, but he did not feel wet. He propelled himself forward, towards a dark shape on the ocean floor, and found that it was unnecessary to swim – or even to imagine himself swimming. But when he paused amidst a field of broken volcanic rock he looked down at himself and saw that he was, in fact, there. He raised a hand to his face and pressed his fingers to his cheeks. He felt the pressure and wondered if, sitting in Deveraux's kitchen, he was actually doing the same thing.

At this thought he felt pulled back, not physically but mentally. He resisted, instinctively feeling he would end up in the kitchen, outside of his dream. The tightening of his mental "muscles" created a sense of disequilibrium and the vision shimmered, threatening to disappear. So he abruptly let go of the question. No, not the question. Questions were okay, they helped guide the vision. But the potent, intellectual desire to *know*. Was he in Deveraux's kitchen? Was the vision real? *No answer now. Move along.* This was not a job for the intellect, which was too active, interfering. *Watch.*

He looked at the black rock surrounding him and wondered why the area felt so lifeless. No plants, no fish, no scuttling crabs. Only himself.

But now some kind of brownish moss spread across the seabed, oozing like ink from small patches scattered here and there, taking on streaks of yellow, red, and black. Soon huge swaths of sand were covered with slimy mats, and from these arose muddy brown lumps looking something like tree stumps that gradually grew towards the surface of the water. Their tops took on bluish tints, their bases a dark shade of purple.

For some reason he understood that the events unfolding before him took place over what would normally seem to him an immense passage of time. *Life,* came the thought, *takes time – though not as much as you might think.* The water seemed penetrated by the quivering vibrations of life itself, stimulating and reinforcing the processes that unfurled the carpet of slime across the ocean floor and raised the muddy towers towards the surface.

Clumps of sponges and frond-like plants appeared, along

with the first signs of movement in the crystalline water: tiny translucent jellyfish and even smaller, twisting wormlike shapes. Minute bursts of movement drew his attention first to wriggling flatworms, the edges of their bodies rippling as they slid through the water, then to spiral-shelled nautiloids propelling themselves above the sea bottom. With a sense of delight he caught sight of a trilobite – a favorite of his since he had found a fossilized one at the age of ten. It swam along the seabed, antennae waving before it. Soon there were so many of these creatures scuttling about he felt almost repulsed, as if giant insects surrounded him.

Now the seafloor looked at once more familiar and alien. No longer the lifeless desert he had seen earlier, there were varicolored coral reefs dotted with mollusks and sponges, scorpion-like invertebrates feeding on what looked like worms with mouths of jagged teeth, clawed, predatory-looking things sliding through the water past great foamy jellyfish and rudimentary squid-like creatures. No fish. And only what looked like prototypes of the familiar plants and weeds he would expect to see beneath the surface of the ocean.

He felt certain that if he were to continue watching, they would appear: fish, plants, amphibians, reptiles, mammals – humans? Evolution – or what he supposed to be the course of evolution – was unfolding before him in the most vivid dream he had ever experienced. But it was more than a dream, wasn't it? He could still feel the plaque with his fingertips, the pressure of the kitchen chair against his backside. If he concentrated he could hear the scratching of the holly bush against the window in the study. He was aware that his eyes were closed, but knew if he opened them the spell would be broken. Sight was too powerful a sense; it would override the inner impressions.

Now there were fish, or something like them. They were like fat worms with lumps where the fins should be, but they possessed eyes and mouths. As he moved through the water he passed variations on these forms, and soon he was seeing triangular, plate-encrusted bodies with flippers and well-defined fins. Long strands of what appeared to be seagrass drifted in the current.

He thought: *I must see what's happening on land*, and found himself standing in a field of brown rock. He crouched down to find patches of algae or lichen growing by the edge of the water, beneath the burning sun. He stared out at the empty expanse of land beyond this, fascinated by the total absence of life. It seemed unfathomable that the land would soon be teeming with an abundance like the ocean's, choked with life.

But the process had already begun. The patches of lichen spread, growing together, looking now more like slimy moss. Tiny insect-like organisms crawled amidst the foamy detritus washing up on the sandy beach. A single crab, pushed ashore by a small wave, scuttled back into the water.

He moved from the beach towards a flat expanse of muddy plain where small, leafless shoots sprouted from beneath the thin ground-covering of slime. Further inland, things that looked more and more like plants had taken hold; the land was dotted with little oases of life. When he looked closer at these he saw insects: tiny millipedes, spiders, mites.

The process of "seeing" was not as smooth as it first seemed. Changes happened as he blinked, or when his attention was distracted by thoughts. He was seeing slices of the evolutionary picture – rapid-fire snapshots that flowed together almost seamlessly. But when he thought of something separate from what was occurring immediately before him – as he did now, when the idea of flying insects came to mind – he experienced a peculiar and fleeting sense of mental gears changing, and he saw what he was thinking of. In this case it was a giant dragonfly gliding over the large, broad leaves of a fern on the edge of a swamp. The sea had receded, and the land was clogged with green plants. Just beyond the edge of the swamp began a forest unlike any he had ever seen, thick with giant trees, pungent with the scent of decay and fertility. Beneath a thick layer of mist, suspended like dry ice over the water, the swamp was alive with wriggling and splashing bodies.

There was again that strange sense that life permeated the very air around him. It was similar to what he had felt in the ocean. Life was insistent, burgeoning like a kind of physical force against – against what? Against non-life? No, that was not it at all. In fact, it was not against anything. It was merely a force: rolling into the cracks and crannies of matter like a surge of tidal water flows around and over and through the channels created by rocks on the seashore, leaving some of itself behind in isolated tidal pools when the wave recedes back into the ocean.

But this begged the question: From where did life flow?

It was all around him now – life, teeming in the mud, bursting up from it in the form of gigantic ferns and trees, darting through the air as monstrous dragonflies, splashing in the water as squirming amphibious bodies. There was something almost gauche about its abundance and variety. Logically, the complexity seemed somehow unnecessary, but it *felt* essential. Or perhaps that was the wrong word. Perhaps it felt *inevitable*. From bacteria to jellyfish, from fish to amphibians, from amphibians to reptiles, from reptiles to mammals…

These thoughts flooded his mind, interrupting the flow of vision. Abruptly he found himself in Deveraux's kitchen. His shoulders ached. He raised his eyes to stare out the window. The rain had stopped, and the first hints of red dawn peeked through gently swaying branches.

19

"Psychometry."

Deveraux's grin spread across his face, reminding Elliott of the Cheshire cat.

"Psychometry?"

"The ability to read the history of an object, such as a stone, or a piece of clothing, a fragment of bone. Psychics have helped police solve crimes using a victim's shirt or something else belonging to them."

"Like the woman who found the lost girl you told me about."

"Precisely. But it has even stranger applications. The scientist who discovered it – or rather, named it – Joseph Buchanan, had an acquaintance who could 'taste' brass in the dark. That is, when he touched a brass object it produced an unpleasant taste in his mouth. In a series of experiments he found people who could do the same with other materials. A younger colleague of his, William Denton, had a wife who was extremely sensitive, and who could 'read' rocks to determine their origin. She even had visions of the past when she held the rocks."

Elliott was interested despite a kind of low-level anxiety, still lingering the morning after. "What kind of visions?"

"Something similar to what you've described. Mind you, she wasn't the only one. Denton experimented on many 'sensitives,' or psychometrists – whatever you want to call them. He'd wrap objects in thick paper and give them to people to read. For example, a piece of volcanic rock might produce a vision of an erupting volcano. A fragment of fossilized bone might result in the image of a dinosaur. He even spot-tested them – waiting a few weeks then giving them the same samples again, always wrapped up and usually without knowing himself exactly which sample he'd given them until afterwards."

"Were they always right?"

"No. But they often were."

The kettle on the stove whistled and Deveraux stood up to turn it off. Elliott watched him pour the water into the coffee filter he'd placed on top of a glass caraffe.

"Cream? Sugar"

"Cream. I'll pour it." He stood up and stretched. The rain had stopped altogether but the sky was still cloaked in gray. He sipped his coffee.

Deveraux said, "We should go to this metaphysical library I know. They've got Denton's book, *The Soul of Things*."

"When was he working? Denton."

"More than a hundred years ago."

"Ah."

"Yes, I know what you're thinking. They must have been less rigorous back then. Hard science was still in its infancy."

"You read my mind."

"Just remember who in this room is psychic."

"How did they presume to explain why a rock would tell one story and not a million others? That is – supposing a piece of volcanic rock gives off an impression of an exploding volcano. That's just one sliver of the experiences it's 'had' in the course of its existence. Why not give off a picture of the person who found it? Or say it spent some time in the ocean, why not a picture of a fish?"

Deveraux smiled. "A very good question. And I don't have a definite answer for you. But the idea is that the mind of the psychometer receives the – I don't know – the stronger impressions over the less dramatic ones – the volcanic eruption over the millions of years simply buried in a lava field. Even if everything the rock has undergone in its existence is somehow recorded by it, a good psychic can tune into the stronger signals, if you will, more readily than the weaker ones."

"An interesting theory."

Deveraux shrugged.

"Even so, why should my rock know so much about the history of the Earth? It can't possibly have been around to 'see' everything I saw. It would've been buried, or broken up, compressed into another kind of rock."

"I've no idea. That's an interesting point."

Elliott stared out the window. The light of day lent an air of sobriety to the proceedings. "I think I should see someone about banging my head on the plane. I should've gotten it checked out right away."

Deveraux looked incredulous. "You're not going to tell me you think you're hallucinating because of a head injury."

Elliott had expected this response. "Why not? Or maybe it's just imagination. Overactive imagination. People have been hypnotized into thinking that they're talking to invisible pigs. That doesn't mean the pigs are really there. My imagination was on overdrive. I knew the rock was supposedly dated to around sixty-five million years ago. The impossibility of this idea stimulated all sorts of thoughts about the evolution of life on Earth. In my tired state I conjured up these images myself, like a waking dream."

He half-expected Deveraux to be irritated by his caution, but the reporter said, "I don't know. I suppose there are problems with the theory I just outlined. But it seems to me that somehow the brain of the psychometer interacts with the recordings on a rock, or a bone, or in the case of that little girl I told you about, a cloth doll."

"You see, that part doesn't make sense. How would the doll know where the girl was? How could it record her impressions if she wasn't carrying it when she got lost?"

"That's a good point. We could theorize that there was some sort of bond between the girl and her doll. I mean, her emotional attachment to the doll impressed some of her essence on it, and created a connection that the psychic could trace."

Elliott was not impressed. "Is there any scientific evidence for such a bond?"

"Well, there is the fact that the psychic was right."

"You know what I mean – have any controlled experiments been done to test the theory that some kind of non-material bond exists between an object and its owner?"

Deveraux nodded. "As a matter of fact, yes. Denton and others. But we can get to that later. The first thing you have to realize if you're going to study the paranormal is that a huge mass of the evidence is anecdotal. Same thing with UFOs and Bigfoot and the Loch Ness monster. People see things in uncontrolled situations. They experience things – like receiving images from rocks – that are largely if not totally subjective. I put my hands on that rock when we first brought it back and I didn't see a damn thing. Does that mean you didn't see anything either?" He did not wait for Elliott to reply. "Of course not. You saw lights on Copper Ridge and all I saw was a big smiley face drawn in the sand. I doubt very much if I could drag you into a lab and get you to see lights again. I even doubt that if we hiked up to the ridge today either of us would see any lights."

"Maybe." He hesitated. "Every time I've had one of these experiences I've been in something of an altered state. Usually I'm very tired, almost on the edge of sleep."

"A trance."

"Something like that. But I've still been somewhat conscious. I mean, part of me is still aware of my physical surroundings as well as my thoughts."

Deveraux sat down across from Elliott. The rock was between them, but they had rejoined the two pieces and covered them with the towel again. One moment Deveraux's attention was focused on Elliott, the next his eyes dropped to the table.

"This is really fascinating, Paul. I don't understand it. I mean, why you? Why now? It's not unheard of that a skeptic becomes a believer–"

"I'm not a believer."

Deveraux smiled. "I almost don't care if you think you are or not. I know you're psychic." He laughed. "You won't mind if I write you up for the next issue of *Strange Truths?*"

"That's not even funny. Psychic or not I have a career to think about. Knight was right about that."

"So what are you going to do?"

"I'm doing it right now."

Deveraux gave him a quizzical look.

"I'm educating myself."

Deveraux's expression collapsed back into the Cheshire grin. "And I'm the teacher. This is rich."

"I'm all ears."

The streets were wet from the night's rain, and water spattered against the sides of the car as they drove. It was early enough that there was little traffic; they reached Capitol Hill fifteen minutes after leaving Deveraux's house, and they were among the first customers at the restaurant. After they had ordered, Deveraux said,

"Did you finish Bill's book?"

Elliott nodded. "Last night."

"And?"

"First of all, it's not really about the paranormal. Half of it's about the methods and value of scientific inquiry. He also spends a fair amount of time talking about the evidence for ancient civilizations before the Egyptians and Sumerians. To round it off he considers the possibility that either *Homo sapiens sapiens* was around a lot earlier than we normally think – that is, more than 100,000 years ago – or that his predecessors were more advanced than we think." He hesitated before saying, "It's not a typical Bill Mathiesson book. He doesn't have all his ducks in a row. You can tell he had begun reading and researching this material only recently. Lots of notes about additional sources he wanted to check out." He sipped the coffee their waiter had just set before them.

"So the book needs a lot of work?"

"If I'm going to do Bill's book justice, I'll have to invest far more time in it than simply writing an introduction."

"And do you want to do the work?"

"I don't know. I mean, of course I do. But of course I'm divided about it. It'll hardly count in my favor if I co-write a book with Bill that contradicts half of what we know about prehistory." He laughed wearily. "Maybe you should write it."

"Ahh... but I'm not a scientist. No one would take me seriously."

"No one will take me seriously either." As he said this he felt a flash of something like despair. Was it true? If he were not in the middle of the situation he would disregard a book like Bill's without cracking its cover. It was highly probable that his peers – in particular his tenure committee – would feel the same way. "I don't want to just give up my career. What the hell else would I do with myself?"

"Write books about the paranormal?"

"I'm not joking. If I endorse Bill's book I could lose my job. It's one thing to talk with you about possibilities, about psychometry and aliens and Atlantis. But when I go from the abstract to the practical I feel sick to my stomach."

"You're not just talking, Paul, you're experiencing. How can you go back on that?"

He rolled his eyes. "We don't know what's happening, Alex. Meanwhile, I've got bills to pay. Hell, I've got to pay back the loans I took out to get my degree."

"Ah, but you've got to look at yourself in the mirror, too."

He allowed his irritation to show. "I don't need that pointed out to me." He stared into his coffee cup.

Deveraux pressed on. "You were awake when you had your visions, even if it was something like a trance state. You said you were aware of the kitchen and everything." Elliott shrugged. "A vision of Mathiesson the minute he died? What are the odds of that?"

"Actually, very good. He was sick and I had every reason to be thinking about him at the time."

"You're just saying that because it'd be easier if you

hadn't had these experiences."

"No, I'm saying it because I can't abandon my training the second some aberration occurs. Like I say, maybe I banged my head too hard on the plane. Or the stress and lack of sleep these past few days has brought on some kind of semi-hallucinatory state."

"Or made you more open to paranormal experiences."

"That's what you want to believe."

"It's not what I want to believe –" Deveraux stopped short. "Okay, I see your point. I'm interested in this stuff and it'd be pretty fascinating if a friend of mine started seeing ghosts and visions. Yes, I'd like to believe that. But that doesn't automatically make it untrue. And you've got your own reasons for not wanting to believe, independent of what the truth may be. Your career, your intellectual convictions –"

Elliott raised a hand to interrupt. "Listen. It's alright. Let's leave it for now." He tried curtailing his irritation by reminding himself that Deveraux was not baiting him, that he was simply interested in what was going on. *And he has a lot less to lose than I do.* "I want to see someone, though. You told me you could get me in to see someone to check out my head."

"So now you think you've got brain damage? You'd rather have brain damage than believe in ghosts?"

Elliott shook his head. "Try to see it from my point of view, Alex. I don't have the benefit of your years of experience. I'm seeing lights in the sky. I'm having intense internal visions, dreams that seem real." He leaned forward and lowered his voice in response to his own spike of anxiety. "I don't know what the signs of schizophrenia or psychotic delusions really are, but I want to at least make sure I'm not showing them now."

His tone sobered Deveraux, who nodded and said, "I have a psychiatrist friend. Met him years ago when I interviewed him about ADD. I'll call him today."

"Thank you."

Deveraux gave a half-smile and leaned in. "So does this mean we can't talk about weird shit anymore?"

Elliott looked at him in disbelief, then gave a short laugh. "Let's just not talk about me."

"What about Bill's book? Tell me about that."

He sipped his coffee, reflecting through his irritation that none of this was Deveraux's fault. He was frustrated with him because his questions kept striking the key nerves. First: Was he going crazy? And: Would he have to give up his job because of Bill's book? The prospect of some major career redirection had been hovering in the back of his mind from the moment Mathiesson handed over his manuscript. Elliott had simply been too star-struck at the time to take it seriously.

"Bill references a lot of popular, speculative works you're probably familiar with: *From Atlantis to the Sphinx*, *Fingerprints of the Gods*."

Deveraux nodded. "Ah, yes. Evidence for an advanced civilization around 12,000 years old. Wiped out in a worldwide catastrophe."

"How about *Forbidden Archaeology*?"

"That's a big one. I haven't read it all. But it's relevant for you. One of the things they hypothesize in the book is that there's a kind of knowledge filter that keeps anomalous finds off to the sidelines, away from the orthodox timelines for the evolution of man. In the 1800s, before that timeline was agreed upon, many discoveries indicated mankind could be much older. But as the modern paradigm solidified, the anomalies were explained away or ignored. And supposedly the same kind of thing still goes on today."

"Back to conspiracy theory."

"Like I said the other day, if it's a conspiracy I'm not sure that it's a conscious one."

The waiter returned with their breakfast: scrambled eggs, bacon and toast.

Elliott felt himself on familiar ground as he said, "There's a simple enough explanation for that. You base a theory on a solid foundation of the best available evidence. If you then find something new that doesn't fit, your first assumption is likely to be that there's a problem with the new data."

"But when enough contrary evidence mounts up it becomes inexcusable to ignore it. You end up buttressing your theory with what you *want* to be true, rather than using evidence alone. The authors of *Forbidden Archaeology* gather together all the scholarly reports of finds from the 1800s through to the present and review the evidence as a whole. That's basically what Graham Hancock does in *Fingerprints of the Gods*. That, in fact, is what most books on the paranormal do, too. They collect the mountains of actual evidence out there. That's why I feel like anyone who hasn't studied the subject doesn't really have any business pronouncing on it. There's so much evidence for ghosts, telepathy, clairvoyance, UFOs – even Atlantis and the Loch Ness Monster. It's overwhelming and confusing. Sometimes even I find it crazy."

Elliott smiled. "I'm glad to hear it."

"But it's there. That's what I find so frustrating when I read interviews with scientists who say things like, 'There's no evidence for life after death, or precognition, or psychokinesis,' or whatever, because it's simply not true. And it's not just anecdotal evidence. There is some laboratory evidence. It's usually not as spectacular as the anecdotes are, but that's probably because it's difficult to make paranormal phenomenon appear on call." He sat back in his chair and gave Elliott a sheepish grin. "I know, I'm on my soapbox. Forgive me."

"It's all the years of holding back."

They ate for several minutes without speaking. The food was greasy and overcooked.

Deveraux said, "So why does Bill reference those books?"

Elliott sat back feeling uncomfortably full. "He takes the rock as a starting point, both for the questions it forces one to ask about how our scientific paradigms are shaped and for the more concrete question it raises: how could something so old have come to be? So he surveys the evidence for the greater antiquity of man. After all, the carvings in the rock look like they were made by intelligent beings, and the only intelligent being we know of who would bother to do something like that is man. So first he looks at the traces of lost civilizations. I'm sure you're familiar with the evidence: the redating of the sphinx, the possibility that the ruins of Tiahuanaco are fifteen thousand years old, the maps of Antarctica that apparently show it ice-free, which it hasn't been for at least ten thousand years."

Deveraux nodded. "I've heard it all before. Convincing evidence for an advanced civilization that existed at least fifteen thousand years ago, one that was probably destroyed in a cataclysm. A comet hitting the Earth or something like that."

"It's intriguing evidence. It's not totally convincing because a fair amount of it's speculation and conjecture. At least based on the books I've been looking at. You have to admit it'd be more compelling if we actually found ruins we could decisively date to the period in question."

Deveraux shrugged. Elliott could not tell if he felt defensive as he said, "It's a bit stronger than all that. Some would argue that we've found exactly those ruins in Tiahuanaco, or even in the Great Sphinx if you only want to go back to around 7000 B.C. And the Great Pyramid at Giza. Millions of blocks used to build it. Many of them weighing up to fifteen tons. Maybe it's not ten thousand years old, but like Bill pointed out, modern engineers can only speculate about how it was built. That's the kind of evidence that's being ignored or disputed simply on the grounds that it doesn't fit the prevailing viewpoint – not because it's inadequate."

"Perhaps. I yield to your greater knowledge of the subject."

"That's very charitable of you. But there's no need. I can't expect you to be convinced overnight."

"You've got to understand, Alex, I'm comfortable with academic papers inching forward one tiny bit of data at a time. Five pages on whether the direction of a curving line on a pottery shard indicates it was produced during one Egyptian dynasty or another. These books Bill uses make some wild, speculative leaps. And they're by non-specialists. No formal training, no peer-review… I can't just take their word for it."

"I'm not suggesting you should, only that you should look at the evidence with an open mind. And you're not giving these guys enough credit. Sure, some of them are sloppy. But some have done their homework. At the very least they raise legitimate questions. You get scientists writing interdisciplinary popular books all the time and you could level the same charges of being non-specialists against them. What you're really complaining about is where the alternative writers land after they make their speculative leaps. Inside or outside the mainstream."

"Yes, well, that's Bill's point.

Deveraux finished eating and pushed his plate to the center of the table. "So where does he go next?"

"He thinks that if you're really open-minded about the age of the earliest civilization you still only end up going back – at most – a hundred thousand years. By the standard timeline, civilization began in Mesopotamia or Egypt around 3000 B.C. Some of these alternative writers push the date back ten or fifteen thousand years. Others push it back a hundred thousand and suggest it was a civilization of Neanderthals, rather than Cro-Magnons like us. But even going back a hundred thousand years doesn't put a dent in a sixty-five million year old rock."

"So the natural next step is to consider that mankind has been around for at least sixty-five million years?"

Elliott laughed. "You say that as if even you're skeptical about it."

"I suppose I am. I haven't come across anything that could explain that." He shrugged. "UFOs, maybe."

"Bill briefly mentions the idea, but he prefers examining other options first."

"There are esoteric thinkers like Blavatsky and Steiner who give detailed cosmologies about the descent of man into matter, millions and millions of years ago."

Elliott nodded in recognition. "One of the books I took from Bill's library is a compilation of cosmologies from various religions and cults around the world. I could only bring myself to glance through it. But I had to learn a lot of mainstream mythology and religion in school."

"What does Bill write about it?"

"He doesn't. He sticks as closely as he can to science."

"And?"

Elliott shrugged. "He still doesn't get far enough back in time to explain the rock."

Their waiter appeared and poured more coffee before they could refuse.

Deveraux said, "I don't know. I've heard stories of human and dinosaur footprints found in a streambed somewhere. Even I think that's a little crazy."

"I'm glad you draw the line somewhere." He swallowed a mouthful of coffee without thinking. "The evidence may exist that man was present on Earth sixty-five million years ago. Bill wasn't convinced he'd found it." He looked at his watch; it was only seven-thirty. "Let's walk off this meal."

As they paid, Deveraux said, "I can think of at least one way to try answering some of these questions."

Elliott stuffed his change into his hip pocket and said, "What?"

"Psychometry."

They stepped outside. A fine mist hovered beneath the gray sky.

20

"Open your eyes wide, please."

Elliott complied, trying not to wince as a bright beam of light shone into first his right, then his left eye. The doctor flicked off the light and wheeled himself back a few inches in his desk chair. He gave Elliott a friendly smile, apparently trying to appear reassuring. Elliott felt a combination of concern – in case something was indeed wrong with him – and mild embarrassment, because he intuitively felt nothing was. If the latter was true, he was wasting the doctor's time to garner a bit of reassurance. But Deveraux had insisted his psychiatrist friend – Peter Hoffman – did not mind seeing him on short notice.

"Any trouble with your memory? Who's the president of the United States?"

Elliott laughed and told him. "No, nothing that I can think of. In truth I've been feeling fine except for these intermittent... I don't know what you want to call them. Hallucinations, I guess."

Hoffman sat back and ran a hand across his bald head. "How about immediately after the accident. Any loss of consciousness? Anything at all unusual?"

"No loss of consciousness. I saw lights outside the airplane window. Just for a second."

"You said it was a difficult landing?"

"Lots of turbulence. The oxygen masks dropped down. Yeah."

Hoffman jotted notes on a pad. "Would it be fair to say

you were considerably stressed?"

Elliott nodded.

"And since then? Any vomiting? Trouble walking? Sleeping? Slurred speech?"

With each shake of his head Elliott felt more absurd.

"You said you hadn't been getting enough sleep."

"That's true. But it's more for lack of opportunity. I've been busy since I got here."

Hoffman glanced at his notepad. "Alright, then. First tell me about the lights in the sky."

Again a flush of embarrassment. "They were silver lights, zipping about… When I think of them now it's hard to bring them into focus. I think they might have been floaters, just somehow I was paying closer attention to them." Hoffman nodded noncommittally and Elliott felt obliged to keep talking. "I was either stressed or exhausted when I saw them. I'd only had a few hours sleep the night before and then Alex dragged me halfway up the mountain to take pictures."

"How did they make you feel when you saw them?"

"Do you mean, like, frightened?"

Hoffman shrugged. "Or happy, nervous, whatever."

Elliott considered this. "I guess… I guess, *curious* mostly. I think we must be on to something when we talk about it as if it's a dream, because with dreams, you know how it is. Strange things don't always seem so strange. When I saw these lights they seemed somehow natural. I didn't react to them as forcefully as I might have had I been fully awake."

Hoffman smiled. "So you didn't think they were UFOs."

Elliott said, perhaps too abruptly, "No."

"Alright. Let's see, then. How about when you dreamed about your friend, Dr. Mathiesson?"

"That must have been a dream. I mean, I woke up sitting

in a chair in the hotel bar. A vivid dream, for sure, but –"

Elliott left the sentence unfinished; Hoffman picked it up for him: "But you were obviously thinking about him a lot, given his situation." Elliott nodded. "Okay, then, the last thing you mentioned is a little more peculiar, yes? Your late night visions in Alex's kitchen. Tell me more about them."

Hoffman's voice was friendly but curiously flat; the same went for his facial expressions, making it difficult for Elliott to ascertain what the psychiatrist was thinking. His own trepidation and embarrassment was, he realized, making him edit himself more than he would normally, in the sense that he did not feel entirely comfortable exploring every aspect of his experiences with Hoffman. His primary purpose in coming was to reassure himself that he had suffered neither a concussion nor the onset of schizophrenia. Now, within the safety of the doctor's office, he felt like a hypochondriac. But he still detected within himself the need for reassurance. So he pressed on:

"I told you about this fossil that Bill found. It's supposed to date to around sixty-five million years ago." He had not mentioned the plaque inside; for the purpose of this interview it was irrelevant. "I woke up at about three in the morning and went downstairs. I ran my fingers over it and started getting visions… pictures in my head of the evolution of life. Something like a television documentary. Very vivid, very intense." He saw them in his mind's eye as he spoke. Remembering them stimulated his curiosity.

Hoffman smiled and said, "Hypnagogic imagery." He said it with the same degree of certainty that Deveraux had said "psychometry" earlier in the day. Elliott was familiar with the term but arched his brows anyway, indicating his desire for Hoffman to elaborate, which he did: "I'm sure you're familiar with the experience, if not the term. You're drifting off to sleep and you experience visual and sometimes auditory hallucinations, usually random, sometimes connected to things that happened to you during the day. Then you pass into sleep."

"What causes them?"

Hoffman's eyes took on a gleam of interest. "Like so many things involving the brain, we don't know exactly. But it's clearly related to dreams. In fact, if we really wanted to play around and test whether you were experiencing hypnagogic hallucinations we'd need to hook you up at the sleep clinic."

"Why's that?"

"Because when you're having a hypnagogic experience there's evidence that you're quite literally dreaming – or at least asleep. Not REM sleep, where you have the deepest dreams, but still... You probably know the brain cycles through different stages of sleep, and each stage produces different wave patterns and combinations: theta, delta, and so on. Well, during hypnagogic states the brain produces theta waves, which indicate a state of sleep."

"So I *am* dreaming!" He felt a curious mixture of relief and disappointment. But mostly relief.

"Technically, yes."

"So no brain damage, no incipient schizophrenia."

Hoffman shook his head and gave a slight smile. He was back in therapeutic mode after the academic diversion. "Those wouldn't be among my first choices, no."

"I'm not used to thinking of hypnagogic hallucinations as being so vivid, so long-lasting."

Hoffman shrugged again; Elliott found the gesture reassuring. "I attribute that to your continued lack of sleep.

Not to mention the stress of having a good friend abruptly pass away when you got out here." He gave a slight smile, almost to himself, then caught Elliott's wondering look. "Excuse me for smiling, it's just that your hallucinations happen to be so... I don't know – intellectual, I guess. It seems clear to me that you've come here for a conference on evolutionary theory and you accordingly hallucinated an evolutionary scenario. On cue." He clapped both hands to his knees as if making ready to stand up. "Anyway, given the circumstances – the stress and lack of sleep – I'd consider it remarkable if you weren't experiencing anything unusual."

Elliott smiled. "Thank you!"

Hoffman raised his brows and said, "However, I'd be remiss if I didn't check for any internal bleeding from your bump on the head." He must have seen Elliott's smile abruptly collapse, because he waved his hand dismissively. "Don't worry, really. I just think, well, you sustained what you've described as a pretty significant blow to the head. You haven't displayed any significant signs of a concussion other than these hallucinations, which seem to have a less dramatic explanation. But you know, in this day and age we've got to cover all the bases."

"What do you recommend?"

"A CAT scan." Without waiting for Elliott's response he pressed the intercom button on his desk phone. "Amy, can you please call the clinic and see if they've got space today for a CT scan? Thank you." To Elliott he said, "We'll do this, if you don't object. I recommend you follow up with your own doctor back home. In the meantime I can prescribe something to help you sleep."

"I don't think I need anything."

"Well, I'll give you the prescription and you can do what

you want with it. In the meantime… Let me suggest something that might sound counterintuitive."

"What's that?"

Hoffman smiled, and Elliott detected a gleam of academic interest in his eyes again. "I suspect your hallucinations are largely due to sleep deprivation and stress. But it's clear that they're *causing* you stress as well, right?" Elliott nodded. "So if anything else occurs over the next few days, just relax into it. Don't let your mind make a big deal out it."

Elliott smiled. "In other words, don't stress out about it."

"That's right. Detach yourself. You're a scientist, right? Well, treat the phenomenon objectively. Observe them. Observe yourself."

"My very own research subject."

"That's right. I'll bet they'll go away on their own once your life settles down again, so take advantage of this rather unusual opportunity to see how your brain works." His tone took on a note of caution. "You know, within reason, of course. If you start experiencing major disruptions in functioning or unusual urges, call me. But I really don't expect anything like that to happen."

Elliott nodded, aware now that his sense of relief was subtly shifting to a desire to be done with his visit. He was about to decline the CAT scan when the intercom beeped and Amy's voice announced she had set up an appointment in an hour's time. Elliott accepted this with a sense that the situation was out of his hands. To Hoffman he said, "I really appreciate you seeing me today."

"Not a problem. No charge." He corrected himself: "Well, that is, no charge for my services. The CAT scan I've got no control over, you understand."

Elliott gave him a wry smile. "I imagine they're not cheap."

"How's your insurance?"

21

"WELL, MY BRAIN APPEARS as normal as it can under the circumstances. No internal damage."

Rachel looked at him sideways as they walked down the gravel trail together. "You *are* crazy, you know." She said it gently, slightly mocking, but he could not take it too hard while her hand was firmly enclosed by his.

"What do you mean?"

"I mean, you have normal paranormal experiences – if I can say that – and you rush off to the doctor thinking you've got brain damage."

"You sound like Alex."

"Well, great minds think alike."

"I'll tell you what I told him: it's not in my training to accept bizarre experiences as some kind of normal part of life."

"I know, I know, it's like what you said the other night. You'd rather trust ideas than experience."

"Did I say that? I must have been drunk."

"No, just confessional."

"But seriously, there are reasonable explanations for what's happened."

"According to your new friend, the psychiatrist."

"That's right."

She stopped walking and turned to face him, letting her hand slip out of his. "You like what he said because it helps you maintain the status quo. It fits with what you already believe about the world."

"What's so wrong with that?"

"Nothing, if you think you already know everything."

He laughed, delighted by her astuteness. "Well you should be happy with Hoffman's advice. He told me not to freak out if I have any more experiences, just observe them, let my natural curiosity have its way."

"Only he thinks they're hallucinations and I think they're real."

"Well, for practical purposes at the moment, it doesn't matter, right? Either way I pay attention to them, see what they've got to tell me." He laughed. "You know, between you, Alex, and Bill's book I've got more crazy ideas bouncing around my brain than at any time since – well, never." He took both her hands and smiled broadly as he experienced a swell of gratitude.

Rachel's cheeks were flushed. Her hair was tied back and the edges of her ears were red with cold. She smiled and said, "You've only got yourself to blame for it. I didn't see any lights in the sky. I'm thick-headed when it comes to ESP. I just attract psychics."

He said, "That much is true," and kissed her. When they broke off and he looked at the park around him with its thick masses of ferns and towering trees he almost felt as if he had been transported to another world altogether, to a time of primeval forests. The mist, still hanging thick in the air, colluded with this impression.

"I love this park. Main streets on every side but you still feel like you're someplace else altogether."

She pulled him gently along. "Except for the traffic noise."

He would have been happy not talking about UFOs and psychics; he was less inclined to play skeptic with Rachel than

Deveraux. What was more, the subjects still generated anxiety about his career. It was increasingly difficult to shake the impression – legitimate or not – that difficult, unavoidable and significant life decisions were in the offing.

"I wonder why this is all happening to you now. Have you ever experienced anything like this before?"

"Psychic visions? Not at all. None that I can think of. Maybe I'm just going crazy."

"That's a very selective madness."

They turned off the main trail and followed a winding course up a steep hill. The sound of the stream below them grew distant.

"I've read that it can happen after a shock," she said. "I can think of one famous psychic who fell off a ladder, and when he woke up he had, you know, impressions about the nurses taking care of him. Then again, I don't think my friend who saw the UFO on the beach had had any kind of shock."

"She was probably very relaxed. I've been, anyway, every time I saw something." He considered this as they walked, which gave him time to catch his breath when the trail leveled off. "Actually, 'relaxed' isn't the right word. It's stronger than that. It's like – well, you're onto something when you talk about the idea of a shock. For one thing, I banged my head pretty badly on the plane. Maybe that contributed to this. But when we hit the turbulence, something in me completely went... I don't know. Something short-circuited and I thought for sure we were going to die. I guess you could call it 'blind panic.' For a moment my entire being was consumed with fear." He smiled and looked at her. "Is this bad form? Not even waiting till the fourth date to tell you just how frightened I can get?"

"Of course not. I was terrified."

"But suddenly the fear vanished and I was flooded with relief. It was like the complete opposite of the fear, so intense that as I sank into it I slipped past what I would say is normal relaxation and kind of, I don't know… I sank into myself. I don't mean I became oblivious to my surroundings. I became *more* aware of them, because some part of my personality had shut down. I was more a receptacle for impressions than an interpreter of them." The ideas had started to flow and he found himself trying to catch them before they slipped away. "I mean, that's what we usually do – we interpret our perceptions at almost the very moment we become aware of them. Or even before we become consciously aware of them. We filter them. It's like there's a computer inside us that rapid-fire determines what we need to know about our surroundings and blocks out the rest. That's what short-circuited when I was overwhelmed by fear on the plane. I guess that's what makes it a 'blind' panic. The computer knew there was nothing I could do, strapped into a hulk of metal, thirty thousand feet off the ground, and it conked out. In those moments after I realized we weren't going to die, when I was experiencing that intense release, the computer hadn't kicked back in yet. I was seeing a little bit of reality that I normally block out."

He paused and looked out at the forest almost without seeing it, his words still running around in his head. Is that what had happened? The phrases that kept coming up when he thought about the problem – "electrical storm," "short circuit" – they were just metaphors. But did they point to some kind of underlying truth?

"Do you think that's what happened when you had the vision of Bill?"

"Not quite. But something like that. I was exhausted, but

I hadn't had any kind of shock like on the plane. I was simply tired, but my mind was filled with thoughts. I was thinking about Bill. I almost felt like he was there before he was there. As I say this I understand that one could say I was perfectly primed for a hallucination. Maybe I was. Anyway, that's what I said to Alex this morning. But I sank into myself. I was in that state in between being awake and asleep – when the computer is less efficient, when it starts to confuse external and internal impressions." He paused, surprised at the turn of his thoughts, at the smoldering sense of discovery he was feeling. "I'm sorry, am I making any sense to you?"

She nodded. "I think so. But keep going."

"What makes sense, maybe, is to hypothesize that the picture of the world we usually carry around in our minds with us is somehow incomplete. I look around me and I think, in a nutshell, 'what I see is what I get.' But what if what I see is merely what my computer is programmed to see? That is, my perceptions are filtered for whatever reason – probably it's more important for me to cross the street safely than to see strange lights in the sky – and after a time, by force of habit, I get locked into the program and think it's telling me the only truth there is to be told about the world. In a way, that's what Bill was talking about in the context of science and methodology, and… Ugh. I'm sorry. I get an idea and I need to run with it."

"Don't be silly. It's fascinating. It would help explain why children tend to have more psychic experiences than adults. Their 'computers' haven't been fully programmed yet."

He kissed her. "You're a genius."

"Thank you."

The patter of raindrops on the overhanging leaves increased in tempo as they walked down the hill. They allowed their momentum to pull them into a jog, and when they got to the bottom they paused to catch their breath. They were in a clearing, and now felt the rain against their skin.

Rachel said, "Keep walking or head back to my place and get out of the rain?"

He looked straight up into the sky and let the drops of water splash against his face, then shook his head like a dog shaking off after a bath.

He said, "It's wonderful, but let's dry off."

★★★

They stopped at the grocery store on their way and picked up deli food and drinks, afterwards walking the four blocks to her house in steady rain. She turned on the heat as soon as they stepped through the door, then sat on the bottom step of the stairwell and pulled off her boots. Elliott also took off his shoes.

"My roommate's away, visiting her boyfriend in Santa Barbara, so we've got the place to ourselves." She stood up. "Let's have some lunch."

He followed her into a small kitchen. The house looked maybe a century old. The hardwood floors were scuffed and worn and the walls needed a fresh coat of paint, but the archways, wainscoting, and other subtle architectural flourishes gave the place distinction and a warm, cozy feel. The kitchen had a gas stove and an ancient-looking refrigerator. He put the grocery bag on the counter and began unloading it.

A towel landed on his head and Rachel said, "This will have to do for the moment. All my extra towels are in the laundry."

He rubbed his hair with the dishrag and smiled at her. She was wearing jeans and a beige wool sweater that was long and loose enough to drop below her waist, but form fitting enough on top to allow for the curves of her breasts. Her cheeks were red, her dark hair wet.

She said, smiling, "Don't look at me like that."

He kissed her and she pressed against him. His thumb slid along the smoothness of her cheek, then his hand buried itself in her hair; his other hand pressed against the small of her back, holding her to him. She gave his lip a gentle bite and whispered,

"Let's at least put the groceries away."

"I'm having a hard time thinking about food," he said, pulling away and handing her a triangle of Brie from the bag.

She said, "I don't know. I'm always hungry after a good walk." She closed the refrigerator door and looked at him, concentration creasing her brow. "In fact, maybe we should go back to the store and get some more food."

In his single-minded state it took him a split second to realize she was joking. She took his hand and pulled him from the kitchen. He followed her up a narrow flight of stairs to her bedroom. A large window overlooked the street, filling the room with gray light. Just above this, the ceiling slanted sharply with the roof. A few clothes sat in a pile by a bookshelf. An acoustic guitar leaned against the closet door. Another stack of books sat beneath a nightstand by the bed. He felt the flow of warm air from the vent by his feet.

Her lips tasted like strawberry and he remembered she had taken a sip of her drink before putting it away. Her wool sweater felt scratchy against his hands and he slid them beneath it, up the curve of her back, across the strap of her bra, letting his fingernails glide gently over her skin. She untucked his shirt and slid her hands over his belly and back. He drew in a sharp breath; her fingers were cold and her touch sent a tingling sensation through his body. Each of them started to raise the other's top off at the same time and they got stuck. She said,

"You go first."

He obliged, lifting the wool sweater over her head and dropping it to the floor. Her breasts pressed against the black lace of her bra and against his chest as she leaned into him and murmured, "I'm cold!" His fingers slid over the strap of her bra and, with a deftness that surprised him, unclipped it. Before it could fall away she tugged at his shirt; he raised his arms and she pulled it over his head. The shock of her naked chest against his was overwhelming. His desire surged within him; when he fumbled with the buttons of her jeans his hands trembled. She took them into hers and pressed them to her lips. Her eyes were soft and deep, their blue a transparent ocean. He felt an intense trust in her, so strong it almost made him weep. Her hands undid his belt and his slid her jeans off. They finished undressing and fell back onto the bed. They wriggled about until they freed the comforter from under them and pulled it over themselves. His hands explored her body, sliding from the nape of her neck down to her soft breasts, fingers caressing her stomach and thighs. He almost laughed, so intense was the shock of reality he experienced. She felt so alive; *he* felt so alive, so clear, once again on the edge of some state of awareness in which he was merely a vessel for his perceptions; they flowed through him, bypassing his intellect, battering him with unfiltered clarity. His fingers probed and kneaded her flesh as if it was the first time he had ever touched another human being. His erection pressed against her leg and when her fingers encircled it he barely retained a sense of himself in the rush of pleasure. As she pulled it gently it took an immense effort for him to whisper,

"Not too much."

She slowed the motion of her hand. He forced himself to concentrate on her skin, faintly salty, soft, warm with life. He raised himself on top of her, propping himself up on his elbows, his erection resting against her stomach. His skin tingled with electricity and life, matching the intensity of his mind. In the strength of arousal it seemed his mind and body were one and the same, only the physical sensations threatened to absorb him entirely. Her teeth biting his neck, the smooth skin of her legs over taut muscles, the soft warmth of her breast in his mouth. For brief flashes these individual perceptions overrode all thought, all the usual automatic efforts his brain might make to distinguish between mental and physical reality. Obscurely, an image of himself plunging his fingers into the dirt on Copper Ridge came to his mind. It surprised him, but, unbidden, thoughts flooded his mind to explain: This was the sensuality of matter. This was the prize for struggling with the unbearable heaviness, the disconnection, the pain of physicality – not just sex, but these moments of complete immersion of self in the world. Matter slowed down and extended sensations, whether of pain or pleasure, emotion or thought... No – more than this – in a sense, these sensations were unique to matter because the force of physical existence so transformed them from their source material as to effectively transmute them. In the state he now experienced them they overwhelmed, blinded, confounded and consumed with intoxicating richness.

She again slid her hand between his legs, and he

reciprocated.

He had never felt so free. The thought consumed him with unusual intensity, almost as if it was itself a physical sensation. He felt like he was losing control. But he restrained himself by focusing his attention on the motion of his hand, on the still-sweet taste of her mouth, and finally on the discomfort in his shoulder as it supported the weight of his body on the bed at an imperfect angle. This concerted effort at detachment succeeded.

Then she pulled him inside her. It was like plunging into warm, thick water, a liquid pleasure radiating outwards and massaging every cell in his body. She moved beneath him and he tried to move in rhythm with her, awkwardly at first then falling into synch. Finally he did lose himself, or perhaps he gave himself up, and for a moment he was gone into something wider and deeper.

In the soaring pleasure he drifted, vaguely aware of his own voice groaning at the release. Through half-closed eyes he saw Rachel smiling, and this stirred within him a sense of something that flickered through his thoughts as love, perhaps, but then again, maybe something more, some expansion of the connection of human love into a multiplicity, a web of interrelations that his satisfied but befuddled form could not comprehend. For a moment he followed this impression through his mind as if it were a will-o-the-wisp, flitting through the tall grasses of a dark swamp, until it slipped away and he became aware of something else altogether.

There was something watching him.

He felt rather than saw it, just outside the shadowed borders of his mind. It had been there... how long? He had sensed it, had sensed its thoughts blending with his own. He experienced fear as a sudden lurch in his stomach, but this was subtly and completely wiped away by complete surprise. *Something else was in his mind.* His perception shifted more intently into this inner landscape, but nothing became clearer. In fact, the opposite occurred. There was now only a sense of vagueness mixed with the traces of pleasure trickling through his body and brain. Whatever had been there was gone. He shook his head. Nothing more than a trick of the mind. He became aware of the weight of his body against Rachel's and slid off her, leaving his right arm around her waist. She kissed him lightly, her eyes half-closed, looking drowsy and contented. He smiled with her, pulled her closer, and drifted off to sleep.

HE AWOKE ALONE. Outside it was twilight, with only the silhouettes of trees visible through the window. It took a moment to remember where he was, but when he did he breathed deeply and contentedly. He rolled over to the nightstand and turned on the light. A note lay underneath it: *Off to work. Late! Stay as long as you like, but I won't be back till after midnight. XXO.* He smiled and lay back in bed, staring at the cracks running jagged through the paint on the ceiling. It felt exquisite to lie naked beneath the comforter, breathing in the scent of her presence.

It was only when he rolled out of bed and his feet touched the cold hardwood floor that he remembered the strange sensation of being watched when he was with Rachel. He turned his mind back to the moment, trying to recall exactly what he had felt. It seemed distant, but real. There were elements of the experience that were becoming very familiar to him: a sense of being in a state of awareness midway between sleep and wakefulness, and of being aware of something that was somehow there and not there, all at once. More hypnagogic imagery? But it felt so real that a part of him simply did not accept it was all a dream. The recognition came to him with a sense of amusement: his common sense was telling him that something strange had happened. His intellect still resisted. The awareness of self-division had never been more plain, but for the moment he observed this with ironic detachment.

He stared out the rain-flecked windows and thought:

Okay, then, why would all of this be happening now? If I am psychic – and even now the idea carried with it a sense of absurdity – *why is it all coming so thick and fast?*

He pulled on his clothes and turned out the light. There was just enough twilight remaining to allow him to find his way down the stairs. In the kitchen he took the brie and an open bottle of white wine from the refrigerator. A loaf of French bread in a paper bag sat on the counter. He sliced himself some of this, added the brie, poured himself a glass of wine, and sat down at the table. He was hungrier than he thought. The cold, mild astringency of the wine sharpened his concentration and brought him fully awake. He flipped through the newspaper while he ate, feeling disconnected from it, part of his mind still working with other thoughts.

When he was done he returned to Deveraux's. Five minutes into the walk a downpour began and by the time he arrived at the house he was shivering and soaked. He showered and changed into pajamas then poured himself a large whiskey on ice and retired to Deveraux's study. He was not tired – several hours of sleep at Rachel's had seen to that – but he could not bring himself to go out again. He pulled a book at random from the stack he had taken from Mathiesson's.

He read for hours, sipping whiskey, feeling like he was taking a tour of the last year of Bill's intellectual life. He was in the perfect frame of mind to appreciate the material now. Outside the cold rain fell steadily, inside he was warm and comfortable in the tattered armchair, glowing pleasantly from the drink. He read through speculations on the advanced astronomical knowledge incorporated into ancient structures at Tiahuanaco in Bolivia, the Giza plateau in Egypt, and Stonehenge in England. He turned to books on world mythology, studying charts of correspondences between the legends of Native Americans, Celts, Sumerians, various African tribes, Australian aborigines... So many tales of "gods" introducing the arts of civilization, agriculture, science, and so on, after a global catastrophe. He reviewed arguments concerning the vast scale of the Great Pyramid at Giza and other construction marvels of the ancient world, like Machu Picchu in Peru and the Oseiron Temple in Egypt. And he saw familiar puzzles in a new light, like how agricultural techniques came into use independently at roughly the same time across the globe: after existing as hunter-gatherers for hundreds of thousands of years, mankind suddenly made the leap to farmer between twelve and nine thousand years ago in areas as diverse and disconnected as Thailand, Northern China, the Near East, and South America.

It all amounted to a very reasonable collection of evidence hinting at the existence of an advanced civilization in prehistory. Not an airtight conclusion, but certainly nothing to be ashamed of hypothesizing. Somehow this civilization had vanished – the evidence seemed to favor a sudden, cataclysmic destruction like a cometary impact. The survivors dispersed to different regions of the Earth and educated indigenous people, who may have considered them to be gods.

Why were there no traces? Well, as Deveraux had pointed out, perhaps there were, in the form of the stone monuments scattered around the Earth. If a large enough asteroid or comet struck and set off a chain reaction of earthquakes, volcanic eruptions, and floods, perhaps even altering the face of the globe and instigating a new ice age, would any hints of civilization remain when the dust settled?

Maybe if they were as massive and permanent as the pyramids at Giza. But otherwise it seemed very unlikely.

What if psychometry really works? Could I figure out what really happened?

He remembered the rock in the kitchen but the thought of attempting to read it again made him realize how tired he was. And a little drunk. Hours of reading in the same chair had made him feel sluggish, uncomfortable and mentally exhausted. It took an effort to push himself up and climb the stairs to his room. But when he lay down in bed he could not fall asleep. His brain continued sifting through bits from his reading: images of imagined cities, cometary impacts, floods washing over the Earth… all jumbled with other random thoughts rambling onto the stage of his mind, none of which seemed real enough to punctuate his restlessness. Even thoughts of Mathiesson and Rachel felt two-dimensional, superficial. He found himself wishing he had an "off" switch.

His mind shifted gears and he began thinking about his career. Immediately he experienced a hollow sensation in his stomach. He had been avoiding thinking about it, but at some point he would have to decide, and at the moment the decision framed itself as an either/or situation. He could either tow the line or let go of it altogether. There were no half-measures, no writing under a pseudonym like Alex. Either he followed the path that seemed to be unfolding before him, in the process abandoning the security of a tenured career, or he betrayed Bill – and perhaps the truth as well.

His stomach rolled, the room swayed gently.

There had been times in college when he had had no money, when the bills fell by the wayside for a few weeks, when he scrounged for food for a few days until the next installment of his loan or his bookstore paycheck came in. But never anything serious, no hardship transcending inconvenience. Now the thought of returning to that state was frightening. It seemed far more serious now that he had a house payment and was looking towards saving money for the future, settling down... A return to instability was the last thing he wanted, poised as he was on the verge of attaining the career in science he had always wanted.

In the midst of these depressing thoughts he became aware of a strange pressure in his head. Not pain as from a headache, but... it was like an unformed thought slowly burgeoning inside, taking shape, waiting to express itself, like words on the tip of his tongue. It was the first thing to pique his interest enough to distract him from the scattered shuffling of thoughts in his brain. He sensed that if he just relaxed his mind, let the stray thoughts fall away, he could grasp it.

He recalled the psychiatrist's advice to observe himself. Here was another opportunity to do so; only now he felt cautious. Something did not feel right in his gut, but he reasoned his way out of it. The reluctance had to be due to stress, to unfamiliarity with these unusual phenomenon in his brain. Only he should be getting used to the strangeness by now...

He forced his curiosity to overturn the unease, and dropped his resistance.

The pressure relaxed as if a bubble had burst, and anxiety trickled into him. He made himself think: *No. Relax. Don't stress about it. See what happens.*

A peculiar, uncomfortable sense of... *invasion.* Restlessness, as if an internal alarm was going off.

But it had to be connected with the distressing thoughts

about his career. Anxiety, fear, losing his job, ending up destitute. And thoughts of Mathiesson. That's all this was. In the hypnagogic state emotions were taking on greater force, taking shape, coming to life. Alcohol had made his mind sloppy, too, and lowered his resistance. This was uncomfortable, but there was no reason to feel threatened.

He observed the anxiety growing, tried detaching himself from it. Images drifted through his mind, so fragmentary that it was difficult to grasp a single one of them. At first all he could make out was that they disturbed him, made him feel soiled, and… now there was malevolence. How strange. It felt so real, so *there*, in his mind, soaring over images of broken cities, smoke rising from the ruins, bodies piled high, and there in his mind a sense of glee, heaps of soiled consciousness returning to matter, ashes, lumps of dead matter dragging down and down and down

Get out!

death, purging, back to matter, right the wrongs, the disequilibrium, their fault, their ignorance keeps us from going back, level the earth, cleanse, and go home

There came into his mind images of clouds of dust layering over green life with barren earth.

covering the mistakes with the refuse of matter, dead matter stripped of life, of the power to harm, humankind the blind parasite, infecting the ether with clumsy groping thought, dragging us down, crippling, civilization, disease, mocking heaven, mankind nothing more than animate clay, no purpose, no intention, barren, like matter itself –

Profound satisfaction roared through him. Death cleansed infected tissue, loosened the grip of matter.

But the pleasure was momentary, confused, giving way to hopelessness and despair.

there is no *escape*

He tried opening his eyes, half-aware of his body, no control over it.

trapped deadweight matter pressing down constricting squeezing

Why why why why?

The flow of images ceased, the last specks of dust expelled from a void. Dead space, floating emptiness, consciousness alone. Aware, powerless.

An ache, a longing so vast, so inclusive it could not be sensed at first because it was all there was. To have back what was gone forever.

Something is inside me again.

It was strange, this sense of recognizing his own voice inside himself, as if he had been outside of himself, watching, and now recognized the inappropriateness of the situation.

The spell broke abruptly. His eyes snapped open.

But the feeling of pressure in his body increased, and with it a concrete sense of the presence of something else, something inside him scrambling to hold on. He had slipped free and it was trying to catch him again. Without thought he twisted inside, exerting a force of will as if wresting free of an unwanted embrace. He squirmed, struggled, clawed his way back into himself, into what he knew, drawing strength from a strange combination of calm and revulsion resolving into relentless determination. This was unacceptable, and he would not allow it any longer. He grasped at the physical – the pressure of his body against the bed, the clatter of rain on the roof, the sour taste in his mouth, even his very awareness of these things – like handholds on a cliff face. And he climbed doggedly, dragging himself up and out, suddenly awake and fully aware, sweating, staring at the ceiling with a feeling of immense gratitude and power.

The phone rang, cutting through the night like an air-raid siren. He was still gasping for breath when he picked it up.

Deveraux's voice sounded unusually crisp. "Paul? Is that you?"

When he replied it felt as if he had not used his voice in weeks.

"It's me. I was sleeping. Having a nightmare."

"Shit. I'm sorry to wake you up. I was just calling to see if you were around. I was going to stay with Christine tonight."

"Fine. No problem."

"Did you have a good time with Rachel?"

"Yeah."

"And?"

"I had a good time with Rachel."

"Ah, well. Better luck next time. I'll see you in the morning. Sorry to wake you up. I hope you can fall back asleep."

He hung up and caught the time on the digital phone. Almost midnight. It felt far later. He rolled his legs off the bed, pressing bare feet against the hardwood floor. The sensation of cool wood induced a profound wave of pleasure, so powerful he laughed out loud. Without thinking he clasped his hands together and squeezed mightily, reveling in the exertion, the sensation of pressure. He suddenly felt invincible.

Why? He did not understand the answer, but it was this: he was back in his body.

It seemed a novelty to reach over and turn on the lamp, to feel the pressure of the switch against his fingers and see the light come on at his bidding. The flash of brightness dazzled him and he laughed in delight. Matter pressing against matter, photons firing from the bulb into his eyes. *Cause and effect. This is what a baby feels like.* Pure delight.

He turned his attention inward and started when he caught sight of something else there, something receding like a shadow in encroaching light.

Just a nightmare?

Of course not.

He probed inside, suddenly aware of the cavernous vastness of his own mind, of nooks and crannies and wide open spaces. Plenty of places to hide. An inner landscape encompassing a whole other world of unexplored jungles and mountains and oceans. And he was familiar with only a small patch of ground a few yards in diameter.

Intellectually, he had always understood: the brain is the most complex lump of organic matter on Earth. It was a cliché to say that human beings only used a tiny piece of it. But this was an abstraction. He felt now that he was seeing this inner vastness first hand. It was as distinct a difference as between reading about the Amazon jungle and actually going there. The analogy was apt, for he felt like an explorer dropped beside the edge of an immense, uncharted landscape. What bothered him most was the recognition that he had no map.

23

HE SENSED THE DIFFERENCE in himself as soon as his fingers touched the surface of the plaque. It was as if a window opened in his mind. He relaxed, his breathing grew deeper, more regular. Suddenly the window expanded and he hovered in a gray sky above a broad expanse of dark water. He was distantly aware of sitting in the kitchen, but the accompanying sensations were muted; it was easy to let them fade to the point of inconsequentiality. He dropped beneath the surface of the water and saw a school of fish visible only as a cluster of shadows in the dim light. He sensed agitation in the water, close to the surface, and rose out of it again. In the distance were flashes of jagged lightning and the roll of thunder.

The thought of "land" came to mind and he found himself over it in the dim light of early evening. He was aware of life and tried to draw his attention towards it.

The effort had the reverse effect. When he exerted his will the internal vision faltered and the kitchen regained a dimension of solidity. He relaxed his attention, allowing the inner experience precedence. *Passivity is key. Slow down thoughts. The more I analyze the more it slips away.*

He retreated to a point where some other part of him seemed to take over. He felt his breathing slow down even further, and with it his mind. The space between thoughts grew; instead of the near-constant stream in normal consciousness, thoughts became like random markers dotting an enormous and otherwise empty field. The part of him he typically thought was him now seemed insubstantial, a piece of something larger.

Images flowed into his mind. Evolution unfolded before him. Precambrian flatworms, jellyfish, broad-leaved plants waving gently in the water like flags in a breeze, superceded by trilobites, red sponges, tubular nautiloids and others inhabitant of the Cambrian era, 500 million years distant. A bizarre-looking creature swam past. It possessed a segmented body as long as his forearm with rows of flat "fins" running horizontally down either side. Multiple eyestalks and a tongue-like tentacle poked out of its head. It was one of the strangest looking things he had ever seen. As he watched it his sense of time slowed and he became aware of the explosion of life occurring around him. Life had begun with a trickle that gathered momentum into a torrent. Its foray into matter was an unqualified success.

Experimentation. There was a feeling that life was "trying out" various forms to see which worked best. A black-eyed sea scorpion swam past, crablike arms and pincers extended. What at first appeared to be plants were actually bulbous collections of cells – perhaps animals, perhaps something in between. Trilobites were made strange by their sheer size and number as they swarmed across the seafloor like an infestation, some almost two feet long. The abundance of life seemed excessive and the small part of him that remained intellectually active made what felt vaguely like an inquisitive gesture.

He immediately became aware of a presence, not an organism in the water, not something inside himself, but something existing at the same time as this glut of life exploded in these primitive oceans. He felt it as a vibration first, an energetic impulse rippling through the ether, and it was only after shifting his attention to it that he became aware of it as an intelligence. Now that he tuned into it he sensed it everywhere; it did not seem to have a discrete existence, instead permeating everything he felt to be living. It was some kind of propulsive force, something in part responsible for the wild diversity of life.

This awareness was so strange that he experienced a perturbation of his mental equilibrium. A bubble of curiosity rose within him. What was the source of this ambient intelligence? Was he perceiving it accurately? Was it an aspect of his own mind or was it outside him? Was it the mind of God?

Almost as suddenly as the questions came up they were quelled by some kind of internal stabilizing mechanism; he was not aware of consciously enabling it, only of a vague desire for his equilibrium to be maintained. There was a clear sense that he was performing a balancing act, that if his thoughts made him top-heavy he would drop out of his trance state and his conscious mind would resume control over his perceptions. He was not ready for this, and the intensity of his questions was transformed into an almost disinterested curiosity.

He rose out of the water and became aware in an unseeing way of some kind of non-material entity existing in the air around him. Its presence was a subtle, non-constrained concretization of energy in the atmosphere, only slightly thicker than air. He had the feeling it could dissipate without effort and reform elsewhere. Why it was there was a mystery. He did not feel in contact with it. It was existing as an image "remembered" by the stone, as part of a film being played back for him.

There were others around him. It was difficult to feel

where one ended and another began, but he had a sense of multiplicity, of bustling activity in the atmosphere. Animated and lightweight, casually formed whorls of energy blending into one another, dissipating and reforming with a kind of playfulness, like children splashing together in a wading pool.

He had no idea how long he experienced this before he realized the clusters were disappearing. Instead of reforming after they dissipated they simply did not return. There was nothing traumatic about it. It was like the children had been called home and the waters they had played in grew still.

He was underwater again, viewing sudden and drastic changes. Barren. A slowing of life energy, a dying-off of material forms. It was not that the seafloor was littered with carcasses, but that great portions of it were empty. Clusters of sponges were few and far between. No trilobites to be seen anywhere. But here and there were signs of movement, of business as usual. Life had not disappeared altogether. It had slowed down. It had suffered a setback.

Then the environment began to recover. A succession of images showed a reburgeoning of forms, some familiar from previous scenes – sea scorpions, trilobites – but now there were also primitive, armor-plated fish. Plants looked more like plants. Long strands of seaweed flowed with the current. Without conscious direction his mind shifted again to perceive the swirling dots of energy that had returned to the scene. The implication was clear: their presence in some way accelerated the pace of evolution. They were now almost visible in the environment, odd bulges in space, slight warpings of visible space wherever they congealed. He approached them but was unable to bring them into clearer focus. It was like trying to catch a ripple of water.

Soon the fish began to look more familiar as well. Plates

of armor shrank to resemble scales. He saw what looked like a coelacanth, its lower fins pushing against the water more like a salamander than a fish. Coral landscapes, bustling with life, stretched towards the surface. He rose out of the water to see a land engulfed by mats of vegetation, wriggling with slime-coated amphibians and millipedes and proto-spiders. Further inland were burgeoning forests.

The air sparkled with the shimmering swirls of energy, but as he watched they again began to disappear. His impulse to follow them was met with a new sensation, something like running into an invisible wall. Wherever they went when they vanished, it was "out of the picture"; the rock had not recorded it. He drifted back under water and sensed decay again. The withdrawal of the energetic presence – beings? – had somehow sapped the creative stream of life. Not terminated it, just slowed it down. The coral reefs were abandoned and decrepit houses. Isolated clumps of mollusks dotted the sea-floor.

On land there was less devastation. And as the shimmering energies returned the electric flow of life resumed. Flying insects buzzed over steaming marshes that blended into massive primeval forests. Amphibians and sail-backed reptiles slipped and wriggled through the mists. Enormous clumps of ferns and moss-draped trees squeezed against each other, choking the landscape in suffocating abundance. Life on land had exploded into being.

He caught occasional glimpses of iridescent movement in the air. More often he was simply aware of the presence of some kind of intelligence existing alongside the unfolding drama. That it was playing a part was obvious, but he deflected the impulse to analyze the question intellectually. The clearest impression was one of pleasure. His mind tingled as he drew nearer to the energy. He was not experiencing the pleasure, however. He perceived their exuberance. "They"? Were these dots of energy truly intelligent and capable of feeling pleasure? Were they some kind of life-form?

This he could not determine. He perceived them mainly as vibrations in the air around him, pulsing with a rhythm that seemed energetically connected to the panorama of life. When these things were here, life picked up on their rhythm and flowed with it, like a surfer uses the energy of a wave to propel himself towards shore. Without their presence, life still evolved forward, vibrating at its own slower pace; with them the pace accelerated, resulting in bursts of growth and complexity. Life adapted and discarded working models with a speed that, in the rapidity of his vision, took on a kind of miraculous grace. The forests expanded and deepened. The oceans took on new life in new shapes: fish grew into familiar forms, crabs and trilobites scrambled over the ocean floor, primitive sharks preyed on them. Sponges and plants smothered monstrous coral reefs. Diversity and complexity seemed the order of the day; the shells of the nautiloids that he had first seen as straight and tubular now spiraled inwards in ever tighter circles. Others were flat and broad, and still others looked like beehives with tentacles poking out of the bottom. Trilobites adopted a new plethora of shapes and sizes.

He moved closer to what looked like a simple shellfish clinging to a mass of coral. Even this seemingly simple creature was actually coordinated and complex. The shell was parted to form a mouth in which minute tentacles waved, collecting microorganisms from the seawater. His consciousness moved closer, slipped inside the animal, became aware of its heart and stomach, of the system of muscles enabling it to open and close its shell, of its reproductive system and the stretch of fibers with which it clung to the coral. He pulled back and a fish darted past, now streamlined and scaly, cutting through the water to snatch up a proto-shrimp.

The tableau overwhelmed with variety. Seeing it firsthand had the paradoxical effect of making it seem more mysterious to him than ever before. It was not merely that he was aware of another influence on evolutionary processes – these swirling energies that seemed to enhance and accelerate novel developments. These influences in fact went some way towards making the numerous explosions of creative development more plausible. It was simply that there was *too much* complexity. Unless these "energy forms" were somehow consciously masterminding evolutionary changes he could not understand how it was all happening. It was like magic. Yet he felt intuitively that "they" were not single-handedly responsible for the process.

When he released these thoughts he was aware that the world was dying again. The light forms had dwindled in number. Waters choked with particulate. Lifeless reefs. The sky above was thick with smoke and ash. Dim light illuminated a muted gray landscape intermittently dotted with the clumsy, jerking movements of animal life, barren trees, mounds of volcanic ash. And then the process began anew. He could not tell what came first – the sensation of life gathering steam or the reappearance of the energy forms – but in little time the earth greened all over again. Ferns first, then clusters of trees burgeoning into forests of ginkgos, palms, redwoods, pines. Insects and reptiles reappeared alongside odd, mammal-reptile-looking creatures reminiscent of hornless rhinoceri. Rats scurried through the undergrowth.

The energy forms were altered as well, hanging thicker in the air, warping and reflecting light like pools of water suspended in space. When they dissipated the process took longer, their congealed energy trickling away in tiny streams rather than simply vanishing.

Another disappearance, then, and another concomitant die-off – but this one comparatively smaller. The earth renewed itself again with an array of spectacular and monstrous creatures. Dinosaurs roamed the land. Great swamps and forests opened onto enormous plains and mountain ranges. Pterosaurs glided in the sky and plate-backed stegosaurs mingled with herds of long-necked Apatosaurs lumbering like elephants through veritable jungles of ferns. Predators stalked the herds, hurling themselves onto the backs of their prey, plunging jagged teeth into necks, tearing off great swaths of flesh with their hind claws. In the oceans were long-necked plesiosaurs, ichthyosaurs, giant sharks. Seafloor flush with life. Immense coral reefs stretching for miles, beds of sponges. An infinite variety of crustaceans and fish.

Compared to the earliest oceans and Carboniferous forests these were all recent arrivals, but in their world he felt so much an alien that it seemed the oldest of all he had yet seen.

Ever-present were the amorphous clusters of energy. They seemed to undergo subtle changes with the passage of time. Where once they danced, evanescent and sparkling in radiant energy, they had become progressively slower, attaining a depth and shape hinting of actual material forms. As the era of the dinosaurs progressed, the forms no longer coalesced and disappeared with the same kind of buoyant effusiveness; once a discrete unit was formed, it stayed together like a blob of protoplasm. Now and again it appeared to adopt the form of a passing saurian as if trying to imitate the structure of the living body. These attempts usually resulted in misshapen effigies containing obvious mistakes – two or three heads, a clawed arm centered on the sloping back of an *Allosaurus*, missing limbs, or an overabundance of legs. There was something grotesquely comical to the process. Whenever the energy plasms managed to sustain a form for any period of time – accurate or not – they stumbled through the physical plane like drunks. When they encountered physical matter like trees or dinosaurs, both forms shuddered under the force of a minor impact and the more ethereal matter acted like a translucent slime. Lumbering reptiles passed through the forms, slowing their pace as they encountered what must have seemed like a thick mass of sludge suspended in the air. Trees were enveloped momentarily as the energy forms passed around them. Occasionally when this happened the pseudo-dinosaurs poured themselves into tree shapes, but such concretizations did not last for long; they seemed inherently less interesting than mobile forms.

By the time the *Triceratops* and *Tyrannosaurus* roamed the scene the energetic masses had obviously learned some kind of trick. Their forms were now more consistent, less misshapen. They moved with a skill approximating that of the creatures they imitated. By now flowering plants colored the landscape, birds flitted from tree to tree, larger mammals scurried underfoot.

When the blobs of energy tried to adopt these smaller forms they were usually unsuccessful; the larger and slower moving dinosaurs apparently made better subjects. There was no questioning their intelligence. They were obviously aware of their surroundings. Their relationship with life was more difficult to understand. In the past their presence seemed to influence the speed and complexity of evolution. Perhaps this still held true, but the stronger impression was that the entities were somehow slowing down.

At first they played with the forms of living organisms like a game of dress-up. Now there was an air of desperation in their activity. At the very beginning of life on Earth they were barely concretized packets of energy, more evanescent and delicate than bubbles. As time passed they became more and more solid. Now these efforts at self-transformation had become laborious. Furthermore, it became increasingly difficult to shake off a form after taking it on. Once the entities had been able to come and go in matter. Now they were getting stuck in it as surely as the massive herbivores around them occasionally sunk into the thick mire of the primeval swamps. The game of dress-up threatened to become permanent.

This recognition struck panic in the entities, compelling rapid, desperate transformations in an effort to remember the trick of dissolving altogether. Their panic infected Elliott. Up to this point he had remained overwhelmingly objective, but the frantic desperation of the things seemed too familiar to resist altogether. Without understanding everything that was happening he felt a kind of sympathy for them. This feeling of being trapped was entirely new to them. Nothing had prepared them for the possibility that they would lose the ability to disperse their energy throughout the universe and flit freely, as pure consciousness, from planet to planet, star to star, to all the radiant galaxies and the realms beyond matter. This was what they were losing as they stumbled awkwardly in the monstrous forms they had congealed into. It was a loss beyond measure.

Plans were taken up and discarded as the entities struggled to escape. These were difficult for him to understand – whatever communication took place between the entitles was beyond him. The few passing glimpses he received were snapshots in a stream of infinite complexity, well beyond his powers of reason. What bits he could process contained shapes and angles, amorphous images and discrete pulses of light.

Then a concerted effort among the creatures, failure, and another effort. A vision of an immense slab of gray stone, an explosion of blinding white light so intense he shrank into himself to escape it, a rabbit hiding in a hole. A glimmer of freedom – only an idea – and another explosion. Then chaos, and the faint, receding scent of death.

24

HE AWOKE DISORIENTED and exhausted and with no recollection of dragging himself back to bed. The gloom set by the early morning light and the steady patter of raindrops against the window depressed him. It took a moment to connect the ache in his lower back to his hunching over the rock to "read" it during the night. The pain nagged whichever way he turned in bed until he finally threw back the sheets and sat up. This was an interesting change from the previous night's experience of exuberance, of the sensuality of the physical world. Now he felt the reverse: the material world was oppressive and heavy, something to struggle against merely to exist in. The effort he made to stand emphasized this: back rippling with pain, head chiming in with a sharp stab over his eyes.

He went downstairs to the kitchen. The stone lay open on the table, the plaque a dull black in the gray morning light. Evidently he had not rejoined the two halves before retiring. Seeing the artifact exposed like this seemed vaguely disrespectful.

He started coffee and sat down at the table, closing his eyes and feeling the heaviness of his body. The visions from the rock felt distant and unreal, dreamlike.

Maybe they were dreams. Maybe I'm delusional.

He smiled at the irony when his intellect – of all things – countered the thought. The evidence went both ways, didn't it? It was hard to imagine a relatively cohesive vision coming to him out of the blue unless there was something to it.

Exactly what that something was – well, that demanded some exploration. He remembered Rachel's comment in response to his suggestion that he was going insane: *That's a very selective madness.*

And that was true. In every way except the psychic one he felt perfectly normal. Of course, that didn't prove anything. This was all so new, and wildly strange.

What if psychometry really works? It could become one of the most important tools science has ever known.

Certainly it would be a mistake to ignore the possibility.

He poured his first cup of coffee and sipped it gingerly, staring at the stone. Bits of images and ideas came to mind like actors congregating onstage, gradually taking the form of the questions he had not allowed himself to dwell on during the vision.

Entities – intelligences – discrete life forms assembling and disassembling in matter. Did they originally exist outside of matter, or as such subtle manifestations of it that they were initially not subject to its laws? They were like sprites or fairies dancing around the universe, coalescing into physical form whenever it suited them, disappearing when it didn't. What happened when they broke apart? Did they retain identity? Did they really disappear or did they instead become something he couldn't see?

More to the point: What were they doing and why?

They had clearly played an important role in the development of life on Earth. Their presence had somehow accelerated evolution. Had they influenced the development of forms? *Not directly. Intelligent. Like all material forms, composed of matter vibrating at a certain rate. Their rate was different from that of the developing life on Earth.*

The image of ripples in a pond came to mind, one set of

ripples emanating from the entities and another from the physical life developing on the planet. When the ripples merged they began to vibrate in concert, each influencing the other and developing a rhythmic relationship that spread back to the original sources and induced a gradual alteration of the original rhythm. Life, accordingly, began to operate at a higher rate. Furthermore, it began, in a sense, to mimic characteristics of the energetic life with which it shared a similar rhythm. It grew more intelligent. Its development became more orderly. Changes in form that should have taken untold billions of years began occurring on a much smaller timescale, sometimes hundreds of millions of years, sometimes less. This was how life evolved so quickly on Earth, through so many millions of forms in such a relatively short period of time. Chance and necessity alone were incapable of transforming the planet in the time allotted – if ever. Life had had help.

But there had been a consequence. A reciprocal effect. The rhythms of the physical forms of life on Earth sprang from matter. These rhythms were far slower, heavier. In its way matter itself possesses innate intelligence. But this is of a type far more alien to understanding than the intelligence of the entities. It is the vast, amorphous awareness possessed by mountains and molten rock, by stars. On its own it would not have developed life in the way that humankind conceived of it. By human standards of reckoning time and development, matter on its own would have stayed where it was, evolving at such an immensely slow pace as to be almost stagnant. But when the entities appeared their presence "energized" matter, activating its comparatively dormant intelligence so that portions of it assembled into organic forms. The consequence for life on Earth was usually called evolution – a movement towards greater and greater complexity.

The consequence for the entities was the reverse. They devolved, gradually losing the ability to ride on waves of light throughout the universe, to assemble and break apart – to exist and not exist – at will. The slower vibrations of physical life on Earth "contaminated" their own vibratory rate, forcing them to slow down, to become increasingly susceptible to material forces until finally, around the time of the dinosaurs, they were almost entirely imprisoned in matter. Their presence had been an incalculable boon – a blessing – for life on Earth; for them it was a curse that cost them their freedom.

The phone rang. Elliott bolted upright in his chair, terrified. His mug tipped over and its contents spilled onto his lap. His hand was trembling so violently as he tried to set the mug on the table that he inadvertently pulled it backwards before letting go; the mug dropped to the floor and shattered. He jerked back from the table and stood up, pulling his bedclothes away from his body in anticipation of scalding coffee burning him. But this was unnecessary. The coffee had gone lukewarm as he sat thinking.

Thinking? That barely described what had been going on. He had started thinking and something else had joined in. *Too many thoughts in there for me to come up with on my own.* Something had been feeding him information. Surprise and fascination accompanied this realization. So, too, strangely enough, did irritation.

The phone persisted. Why the hell was Knight calling him at eight-thirty in the morning?

He reached for the set and paused in mid-thought, suddenly aware of the smooth plastic of the receiver beneath his palm.

Why did he know it was Knight on the phone? It had to be Alex or Rachel. But no, it was Knight, it was definitely Knight. He picked up the receiver.

"May I speak to Paul Elliott, please?"

It was indeed Knight. A clear awareness rose up in Elliott: Knight was nearby and planning to come over. "Bob, hi. This is Paul."

"I hope I haven't woken you up?"

"No."

"I was just in the area and I thought I might stop by to collect that manuscript. Have you had a chance to copy it?"

"Yes. Alex copied it at his office."

"Splendid. Shall I drop by in twenty minutes? Can you give me the address?"

Elliott did so. He hung up with a sense of inevitability.

25

WHEN THE BELL RANG he had just finished putting on fresh clothes and dumping the pieces of mug into the trash. Knight wore a full-length, black overcoat and a brown fedora hat. His bright smile gave the impression that he had been up far longer than Elliott.

"Come in. I'm starting some more coffee."

"That's very kind. Thank you." He removed his jacket and hung it on the coat rack by the door. He rubbed his hands together for warmth and said, "This place seems cozy."

As they walked into the kitchen Elliott said, "I imagine anything would seem cozy compared to the mess outside today."

"Ah, Seattle in October. This is what we've come to expect." He nodded as Elliott pointed to a carton of cream in the refrigerator. "I suppose we should be grateful for the few nice days we've had in the past week."

Elliott poured two cups of coffee, picked up one and said, "I'll let you add your own cream so I don't overdo it. Sugar's right there."

They took their mugs into Deveraux's study. Elliott offered Knight the armchair and swiveled the desk chair around for himself.

Knight sipped his coffee and smiled. "That's very good. Thank you." He was dressed well, in gray slacks and a matching gray vest over a white shirt. He looked immediately comfortable, if a little out of place, in Deveraux's tattered and faded green armchair. He pointed to a stack of loose papers on the coffee table. "Is that Bill's manuscript?"

Elliott nodded. "That's my copy. I think the pages are out of order since I've been reading it here and there over the past few days." He reached behind him and took a large brown envelope from the desk. "This is the copy Alex made for you." He passed it over to Knight.

"Thank you." He set the package on the table and tapped the pages of Elliott's copy. "Have you finished it? What did you think?"

"It's very interesting. In a way it's quite distinct from his other work, but it's obvious that he wrote it."

Knight understood. "He has a distinctive style, doesn't he? Very warm. His character comes through."

"That's right."

Knight picked up a handful of pages and leaned back in the chair, scanning them. "I assume it's along the lines of his talk. The limits of science and all that?" He did not look up as he spoke, creating the impression that he was a busy professor grading a paper. He gave a groan. "Good Lord, this is worse than I thought." He gave Elliott an incredulous stare. "The whole 'lost civilization' argument?"

Elliott felt a flush of embarrassment that made him irritated with himself. "Bill suggests it's an area of investigation that mainstream science has ignored."

"Who built the pyramids? Like in his lecture?"

"And the sphinx, and Teotihuacán and so on. He asks the questions, yes. He wonders if we've really got an ironclad case about how they were constructed with the technology available at the time."

"He doesn't think it was spacemen, does he?"

Knight's sarcasm was unsurprising. "He doesn't say. He

simply identifies some of the problems with the mainstream scenario and suggests they be addressed. He said the same thing in his lecture."

"What else does he talk about?"

Elliott picked up his coffee. "I hesitate to say. I know you're a skeptical audience – which is fine. It just seems better if you read it in Bill's words rather than having me try to distill it after one quick read."

Knight nodded, drew a deep breath and returned the manuscript to the table. He sipped his coffee. "Have you given any thought to my advice?"

"About editing the book? I've thought about it."

"And?"

"I appreciate your suggestion. But you must understand I feel an obligation to Bill."

Knight shrugged and nestled back into his chair, staring into his coffee mug. Finally he said, "Forgive me, Paul. I understand what you're feeling and I admire you for it. I really do. But you don't owe Bill anything. You two were close. I know it's flattering that he asked you to do this. But I have to ask again: do you think publishing this book will do Bill's reputation any favors? It won't help yours, that's for sure. Oh, I suppose if you play your cards just right and distance yourself from the material you might come away unscathed. But that seems rather unlikely." He gave a tight-lipped frown as if thinking about a difficult problem. "Let me ask instead: how do *you* feel about what Bill's written? Aside from the technical questions about the age of the pyramids and so on. What would you think if you were reading it without having known him?"

Elliott hesitated. "It's hard to say without getting into the technical details; they form the basis of the argument. How were the pyramids built? What's the evidence for an advanced civilization predating Egypt and Sumer?"

"You're evading the question. If you read Bill's book without having known him personally, how would you feel about it?"

Elliott opted for honesty. "I would very possibly reject it out of hand. I probably wouldn't even pick it up in the first place."

Knight nodded, satisfied. "Exactly."

"But setting aside career issues, that's not much of an argument, is it? About whether or not certain ideas have any merit? Was there an advanced civilization in the past, are paranormal phenomenon and UFOs real?"

Knight interrupted. "Good Lord, he doesn't get into aliens and ESP, does he?"

"Not really, but he might as well. His point is that as scientists we set arbitrary limits to our field of inquiry."

"Of course we do. A microbiologist studies some specific aspect of cell biology, an archaeologist a particular period in history."

"It's an obvious point, I know. We narrow our focus in order to get something done. But we set metaphysical limits, too. And we fall in love with our theories and resent anyone – particularly non-scientists – raising objections to them. That's why we're so quick to dismiss any suggestion that, for example, we don't know how the pyramids were built. We deem it ignorant and insulting. We act like we've cornered the market on the subject and its nobody's business but our own to critique it."

Knight fidgeted in his chair. He said, "You're arguing that scientists are human. I couldn't agree more. But the problem with what you're saying is that I – and I presume the bulk of my colleagues – don't feel we need to re-evaluate the evidence for our views on prehistory. I don't critique alternative archaeologists because I resent them. I do it because I think they're wrong."

"But what if our feelings keep us from seeing the data objectively? I look at some of the evidence in Bill's book and feel a little embarrassed that I hadn't really considered it until now. I don't know if the scenario it hypothesizes really existed, but there are enough coincidences in the past to at least consider the possibility that some prior civilization dispersed its knowledge to the Egyptians and Sumerians, perhaps even to South American cultures. The simultaneous origins of agriculture, the common myths, sophisticated and shared construction techniques, advanced astronomical observation... The list goes on and on."

Knight smiled as he sat back in his seat. "And I could give you explanations for every item on your list and not have to change my basic picture of the rise of civilizations."

Of course he could. Elliott could give himself the explanations; he was more than just familiar with them. They were part of his own fundamental understanding of prehistory, of an inner template built through years of study. He was only challenging the paradigm now because of a unique confluence of factors: his relationship with Mathiesson, his own experiences, and his emerging understanding that his old way of doing things was somehow less efficient, less inclusive of evidence, less rational than he had always assumed. In a way, Knight was in a different world. And he was perfectly comfortable there. Still he said, "But they're not true explanations. They're hypotheses. For example, we hypothesize that at a certain point in the development of a society both language and agriculture become necessary, and so they just come about, as if on cue. That may be, but it's an educated guess, not a fact. But we settle on it as if it were a fact because we don't want to think about an advanced civilization colonizing the world in prehistory. It's embarrassing to think we could be missing such a massive piece of the puzzle. Maybe it even bruises our egos to think there was an advanced civilization in the distant past and that we're not the pinnacle of cultural evolution."

Knight was shaking his head well before Elliott finished. "I disagree, Paul. Setting aside your enthusiastic forays into psychology, I'll remind you that as scientists we go for the most straightforward explanation. Occam's razor and all that. You know this. The current way of thinking makes the most sense given the evidence at hand. As I said to Bill during his lecture – I don't think there are any great mysteries in prehistory to be solved."

Elliott was not sure how to respond. In one sense there was little to say. He thought one thing, Knight thought the opposite. *And ne'er the twain shall meet.* Nonetheless, he tried, irritated with himself as he fumbled for words. "That's... We're not playing on the same field, are we? If I happen to think that there are genuine problems with the current paradigm then your explanation is no longer the simplest one available. Maybe from my perspective it's simpler to posit a single 'mother' culture that diffused its knowledge throughout the world."

"Atlantis?" Knight's tone was dismissive.

"Maybe. What difference does it make what you call it? The same observation applies to science's views on paranormal phenomena. They don't exist. The so-called simplest view is that they can't exist because they seem to flaunt materialistic laws, so they must be the result of misperception, ignorance, and fraud."

"And so they must."

"But from the point of view of someone who's seen a ghost or UFO or had a dream that foretold the future, science's simplest explanation is hardly robust. It's more likely to be wrong."

Knight gave a theatrical sigh of resignation. "My dear boy, if you're going to start preaching to me about ESP and occult mysteries I'm afraid there's little hope for you. You've got to draw the line somewhere. Think about that."

"I *am* thinking about it, Bob. Isn't it possible that our philosophy of materialism, of reductionism, is just one of those arbitrary limits we set? It makes sense – we can most easily study what we can see and hold in our hands. Break it down into its smallest bits and see how it works. And if we don't look too hard it seems like the material world is all there is. But what if it's not? What if the sum of something really is greater than its parts? Just because we need to see the world a certain way doesn't mean the world has to play along.

"You scoff at paranormal phenomenon, just like I've always done. Why are we so afraid of it? Because if a single case of mind over matter is proven true it undermines the entire materialistic argument. If I can read your mind or have a vision of the future then I've somehow managed to perceive a realm outside the material. The world becomes broader, deeper. The exclusivity of materialism becomes unnecessary." He thought of his visions of the past, of the apparent influence of the entities on the course of evolution, and said, "Even the most basic notions of Darwin become unnecessary. If there's some kind of intelligence other than our own out there, operating unrestricted by material law, then –"

"Like God?" Knight's interruption was calm and deliberate, giving the impression that Elliott was digging himself into a hole and he could only stand by helplessly and watch.

Elliott saw this, but nonetheless said, "Why not? I don't personally think it's as easy as that. But there's no reason why a religious-minded scientist, after observing the intricate actions of, I don't know, a virus invading a cell and replicating itself, shouldn't step back from his lab bench in awe, thinking, 'Isn't it amazing how God works?' The only people who have a problem with that are those with a different philosophy, the ones who step back from the bench and say, isn't it amazing how Nature works, all by itself and without any help from some supernatural agency? Religion is accused of its 'God of the gaps' but science has its own 'materialism of the gaps.' We don't know all the answers, but when we do we're certain they'll be based exclusively on physical laws. Religion and the institution of modern science are both faith-based when it comes to metaphysics. They both succumb to dogma in the face of the fundamental questions, and they both suffer accordingly."

Knight sat back in his chair and crossed his legs. "And how exactly is that?"

"They stagnate. They refuse new answers based on the presumption that they've already got all the answers they need. One of our greatest strengths is also one of our greatest weaknesses. Not just as scientists or theologians, but as human beings. We want to know, to find answers at all costs. We want our understanding of the world set in stone, whether through arrogance or a desire for power or security or whatever. So we prod ourselves on to fantastic achievements – civilization, for example. But once we think we understand something we stubbornly cling to the knowledge, as if letting go would somehow make us slip backwards into chaos. Send us back to a new dark age. What's more, we invest so much of ourselves in our paradigms that we take it personally if they turn out to be wrong. So we dig in our heels and refuse to change, even in the face of overwhelming evidence. We resist new ideas, new paradigms and don't seriously question the old ones."

Knight said, "But you're wrong, Paul. What we do in science, you seem to have forgotten, is put ideas to the litmus test, debate them as objectively as we can, and discard the losers."

"Not quite. We say that, but then we turn around and dismiss evidence for the paranormal or some other 'fringe' idea based on personal bias rather than evidence. We debate acceptable ideas, not unacceptable ones. We debate a fifty-year difference, not a thousand-year one. There are boundaries within boundaries. As soon as I suggest Atlantis existed ten thousand years ago I'm kicked off the playing field altogether. Science is a self-correcting process, but only to a point. It's hindered by the fact that human beings practice it, and what they want – what they need – to believe determines the boundaries of the playing field. Outside those boundaries you're labeled a crank or a non-scientist."

Knight said with irritation, "What do you recommend then, Paul? That we abandon science?"

Elliott felt a flash of frustration. "Of course not. Science isn't the problem. Science as a tool doesn't claim there's nothing out there that doesn't obey material processes. It's the scientists who get caught up in the metaphysics of materialism who say that. Science is a perfectly reasonable attempt to understand the world. But the assumptions modern science rests on are metaphysical. What do I recommend? That we pay more than lip service to this idea and actually start asking ourselves why we believe what we believe. If we come up against a brick wall, some kind of fundamental assumption that we cling to dearly, then we take ourselves to task for it. If so-and-so says they've seen a ghost we don't just say, that's impossible, ghosts don't exist. We say, maybe they did see a ghost. We ask, what could a ghost be? Maybe we first explore the problem from the angle of materialism and then try to stretch our minds beyond that boundary to ask more questions. The complexity of the universe is beyond reckoning at this point, so why on earth do we need to jump the gun and insist we've got the fundamental answers? It's quite possible that we have *no idea* about the fundamental answers yet. All we really have are preferences about what we'd like them to be."

He sat back, surprised at himself for going on so long. Surprised, even, to hear himself saying as much as he was. Knight in turn edged forward in his chair and said,

"Listen, Paul. You'll forgive me if I don't agree with what you're getting at. To my mind, we have adopted the doctrine of materialism for the best reason possible: it's what all the evidence points to. I think you know that, and I think you're too swept up in emotion over Bill to recognize it at the moment. I know you'll find that attitude patronizing, but I don't mean it to be. You're human, though, just like the rest of us, and your judgment is clouded right now. And tread carefully. What you're talking about isn't merely misguided. It's the kind of thing that will cause you trouble with your tenure committee. Nothing you've said is going to help you get published where you need to get published. Your attitude is, shall we say, professionally unsound."

Elliott was suddenly reminded of Knight's relationship with the chair of his tenure committee. Nichelle Davies was his former student and was undoubtedly proud of her association with one of the most famous men in the field. With sudden clarity he saw that at a word from Knight he could be denied tenure.

Knight continued, "And think about what I said about the book. You'll have plenty of time while you're revising to consider what good publishing it will do." He stood up and reached for the packet on the table. "Thank you for copying this for me. It promises to be an interesting read."

Elliott followed him into the kitchen. He took Knight's mug and rinsed them both out in the sink, feeling dismay at their inability to arrive at any mutually satisfactory conclusions regarding their differences. It was depressing to realize that they had not participated in a true discussion; they had merely stated opposing positions. It seemed impossible that their views could ever blend together; they seemed like magnets with identical polarity, forever repulsing the other's point of view.

Why did this have to be so? If objectivity was the name of the game, then both of them should have been able to discuss their differences more reasonably. Knight was not willing to open himself up to these... aberrant possibilities any more than Elliott would have been a week ago, before seeing visions of lights and doppelgangers and unknown history, and before reading Bill's book. But for that matter, some of the force of Elliott's own argument arose from his mounting dislike of Knight. Perhaps even as a reaction to his own uncertainty about everything. *So much for objectivity.*

Then there came a sinking feeling... Had he said too

much to Knight, a man who likely had undue influence on his academic future? Their conversation could end up being much more than an intellectual exercise if Knight chose to put in a negative word with Nichelle Davies. It was standard practice at his college to request outside evaluations for tenure – to send out a candidate's CV to sources outside the college proper for supposedly objective reviews. Given Nichelle's connections with Knight it was quite possible she would request an evaluation from him. Tenure decisions always possessed an element of arbitrariness. Elliott knew he was a reasonable candidate, but no one's academic record was perfect. He could have published more, or in better journals. He could have cozied up to Nichelle Davies and the rest of his tenure committee more effectively. What often tipped the scales was a good word from the right person. Or a bad one from someone like Knight.

He turned to find Knight examining the rock. He was so focused that it was a moment before he glanced up at Elliott. "This is interesting. What is it?"

Elliott crossed to the opposite side of the table. Why hadn't he wanted to discuss the rock? Maybe he should have started with it instead of spending so much time talking about the limits of science. The rock could teach more about that subject than a hundred books. "Something Bill inherited from Gene Attenbaum, who found it in some very old strata."

Knight traced his fingers along the surface of the rock. "How old?"

"Sixty-five million years."

Knight let out a low whistle. "You've been holding out on me, Paul." He pulled out the chair and sat down. "This is why Bill changed his mind about everything."

"I think you're probably right."

Knight studied the rock, drawing his index finger along the fossilized impressions, then turning to the half of the stone that did not contain the plaque. Elliott watched in silence, expectantly. In that moment he accepted the absurd possibility that the rock really was sixty-five million years old, that the plaque in it was a kind of storybook relating a hidden aspect of life on Earth.

"This was his justification for letting go of his better judgment." Knight stood up. "Would you mind if I take some pictures of it? I've got a digital camera in the car." He turned away before Elliott had time to answer.

Did he mind? Why not? He had given up the idea that he could convince Knight of anything. Maybe the rock would do it for him.

Knight returned holding his camera. "You don't mind?"

"Be my guest."

He took several shots of both sections of the stone. "It's fascinating, I have to admit. Ingenious, if it's a hoax." He lowered the camera. "Any details about where it was found?"

Elliott pointed to Knight's copy of Bill's manuscript. "He discusses it in there. I also have one of Attenbaum's catalogues listing it."

"May I take a look?"

Elliott retrieved it from the study, found the relevant page, and handed it to Knight, who produced a notepad and pen from his vest pocket.

"Have you had a chance to look into it yourself?"

"I haven't tried to verify it, no, if that's what you mean. Not enough time on my hands."

Knight smiled. "No, of course not." He returned the notepad to his pocket and extended his hand. "I'll let you know if I find out anything interesting about it."

Elliott was surprised at Knight's complacency. He said, "What do you think?"

As they walked together towards the front door Knight said, "Do I think that rock is sixty-five million years old? No, of course not. But I'll look into it, like any good scientist should." He pulled on his coat. "And maybe I'll find something to make you change your mind about these opinions you've taken up. Maybe I can even make you think twice about publishing that book. Really, Paul, it won't do anyone any good."

"I'll keep that in mind."

Knight put on his hat and reached for the door. With his hand poised on the handle he said, half to himself, "I wonder why Bill was holding out on me? Why do you suppose he didn't share this with me while he was still alive?"

Elliott was surprised to see that Knight appeared genuinely hurt. Mathiesson had not taken him into his confidences. They had been colleagues and, in a way, friends, for over a decade, but Mathiesson did not share with him what was obviously a watershed in his life. Knight was seeing this clearly for the first time. Elliott felt a rush of sympathy for him, but the answer to his question was obvious. "I suppose he knew you'd be skeptical. He wanted to get his facts in order." When Knight remained silent he added, "He must have felt vulnerable. He was trying to build a bridge between one paradigm and another. And in the beginning it must have seemed pretty fragile. To share it too soon, before he understood enough himself, might have caused the whole thing to collapse."

Knight smiled warmly and opened the door. "Thank you for saying that. Just keep it in mind while you think about publishing the book."

They shook hands. Elliott closed the door behind him.

26

"I don't know what to talk about first. Normally it would be about Rachel, but this might be a rare instance where my lasciviousness takes a backseat to intellectual curiosity." Deveraux grimaced as he ground the gears starting up again from a crosswalk, then sighed as he immediately had to stop for a red light.

"I'm glad I can bring that out in you."

"Tell me more about what it's like to read the rock."

"I don't know what to make of it myself. I'm in a kind of trance. Somewhere between being asleep and awake. I'm sure you've experienced something like it yourself when you're on the verge of sleep – your friendly psychiatrist Peter thinks it's a hypnagogic state. You're almost asleep and your brain tosses around random thoughts."

"A kind of clearing house for the day's impressions."

"Yeah. Only when I read the rock it's more consistent, more vivid… It's like a sustained hypnagogic state. Usually you pass through that state quickly on the way from normal consciousness to sleep. Imagine if you paused there, on your way, and were aware of what was going on, not in a disoriented, dreamy kind of way, but in a state more like everyday consciousness."

"You make it sound like a waking dream." Elliott nodded. "But then what's to say you're not really dreaming?"

"I don't know." They drove up a steep hill with the freeway on their right. Elliott stared out the window at the rain, recalling a newspaper report about a blizzard in Ohio.

"During the experiences there was no questioning their validity. It was the same thing when I saw Bill in the hotel."

"Ahh, but that's like a dream too, isn't it?"

"I thought I was the skeptical one."

"Don't get me wrong. I'm already convinced something's going on. I just want to understand better how it works. The library's just past that row of apartments over there." Deveraux zipped through a light, slowing abruptly at the sight of another car pulling away from the side of the road.

"I don't know what to make of it. But at the time the experiences actually seemed more real, more vivid and intense even than..." He spread his hands to indicate the world around them. "Than all this."

Deveraux simply nodded as he concentrated on squeezing into the vacated spot.

Elliott followed his own train of thought as they walked through the light rain. What did he mean, more real? As they walked his senses were directed outwards, but there was something almost feeble about his perception. He barely took in the wrought-iron gates and the cherry trees lining the damp sidewalk. He was aware of them, but they possessed only a two-dimensional reality. When he actually focused on them they seemed poised to gain a third dimension, a kind of depth that made them seem more real and more meaningful.

But the "depth" that he became aware of when he focused his attention on a cherry tree, for example, was actually more than spatial depth, more than a sense that the tree was an actual physical object that existed in three dimensions of space. There was also a sense of it as a living thing, something with a history and a future trajectory. There was a sense of his connection to it, of his awareness of the tree somehow engaging him in something like a participatory relationship with it. And this, he recognized, almost gave him the impression that the tree itself possessed a kind of awareness, one that somehow touched Elliott's but which was vastly different – meaning that its web of relationships, those things of which it was aware, with which it was connected, and its very way of existing in this web were almost totally foreign to him. Only in this brief moment did they overlap, and only now because Elliott had actively shifted his own awareness to the tree.

Was this a trick of the mind? Was he in some way anthropomorphizing the tree, granting it an awareness it did not really possess merely by shifting – and thereby transferring – his own active attention to it? Perhaps. It did not seem so. In fact it seemed quite the opposite – that he was actually expanding his own awareness to include a recognition of the tree as a sentient being. But he could not see a definitive answer to the question. And the same line of reasoning applied to the issue of whether his visions were an accurate reflection of reality or merely waking dreams. When he was experiencing the visions, it felt as though his attention was more focused, his awareness magnified, just as when he actively concentrated on the cherry tree. If this was actually the case, one could argue that in such a mental state he was taking in a greater amount and a more tangible kind of information. Following this line of reasoning one could hypothesize that information gained in this fashion might more accurately represent reality than everyday perceptions.

Then again, it might all be a dream.

He could not shake a feeling of frustration as they stepped inside a small brick building. Elliott followed Deveraux up a narrow wooden staircase and down a hallway lined with various offices for massage therapists, acupuncturists, and herbalists. At the end of the hall they entered what looked like a bookstore: rows of shelves were lined with new books. A desk with a cash register sat just offset from the middle of the room. As at Rachel's bookstore the air smelled of incense. Deveraux said,

"The library's in back."

They said hello to a woman reading at the desk and went through a doorway at the back of the store, down some creaking wooden steps into another large room lined with books. The smell of incense was replaced by the musty odor of old books. The library was a single large room. Many of the shelves had glass-paneled doors on them, some with locks. Their footsteps sounded heavy on the hardwood floors after the carpet in the bookstore. At the far end of the room was a large desk set against the wall. Sitting behind three tall stacks of books was a thin, older-looking man with a round face hidden behind glasses and a heavy beard. He looked up at them as they stopped in front of the desk and said calmly,

"Alex. How nice to see you."

"And the same goes for me, Marcus. Meet my friend, Paul Elliott."

Marcus stood up from behind the desk and shook Elliott's hand softly. He was quite thin; this might have been accentuated by the way his shirt was tucked tightly into his jeans. His beard was reddish-brown, slightly darker than his thick head of hair, and it worked with the shape of his face and the small glasses he wore to make his head seem too large for his body. Elliott could not quite guess his age. Perhaps in his fifties, but there was a sense of energy to him that indicated he might be younger.

"A pleasure to meet you, Paul. What brings the two of

you here?"

Deveraux said, "Research, of course."

"What are you writing about today?"

Deveraux glanced at Elliott before saying, "Er... Nothing exactly. Not quite yet. We're here on an exploratory mission. On behalf of Paul, really."

Marcus transferred his smile to Elliott. "And what line of work are you in, may I ask?"

"I'm a paleoanthropologist at a college in Ohio."

The librarian seemed genuine as he said, "That sounds like it could be quite interesting. I was once on the academic path myself, thirty years ago. But I got sidetracked."

"What happened?"

Marcus smiled and his eyes strayed from Elliott's. "Ahh... I fell in love. Silly, really. But it was the early seventies. I was a hippie. The counterculture and all that. I gave up my ambitions to be an English Professor and followed my heart to start a commune in upstate New York. It even worked for a while. By the time we fell out of love I was already on to other things."

Elliott asked, "Such as?"

Marcus spread his arms, indicating the room around him. "This is the legacy of the sixties that stayed with me. I stopped the drugs, for the most part, but kept at the expanding consciousness stuff."

Deveraux said, "It's a shame you can't get a degree in esoteric wisdom."

Marcus nodded. "Quite. Though I'm not sure the pay would be any better. Now, what can I help you with?"

"I was telling Paul about Denton's book on psychometry. I took it out a few years back to do a piece on psychic archaeology."

"Well I'm afraid you can't take it out anymore. It's over a hundred years old and has started falling apart. Follow me." He stepped out from behind the desk and walked to the far end of the room, stopping at one of the glass cabinets that had a lock on it. He produced a ring of keys from his pocket, inserted one into the lock, swung open the door and crouched down by the bottom shelf. "Here we go." He lifted four books from the case and set them on a nearby table. Three of the books looked their age: well-worn, with creased and faded brown and black covers. The odd one out was a paperback that looked much more recent. Marcus said, "*The Soul of Things*. Published around 1880. Unfortunately they've only reissued the first volume," – he tapped the paperback – "so these others are quite rare."

Deveraux looked surprised. "I didn't know there was more than one volume."

"There are three."

Deveraux scanned the bindings and picked up one of the volumes, saying, "Volume two." He thumbed through it then gave Marcus a plaintive look. "We really can't take it out of here?"

Marcus raised his eyebrows slightly and smiled. Elliott had the impression that this was not the first time Deveraux had asked him for special treatment. "Ah, Alex," he said. "A simple 'no' is never good enough for you, is it?" But something in his tone made it clear he would let them take the books.

Deveraux said, "Great. I'll buy you lunch to show my gratitude."

Marcus replaced one of the older books in the glass case while saying, "You can take the newer version of the first volume." He stood up and added, "How generous of you to buy me a lunch that you will no doubt charge to expenses."

"Ha! I haven't sold the story to anyone yet, so it's all on my own dime for now."

Marcus pretended to be impressed, narrowing his eyes and nodding. "Well, well, well. And when do you think you'll have it written?

Deveraux pointed to Paul, who was watching the exchange with amusement. "That all depends on him."

Marcus turned to Elliott, looking genuinely intrigued. "Well, then, this should be an interesting lunch. Let me get my coat."

★★★

Over hot sandwiches Elliott repeated his story. Marcus was a gratifying audience: attentive and patient, particularly as Elliott struggled to express the variety of impressions and the manner in which he had received them. As he spoke he realized that part of the problem was that he simply did not have the right vocabulary – language itself did not seem entirely capable of accurately conveying internal processes. He was constantly falling back on metaphors that could only approximate descriptions of his mental states. He said as much, but Marcus nodded periodically with understanding, giving him the impression that the librarian might have a better idea of what was going on than Elliott himself.

When Elliott finished, Marcus said, "That is really, really fascinating. Thank you for sharing it with me. It's rare to meet someone with such an elaborate and lengthy kind of vision like that."

Deveraux interjected, "But you *have* met others with stories like Paul's?"

Marcus sat back from the table and crossed his arms. He

looked down at his chest for what felt like a quarter-minute before saying, "Well, not exactly like Paul's. I've known people who could psychometrize a piece of clothing, for example. I've reliably heard about people who get impressions from volcanic rock and that kind of thing. But usually the kind of sweeping vision you've had, Paul, comes channeled. Through a medium. And as I understand it – I've never personally experienced it, mind you – a channeler isn't usually receiving detailed visions but is basically reciting, or being used to recite, messages from spirits. You know, discarnate entities like disembodied human souls, or aliens."

Elliott experienced a flash of skepticism. "Aliens?"

Marcus was unfazed. "So *they* say, anyway."

"What do you mean?"

Marcus smiled. "Well, that's the thing. They say they're aliens or angels or spirits, whatever, but how do we know? That's the question. Why should we take it on faith from them that they're who they say they are? Moreover, why should we automatically believe what they say?" He leaned forward again and rested his elbows on the table. "One of my favorite stories in that regard is of a shaman-in-training, Michael Harner, who had a vision of giant black dragons who told him they had created all life on Earth. When Harner came out of his vision he told the story to one of his mentors, who replied, with amusement I imagine, 'Oh, they're always saying that.' I hasten to add that this doesn't mean that the dragon's didn't create life – who knows? But I take it as a reminder that you can't swallow this kind of experience hook, line, and sinker. There's meaning to it, but we can't, in our eagerness to find that meaning, settle for the first apparently comprehensive story that comes our way. The fact is, there are too many stories out there that seem to answer all the cosmological questions that need to be answered. They can't all be right."

Elliott had listened intently, and now he sat back and drained his coffee before saying exactly what he felt: "That sounds very confusing. And a little disappointing. You make it sound as if I could be delusional."

Marcus shook his head. "Not at all. I didn't discount your experiences. I'm just telling you to be careful about taking them at face value. You mentioned just now that you didn't have the right words to describe everything. Imagine your brain, when it's receiving the visions, doesn't have the right visual vocabulary to express the impressions it's receiving. It does the best it can and it ends up using metaphors. It's kind of like when you dream that you're walking down a street and you hear a car alarm that persists no matter how far away from it you walk. Then you wake up and realize it's your alarm-clock. Your brain is receiving an objective impression, but it's not in the proper state of awareness to interpret it correctly." He took a bite from his sandwich, which sat largely untouched on his plate – it was no wonder he was so thin – and said from the side of his mouth, "If our friend Alex here had read the third volume of Denton's book he would know what I'm talking about."

Deveraux adopted a pained look. "I told you, I didn't know there were three volumes."

Elliott said, "What's it got to do with what you're saying?"

"Volume Three is probably the strangest of the bunch. Denton has his psychometers giving impressions of places like Jupiter, talking about the inhabitants and their cities, that kind of thing."

Elliott said, "That's absurd."

Marcus nodded. "I agree with you. When you first read that it calls into question any impressions you get via psychometry."

Deveraux said, "It makes it all seem like wild imagination. Flights of fancy."

"But then if you're honest you have to consider the times when psychometry actually does work. I've told Alex about archaeologists who've used psychics quite successfully to help them figure out where to dig. And unless Denton is lying elsewhere in *The Soul of Things*, his subjects were often right on target. Other researchers have had similar results. So it's a problem: sometimes psychometry works and sometimes it doesn't. In fact, not only does it not work sometimes, it can give wildly mistaken impressions about, for example, distant planets."

Deveraux smiled. "Unless of course there's a lot we don't know about Jupiter."

"So what am I to make of my own readings? They seem to fit more into the Jupiter category."

Marcus shrugged. "I don't know. On the one hand, yes, they do deviate from modern-day theories of history. On the other hand, much of what you've told me sounds like it would fit in with certain esoteric wisdom traditions. You must have heard, if only peripherally, of the cosmologies of teachers like Blavatsky? Cayce?"

"Only passingly, and only recently. One of the books I took from Bill's study was a compilation of that kind of thing."

Deveraux said, "Paul has been pretty by-the-book as far as his education goes."

"No matter. But you know that every religion – every mythology, in fact – has its own cosmology, its own explanation for how the universe was created, how mankind came to be, that sort of thing. Madame Blavatsky was the founder of Theosophy. She gave us a detailed description of the descent into matter of something that would eventually be mankind. She claimed to have received this information by esoteric means – and she probably did, at least in part – but in truth even her system bears similarities to several others. You've given me a kind of cosmology that partly resembles many others with which I'm familiar."

Deveraux said, "Such as?"

"Well, like I said, Blavatsky's, certainly Edgar Cayce's. But also a lot of the channeled material I've come across. For example, I once sat in on a session with people channeling aliens who claimed to have escaped to Earth following the horrific collapse of their own galactic civilization. When they got here they genetically modified apes to create human beings and then implanted part of their souls into the new bodies, because their own bodies were unsuitable to the Earth's environment."

Elliott shook his head. "I'm sorry, but that sounds like 1950's science fiction."

"Again, I'm inclined to agree with you. But there are similar thematic elements in your own vision. Namely the idea that some outside, non-human influence arrived on Earth and interfered with the natural development of life. And who am I to say that there's no objective truth to these stories?"

"But you pointed out yourself that they can't all be true."

Deveraux said, "But they're coming from somewhere. Either the wild imaginations of channelers and, in this case, you, Paul, or from somewhere outside, some kind of objective source."

Elliott said, "But what kind of objective source are you talking about? Marcus, you used the example of a dreaming brain interpreting what is objectively an alarm clock as something altogether different – a car alarm, for example. Fine. But what's the objective source – what's the alarm clock – that my brain, and the brains of all these channelers, is getting its signals from?"

Marcus clapped his hands together and leaned forward. "That is basically the question that mystical traditions and religions – even philosophers – have been trying to answer from day one. What is the true nature of reality? Because that's what you're asking, Paul. As soon as you start trying to answer that question you've joined a long line of seekers trying to ascertain the secrets about how the universe works."

Deveraux said with mock gravity, "Paul... I never knew..."

Marcus smiled. "Actually, Alex, you've known all along. You know as well as I do, Paul, that science is just another tradition trying to answer the same question."

Deveraux said, "If perhaps in a more close-minded kind of way."

"Well, yes and no. Science has limited its field of study to the material universe and consequently limited the answers it can come up with. But we all know how close-minded some traditional cultures and religions can be. Whether because of power, or some desire to maintain the familiar status quo. It's human nature, really." Marcus shrugged and took another small bite from his sandwich. "I'm not sure that's the point. I think what's important is that there's some profound impulse in all of these traditions, including science, to understand the universe and our part in it. If you settle on one truth, and if you're honest, you'll discover sooner or later that it's full of its own kind of assumptions and contradictions. If you want to keep moving forward you've got to open your mind to other possibilities, including the one that you might never find the exact answer." He smiled suddenly and said, "Sorry, didn't mean to go on so long."

Deveraux said, "Not at all, Marcus." He turned to Elliott. "I've never gotten so much out of him before."

Marcus wiped his beard and said good-naturedly, "That's because you're always using me for something, Alex." He noticed, perhaps for the first time, that everyone else's plates were empty. "Ugh, what time is it? 1:30? I should get back to the library. Sorry to have monopolized the conversation."

At the counter, as Deveraux paid, Marcus said, "What are you two doing tonight? Nothing? Well, then allow me to suggest you accompany me to a reading. There's a woman I know who claims to channel angels and spirits of the deceased. About once a month she'll do a group reading, kind of an informal lecture depending on who comes through."

Deveraux said immediately, "Wonderful!"

"I'll have to call her of course, and make sure she doesn't mind a couple more people. She holds them in her house, which is a little small, and she'll want to make sure you don't bring any negative energy with you." He smiled again. "I can vouch for you, right?"

Elliott said, "I'm certainly not one to cast any stones at this point."

Deveraux slapped him on the back. "That's the spirit, Paul." He turned to Marcus. "Count us in."

27

"THIS IS ETHEL WHITE. Ethel, this is Alex, and this is Paul."

They shook hands as Marcus introduced them. Ethel was a plump, gray-haired woman a few inches shorter than Elliott. She looked to be in her early sixties. Her hair was cut short and the tight curls made it seem to fit unevenly on her head. The look did not flatter her plain features. She seemed entirely normal as she took Elliott's hand in hers and shook it lightly.

"A pleasure to meet you both." Her voice had an odd lack of definition to it, slightly nasal mixed with a sing-song quality.

"Thank you for having us," Elliott said. "It's my first time at something like this." The words sounded banal to him the moment they came out, as if he was admitting something he should be ashamed of.

"I hope you'll find it interesting. I never really know what I'm going to get. Though I feel like it'll go well tonight." She smiled. "You're the last ones here. Shall we go into my sitting room?"

They followed her into a brightly-lit room with eight folding chairs set in semi-circle facing a beige lounge-chair. A small chandelier hung from the ceiling and a bookshelf was placed beside the chair. A stick of incense was set in a wooden holder atop it and the smell of jasmine filled the air.

Ethel said, "I'll be with you all in just a few minutes," and left the room through a different door, closing it gently behind her.

Marcus said, "Hello, Eric, Ann."

As Marcus started talking Deveraux leaned over to Elliott and said quietly, "What do you think?"

"I don't know what to think. If you'd told me I'd be doing this when I came to Seattle for a scientific conference on human origins I'd have laughed in your face."

Deveraux grinned. "And yet, here you are, seeking the answers to human origins."

Marcus' voice interrupted. "Alex, Paul. I'd like you to meet another couple friends of mine."

They shook hands with Eric and Ann. Just then Ethel returned and sat down in the beige chair. She had not changed, and her loose fitting white pants and maroon blouse seemed much too unassuming for someone about to channel angels. She nodded to a middle-aged man sitting at the end of the row, who dimmed the overhead lights to a level approximating twilight

Ethel said, "Thank you all for coming tonight. It's wonderful to have so many inquiring souls in the room with me." She paused and breathed in deeply. A relaxed smile formed on her face and she closed her eyes halfway as she exhaled. She was silent longer than Elliott would have expected; she seemed to be slowing herself down. Elliott observed that her audience was reverentially silent, waiting patiently for her to speak. She inhaled and exhaled slowly again before saying, almost as a sigh, "So much energy in the room tonight. Good energy, loving."

Elliott could not decide exactly how much she was affecting an appearance of relaxation, or of entering a trance state. His skepticism arose spontaneously, without intention.

"And others. I'm feeling others around us, too."

It was difficult, too, to take her seriously when her soft,

slight voice seemed so incongruous with what he expected from someone in connection with the "great beyond." But he found his attitude irritating and intrusive, and he began to consciously sidestep his objections as he had done with the rock in Mathiesson's basement. He was getting better at this. As she continued talking, her voice growing quieter, her pauses longer, he began to relax, to quiet the internal voice of skepticism and dissent, so that he could almost see her purely, objectively, without a parallel stream of commentary passing judgment on her.

But when she spoke again his efforts were completely derailed. Her voice had changed to affect an odd kind of accent, a combination of Middle Eastern and Indian, with oddly placed pauses between words, almost as if she was on a respirator and had to pause frequently to draw in fresh breath. "I see... so much... light here tonight... This is good... good. Welcome... Welcome, all of you." Her eyes opened and surveyed the room as if she was seeing it for the first time. She gave a contented sigh and said, "Before I let you ask... questions... I feel your eagerness! But before that, I want to talk about something... something you already all know, but have forgotten..." As she said this she shook her forefinger at the audience, playfully admonishing. "You have forgotten because you are... no, not sinners... I hear those of you who think that... You are not bad... you are... distracted. You are children in a toy store at Christmas... There is so much to see in this... playground that you call Earth..." Her eyes drifted closed as a smile rose up, and she sat back in her chair. "But you are here to learn... It is only right that you should not know all the rules yet."

Elliott's skepticism overruled his efforts to quell it, surprising him with its intensity. Her presentation was offensive and insulting – how could she expect him to be conned by her? A poor actress who can't even nail a discernible accent.

"You exist in what you would call… cocoons. And the funny thing, the thing we here, watching you, are so amused by… is that you have made these cocoons, you have woven them yourselves with your hopes, your fears, your dreams and nightmares, and… you climb inside them…" She smiled deeply, her eyes closed, and extended the pause for several seconds before continuing, "You climb inside them and then forget to come out! You forget that your birthright is to become butterflies! The most beautiful butterflies in the universe!" The corners of her smile drifted down. "We laugh, but we mean no harm… In fact, it causes us great sadness to see your suffering… We feel your pain, we can even reach out and take a little bit of it away… if you will let us… I see some of you here tonight who know how to do this… Let it be known that all of you have this power to let go of… fear. And we can help… But it is you, finally… ultimately… who must break out of your cocoons…" She smiled again and her voice grew light. "And you will, you know. And as each of you does, there will spread like wildfire from one individual to those around him or her… the freedom of love that will… in turn… help the others break free…"

Elliott scanned the attentive faces in the audience and felt a flash of contempt for them as they lapped up Ethel's vague, quasi-religious pabulum about everyone being lost children of God. He felt himself withdrawing further, even detecting irritation with Marcus and Deveraux for dragging him here. He looked at Deveraux, hoping to exchange a grimace, but the reporter was focused on the medium.

After several more minutes of speaking, Ethel said, "Now

let me take… some questions. I know you have many… and I hope to guide you to the answers you seek."

Ann raised her hand and Ethel said, "Yes, child. What do you wish to know?"

"I'm hoping you can help me understand the recent difficulties I've been having with my business. If you can give me some guidance about how to make things run more smoothly." She spoke with deference and – so it seemed to Elliott – alarming naiveté.

Ethel nodded but remained silent. After a quarter-minute she said, "Fear." She paused. Elliott's irritation increased. "You have fear inside that your work will fail… that your plans will not come to fruition." Ann nodded her head eagerly. "This fear holds you back, child… It is the problem of mankind. The choice between fear and love… one causes you to withdraw, the other to reach out to embrace the universe. And when you embrace the universe the universe embraces you… You are afraid of reaching out to the people who come to you in your work… You are afraid they will reject what you offer them… They sense this fear – we are all children of God, we are all connected… They sense this fear, although they do not know where it comes from, and what happens then, you see… is that they feel fear… And feeling fear… they run. They run from you." Ethel's smile seemed to Elliott a combination of contentment and gentle condescension.

Ann nodded and said quietly, "Yes, yes. I know what you're talking about! How can I do this? How can I let go of the fear?"

"Sweet child… Sweet, sweet child! Thank you for asking… That is the first step towards loving. You must learn… to catch it –" Ethel reached out her hand and closed it into a fist – "catch it like the irritating insect it is… and then… let it go." She opened her fist and stretched her palm out to the audience. "You will see it then… for what it is…" She smiled. "And when the insects stop buzzing… you will notice the love that permeates the very air… around you… You will breathe it in… easily… with great joy…"

Elliott felt himself starting to stand up. He caught himself in time, but his frustration was overwhelming. This woman had nothing to do with him. She was a charlatan, a bad actress with a smattering of knowledge gleaned from the self-help section of the bookstore. She did not have visions of the past, she did not speak with angels. She was wasting his time. Sitting here listening to her was, he realized, making him feel crazy for having visions. All his old skepticism came rushing back to him, driving out the careful considerations and tentative conclusions he had reached over the past several days. Somehow this woman's obvious insincerity was contaminating him. It made him see quite clearly that he had been deluding himself. If he was lucky he was only having some kind of waking dreams. If he was unlucky he had a tumor or something in his brain that was distorting his fundamental sense of reality.

I will not give up my career for this shit.

He realized he was sweating, though the room had at first seemed comfortably cool. Now it felt oppressive and claustrophobic. In his agitation he was taking in deep breaths. He forced himself to open his mind again, to relax. Someone else was asking a question now but he deliberately ignored it, as well as Ethel's response. Instead he closed his own eyes partway and concentrated on taking deep, even breaths. He realized that he was having some kind of anxiety attack and this confused and frightened him. What was happening? Had he simply let his irritation get the better of him, let it catch flame, kindled by anxieties about what was happening to him that he had not yet faced? It seemed possible. There was something irrational in his reaction to Ethel and her audience. He would have understood a more dismissive attitude, but not the outright hostility he was feeling.

Gradually, he shifted his attention outwards again, not to Ethel's specific words but rather to the tone of her voice. Her pauses had become less frequent; she spoke almost fluidly now. His claustrophobia diminished as his sense of the space in the room expanded. He became aware of the people next to him, first through a subtle sense of their breathing, filling the air around him, a rhythmic pulsing melding with the flow of Ethel's words. This was followed by a deeper sort of awareness, of this room full of individuals, of individual minds, tenuously connected by their focus on Ethel. The medium, too, was part of this group; there was some process taking place, something too subtle for Elliott to immediately grasp, and as usual when he tried to focus on it his awareness of it decreased. Intention was not helpful now, at least not the kind that fueled everyday consciousness. Passive attention was the key: allowing the impressions to flow over him without the distractions of analysis and interpretation. This was a kind of balancing act at which he was slowly becoming more adept.

He was vaguely aware of the minds around him – including Ethel's – as trickles of water flowing tentatively towards one another. His awareness was not so clear that he detected individual personalities – he did not sense Deveraux, for example. Only Ethel's mind was somehow distinguishable from the general flow, giving the impression of a warm brightness. But he was conscious of a sort of background noise and imagery that he understood quite automatically to be the thoughts of those present in the room. He could not disentangle these from one another; they were like ambient noise in a crowded restaurant. He was aware that they were beginning to merge, to flow together, and was curious to understand what would happen as this transpired. But his own consciousness of what was happening was somehow keeping him subtly out of synch with the process; he was the observer, and as such he could not entirely participate.

This he took to be the source of his sense of a broken rhythm, an interrupted flow of awareness. It was his mind that was not joining the communal flow. But he was reluctant to let go entirely. It was enough to have come this far, to be aware at this level of the subtle process occurring within the group. To let go of his individual consciousness altogether would entail letting go of that part of him that would remember whatever happened next.

So instead he shifted his attention gently to the discordant rhythm. He had a vague idea that he could perhaps consciously alter it, make it move in synch with those around him without abandoning his individual awareness. He had a sense of tracing it backwards as if he was following a stream uphill to its source, felt himself getting closer and closer until –

– until he became aware that the source of the rhythm was not, after all, *him*. It was something else altogether. Like him, it stood just outside the general stream of minds in the room, somehow vibrating in an awkward rhythm that allowed intermittent contact with the group flow.

And it was aware of him.

He mentally recoiled as he felt it probing him. But his

initial flash of fear – had it lasted any longer he would have abruptly lost his awareness of the group mind and returned to normal consciousness – gave way to curiosity. This thing was aware of him, but its probing was clumsy, giving Elliott the impression that it was only partially aware itself. He had the image of something like an amorphous pseudopod, an octopus, perhaps, tapping a tentacle against a rock to ascertain if it was in fact a mussel that could be opened. But he did not feel threatened; the probing seemed motivated by a curiosity not unlike his own. His predominant sensation was wonder. And he sensed that his own awareness of the creature made it aware that it had found something worthy of attention.

At the same time he became aware of other presences in the room, discrete but somehow fluid and intermingling. He had the impression of them drifting through the room, dipping into the stream of the group mind, sipping from it, then slipping out again. Their driving force was a kind of… thirst. Of hunger. He was aware that their focal point was Ethel, that they were then – that they must be what people called spirits – and simultaneously felt surprise at both their presence and at the thought that Ethel was, in fact, a genuine medium.

The light in the room seemed dimmer than it had previously; now he was not even sure if his eyes were fully open when he saw shadowy shapes coalesce into what appeared to be human forms, standing near Ethel. The faces were blurry, but they began to take on individual characteristics. The taller of the two on Ethel's right was gray-haired, his face a pasty white and wrinkled with lines. His eyes were oddly indistinct; at first they did not appear to be looking at anything. Then slowly they gained a kind of personality, a focus, animation. They seemed to be staring at Elliott. The corners of the spirit-mouth moved up into what looked like a smile and the mouth opened.

Elliott felt himself frozen. Several forms had solidified around Ethel now. One of these was an elderly lady who reminded him of Ethel herself. Another appeared to be a child, a boy of perhaps twelve, with a crew-cut, a t-shirt and loose-fitting shorts, though its legs seemed to fade without reaching the floor. This one was whispering in Ethel's ear. Ethel herself was a solid but mostly dark mass sitting upright in her chair. In fact, all of her surroundings were shadowy and indistinct. Elliott tried but could not turn his head to inspect the rest of the room.

The spirit that had appeared to smile at him moved as if to cross the room towards him and he felt a sudden jolt of fear. As if in response the spirit form flickered and blurred. For an instant the face contorted with what appeared to be malevolence; it happened so quickly that it was hard to be sure. Elliott felt an unpleasant scratching sensation ripple across the surface of his body, sandpaper on skin, and a burning desire to move. But he could not. The figure remained stationary next to Ethel. After a moment it bent to speak into her ear; the boy had vanished.

Elliott felt a peculiar kind of pressure in his head, an odd sense of ideas forming and a desire to speak them. But he could not; it was as if the words were on the tip of his tongue but he had forgotten them. Automatically his attention turned inwards and he became aware again of the gentle prodding of something that was somehow outside and inside him at the same time. This was what was trying to speak. The pressure of ideas was coming from it, and he knew that if he could somehow let go he would understand what it was trying to say.

But he did not want to do this. He felt an instinctive fear, the same kind that had gripped him when he first sensed the thing's presence – the same kind, in fact, that had come over him when he had experienced a similar kind of intrusion just as he was falling asleep in Rachel's bed. Only this time the fear did not go away. Combined with the visions of spirits surrounding Ethel White he felt overwhelmed.

Wake up!

His eyes snapped open. Ethel's voice could be heard distinctly:

"Your father is here with us now, and he wants you to know that your son is with him, that he's looking out for him."

Elliott glanced around the room. Everything seemed exactly as it had before he had entered his trance. Or had he simply fallen asleep? At the moment the question was irrelevant. He was flooded with a sense of relief, exactly as if he had just woken up from a nightmare. He now found Ethel's voice comforting; her words were an anchor to solid reality. He listened with relief as she finished conveying a message from the deceased father of someone in the audience. Her voice was her own now; somewhere during the session she had shed the personality of the "higher spirit." Now it appeared she was merely a messenger rather than an active channel.

After a long pause she said, "I guess that's all for now." She took a deep breath and smiled, surveying the audience. "Let's all just breathe deeply for a few minutes and relax. Imagine a warm, white light shining on all of us here, washing over us, cleansing our auras… That's good. I always find it wise to purify after a sitting. So much energy there, it can sometimes seem… agitating." After several minutes she nodded to the person who had dimmed the lights at the beginning of the session. "Stephen, if you don't mind."

Elliott felt the complete return of normal consciousness as the lights rose. For all intents and purposes, he thought, it was exactly like waking from a dream. He had simply been dreaming for part of the session. This made perfect sense: he had been participating in a séance so it was only natural that his mind should toss up images of spirits, that his subconscious should be informed by Ethel's words. He had seen an elderly man and a boy around the time she claimed to be speaking to just such a pair. He had heard the words and his imagination had obliged by conjuring up a picture for him. Just like Marcus' description of what a dreaming brain might do with the sound of an alarm clock.

He stood up at the same time as Deveraux, who said, "Well, that was interesting."

Several small groups of people had formed and broken into conversation. Elliott felt compelled to leave. The thought of walking outside in the fresh air and rain was intoxicating, the perfect antidote to the claustrophobia he had experienced in the room. At the same time he realized it would be rude to leave so abruptly. He looked around the room. Marcus was speaking with his friends. Deveraux stretched his back and said,

"What did you think?"

Elliott was considering what to say when he felt a gentle tap on his arm. He was surprised to see Ethel White looking up at him, the scolding look on her face tempered by her gentle tone as she said,

"Why didn't you tell me you were a medium?"

28

Elliott felt as if she had kicked him in the stomach. He stared at her, unable to answer.

Ethel said, "They knew, too. I had the feeling that they wanted to talk through you, but you didn't let them."

Deveraux looked from Elliott to Ethel and then back again.

"Is that true, Paul? What did you see?"

Ethel said, "I wonder, did you see anything? I don't often see, I merely sense. Just now I felt that something was going on with you. It was an unusually strong session. I wonder if your presence wasn't somehow amplifying the effects." She seemed to realize for the first time that Elliott looked unsettled. She put her hand on his arm and said, "Why don't you stay after, dear, have a cup of tea. Just let me say goodbye to my guests." She squeezed his arm and moved away.

Elliott said, "I thought I was dreaming."

Deveraux shook his head. "You should know better by now."

"This is all getting a little too strange for me." He sat down again.

Deveraux opened his mouth to speak but apparently thought better of it. Marcus joined them, saying, "So the mystery deepens. Ethel told me to take you into the kitchen to make some tea. What's going on?"

They followed him out the door that Ethel had gone through before the séance. Elliott said, "Actually, I could use something stronger."

The kitchen was cramped. A small table with four unevenly-stained chairs sat in a nook overlooking the street. It was dark outside but the rain could be seen passing through the glow of the streetlamps. The room felt too warm. Elliott took a seat close to the window and pushed aside a stack of well-used cookbooks as Ethel walked in. He felt himself flinch as she sat down across from him.

"That bad? You seem like you're a natural."

He said, "How did you know?"

"I'm not sure. I just felt it. I didn't see anything, but I felt your energy – it comes through as a kind of glow inside me, with your own individual character attached to it."

"I don't understand."

She smiled. "That's okay. I was very confused when it first happened to me."

Marcus was looking through the cupboards. He said, "I think our friend would like something more than tea at the moment, Ethel."

"Above the refrigerator, Marcus." She said to Elliott, "But not too much, Paul. You don't want to cloud your mind."

"I don't know how I could get more confused than I am now."

"Tell us what you experienced."

He told them in detail. As he started talking Marcus set a glass in front of him. His first sip of whiskey burned his throat and warmed his stomach.

When he finished Ethel wrinkled her brow and said, "Something was trying to speak through you. This can't be the first time this has happened to you, can it?"

When Elliott hesitated Deveraux said, "Paul's been having an interesting week." He summarized Elliott's experiences with the rock and his vision of Mathiesson. When he was done he looked sheepishly at Elliott and said, "Sorry, Paul, but we need to get advice from an expert."

Ethel laughed. "I'm hardly an expert. But I can tell you this. When I first started getting messages it felt almost exactly as you describe, like thoughts were forming in my head that I knew weren't my own." She smiled shyly. "I was a secretary at a law firm. My education went about as far as it needed to get me to type and proofread memos. It was a good job for a young woman at the time. Thank you, Marcus." She took her teacup from him and sipped from it. "In my mid-twenties I started having quite vivid dreams. Usually I was in a classroom listening to someone speak about the different levels of the mind or the non-material forms inhabiting the galaxy. It was all very confusing. I wasn't much of a reader, certainly not of that sort of thing. But after a few of these dreams I decided to write them down immediately upon waking up – sometimes at three or four in the morning. I figured I could at least try to make sense of them better in the morning.

"What happened was that shortly after I started writing I felt the same kind of pressure in my head that you described. Only it wasn't to make me speak, but to write. I felt the urge, as I wrote, to let go of my hand, so to speak, to stop telling it what to do, and so I gave into it. I let my hand go limp. But it kept writing. And it wrote out the lessons from my dreams."

Deveraux said, "Automatic writing."

Ethel nodded. "The entity claimed to be my teacher in another dimension. It said I had chosen my current incarnation, with its rather dry administrative occupation, so that I could focus on my intellectual and spiritual development." She colored as she laughed. "Basically it was saying I wasn't very clever and it was there to smarten me up!"

Elliott asked, "What happened to it? Is that what spoke tonight?"

"No, it left me after a few years. I guess it felt like it had done its job."

Deveraux said, "So what were you channeling tonight? Apart from the, er… spirits?"

"That was an angel." She glanced at Deveraux and Elliott from behind her teacup. "Don't look so surprised. Angels are all around us. Even you two."

Elliott said, "I'm hardly one to feel skeptical. But that doesn't mean I don't."

She shrugged. "I suppose that's for the best."

"You asked if this was the first time this happened to me. Something like it has actually been happening quite a lot lately." He looked at Deveraux. "I haven't had the chance to tell you everything. I haven't even had the time to process it myself." He thought of that morning at the breakfast table when it had seemed that something else was prompting his thoughts about the nature of the entities. He thought also of the nightmare the previous evening, and of the sense of something being inside his head while in bed with Rachel. But there was more, he realized. As he considered these incidents more came to mind, coalescing because of a similarity he had not recognized before. There was the moment in the Thai restaurant with Deveraux, Christine and Rachel, when his stray thoughts had slipped away from him and his consciousness seemed to float independently over the vastness of the surrounding area. Of course there was that peculiar moment on Copper Ridge, even before he had seen the lights, when the forest floor seemed to come to life around him. Even when he had first embraced Rachel outside her house it had seemed that his consciousness was hovering in a kind of mid-state, somewhere between the familiar parameters of reality and something incalculably vaster and deeper. There were undoubtedly other incidents that would occur to him if he continued this line of thought, but he interrupted it to say,

"My mind seems, lately, to have adopted a taste for independence. Sometimes it seems something else is thinking thoughts for me – something happened when I was sitting at the breakfast table this morning that I can tell you about. But at other times it seems like my consciousness slips away – not literally. I don't mean I'm having out-of-body experiences, but I seem to have these moments where I dissociate from the… from the immediacy of the present moment. Where my consciousness seems to take in a different tenor of reality. It's a little difficult for me to explain.

"But for the first question: has it happened to me before? Yes, many times over the past week that I can think of. This morning as I was considering my vision with the rock I slipped into some kind of… I don't know, a reverie I guess, that seemed informed by something else. I started getting ideas about these entities that I would definitely not have considered on my own, things I didn't even really understand, about – I almost blush to say it because it sounds a little absurd – about vibratory rates, about how sympathetic vibrations between the entities and life on earth somehow affected the development of both. When the phone rang I snapped out of what I would call a trance so abruptly that I spilled my coffee and shattered your mug." He directed this last comment to Deveraux and added,

"Sorry."

Ethel nodded. "What else?"

He related the nightmare of the previous night. "At some point it was suddenly clear that these thoughts of being trapped in matter were not my own." He considered this then said, "Although I could sympathize, in a way, because I've felt a somewhat similar kind of emptiness, I guess you could call it a sense of meaninglessness, at certain moments in my life. All of us probably have. But this was of a different caliber, like it came from a wider, more profound breadth of experience and understanding. There was a sense of loss, so intense that… I don't know. It was overwhelming.

"This sounds kind of ridiculous to me even as I say it. I mean, I know if you were a more skeptical audience you could easily say I was just having an unusually powerful nightmare. So I don't feel like I can actually convince you with words. I just felt strongly that the thoughts were not my own. Maybe I sensed another presence inside me, though I don't recollect anything so distinct."

Ethel said, "Personally I don't need any more convincing. You sound like you've got the makings of a channeler."

The comment frustrated Elliott. "What exactly does that mean? What could I be channeling? And why would I be seeing spirits, too? You said you don't see anything. I saw images of the people you were talking about. What's more, one of them started to approach me. When I resisted it flashed me a glare that was – I don't know – I guess you could say it seemed evil."

Ethel said, "You were afraid."

"That's right." He sat back in the chair and looked away. "Of course I was. I still am. My visions involving the rock were more… passive. I felt like I was watching a movie, basically. It's entirely different to think that something's paying attention to you."

Ethel placed her hand gently on his arm. "The fear attracts other entities. You'll have to learn to control that. It's very important if you want to open up to this."

"That seems to be happening whether I want to or not."

"I know. It can be frightening. But you have more control over it than you think. Besides, the truth is that spirits are around us all the time. Negative entities, too." She smiled. "And angels, of course. It's just that not everyone can see them."

Deveraux said, "So consider yourself lucky, Paul."

"You just have to have faith that things will work out." Ethel squeezed his arm and smiled reassuringly. "Trust in the universe. I know that probably sounds trite, but it is fundamentally a good place."

Marcus said, "I agree with Ethel, but there are still things you need to look out for. There are negative forces out there, right Ethel? And once you start paying attention to them, they notice you, too."

"They notice you all the time. Spirits are everywhere, and they influence our thoughts, our impulses. In a way they're already inside us. But Marcus is right: once you start focusing on their presence, they become aware of this. Many of them want to communicate to us. Through us. And occasionally you'll come across a bad apple. They're out there in the spirit world as well as this one."

Deveraux said, "What do they want?"

"They like our energy. We have lots of it. Concentrated."

Marcus smiled, "And we leak."

"I don't follow." Elliott was experiencing a sense of disconnect. He found the conversation both fascinating and absurd.

Marcus said, "We're full of holes. Ethel's right to say that we're like concentrated bundles of energy. Picture a universe composed of energy vibrating at different rates. The slower the rate, the thicker the matter. We're concretized energy." He sat back in his chair and smiled. "Does that make sense? It won't sound surprising if you're familiar with modern physics. $E=mc^2$ and all that. But we're not used to applying this sort of understanding to ourselves. Everything is energy, even consciousness. We ourselves are a blending of energies vibrating at different rates: consciousness and denser physical matter. Some say, and I'm inclined to agree, that all matter is permeated with consciousness – the denser the matter the more sluggish the consciousness.

"You can take your pick of metaphors, but here's just one: the universe is like an ocean of energy, and discrete packets of energy are dense little whirlpools in it. Physical matter vibrates, but very slowly compared to, for example, light or consciousness. But it's all energy. And this is why everything's connected. Furthermore, there's an ongoing exchange of energy between different vibratory states. On the one hand you've got the second law of thermodynamics, which talks about the dissolution of energetic states to stable ones. But there's also a creative force that runs counter to this. I would call this creative force *consciousness*." He smiled. "But that's just my opinion."

Elliott said, "Whose consciousness?"

Marcus laughed. "You have a knack for penetrating questions. Some say God's; others posit something either more or less ambiguous. Some say yours and mine."

"Meaning?"

"That we all participate in the creation of the universe.

That our awareness of the universe is in some way not merely passive observation but constructive force."

"I think I'm going to need another drink."

"Hah! But I've gotten off the point, haven't I? Not surprising. I started by saying that we leak. What I mean is that for some reason it seems that, well… Let's fall back on metaphors again. Instead of an ocean let's make the universe a desert of diffuse energy. Physical matter like you and me, we're like oases in this desert. Denser matter – a rock for example – is more stable and consequently doesn't leak energy the same way we do, although everything does leak. Everything breaks down ultimately, freeing what was once focused energy to take on new forms. But apparently for some denizens of the spirit world the particular blending of energy that occurs in the living human form is appealing and, alas, accessible."

Ethel said, "Marcus, dear, you're making it sound like spirits are some kind of parasite."

"That's true. Maybe not all of them, but who knows? Maybe even the good ones are sipping surreptitiously from your energy while you interact with them. At any rate, when I say we leak it's because our forms are unstable. This instability is fundamentally a good thing. It's another word for freedom. Something that is entirely stable has no potential, no possibility of evolution. But at the same time our instability leaves us vulnerable to anything that can exploit it. We have cracks in our façades through which our energy can escape, and through which things can get in."

Deveraux asked, "Are you talking about possession?"

Marcus nodded. "Sure. That, and other less dramatic phenomenon. Mental and physical illness can be caused by entities sucking away our energy." He gave a small laugh.

"Yeah, I know, that sounds hopelessly medieval. So does possession, of course. But it seems that in some instances, perhaps when an individual's personality or ego isn't particularly well-defined, some sort of non-corporeal – or less corporeal – entity can invade, subjugate the personality, and take over the physical form."

Elliott was still experiencing a blend of skepticism and fascination. He said, "And this is what you suggest I open up to, Ethel?"

She wrinkled her brow, thoughtful and concerned. "Marcus is right to warn you of the dangers. Maybe 'complications' is a better word. But I've been able to fend for myself and I bet you can, too. It sounds like you encountered something negative just now and yet you pulled yourself out of your trance." She looked at Marcus with a hurt look – Elliott could not tell if it was playful or not – and said, "Besides, if we didn't have those cracks in our makeup then nothing good could get in either."

Marcus smiled at her affectionately. "I entirely agree. I'm just rambling as usual."

Ethel continued, "And if my angel wants a few sips of my energy I'm happy to oblige. It's the least I can do." She said to Elliott, "Now you, my dear, have to figure out what *you* want to do. You're developing your psychic faculty. It probably started spontaneously for some reason but now the ball's rolling."

Elliott said, "It might have started when I banged my head in the airplane."

Ethel shrugged. "That might be. It can start like that. There's a kind of... I don't know how to put it... rewiring that takes place. It can develop. Maybe it's been going on for a while. You still have to learn to see, to pay attention to things you might normally ignore. That's how you can develop the techniques."

Marcus said, "It's a process of revaluing perceptions. We're programmed to filter out unnecessary data. Imagine driving down the street listening to the news. Someone walks in front of your car and you slam on the brakes to avoid hitting them. You wouldn't be surprised to find that you'd missed what was being said on the radio. Your brain directed all its energies to the emergency. The physical world typically commands most of our attention, unless we're half-asleep or already dreaming. But in a trance state the usual external stimuli are muted. You filter them out for a change, allowing your brain to pick up more subtle signals."

Deveraux said, "Which explains why I didn't see anything on Copper Ridge."

"The trick is learning to control the filters, Paul. Which is something you've already started to do."

Ethel nodded. "It's seems you have lots of opportunities. This rock, for example."

Marcus said, "Tell me more about that. Where's it from?"

"I haven't had time to investigate that as much as I should. A place called the Morrison Basin. I'm not familiar with the geology of the area but the professor who found it had reason to believe it was sixty-five million years old, based on the strata he dug it out of."

Deveraux said, "Perhaps we should make that a priority."

"Why? To prove it?" Marcus sounded skeptical. "I agree in one sense that that's an important question, but it seems Paul's been having these experiences regardless of the rock."

"Fair enough. I'm getting ahead of the game here. Sorry, reporter's instincts."

Elliott said, "No, it's a good idea. Basically everything that's happened to me has been entirely subjective. It's reassuring in a way to sit here and talk this through with you, but I wouldn't mind something more tangible to get hold of. It's like Bill said to me before he died. He said he'd spent his whole life as a scientist and all his answers still needed to be empirical, something he could hold in his hands. I can't shake that desire myself."

Marcus shrugged. "Forgive me if I sound cynical, but good luck finding that absolute proof. You're joining a long line of eminently capable people who've tried."

Ethel tapped Marcus' arm. "Tut, tut, Marcus. You *are* being cynical. Proof comes in all shapes and sizes."

"Not the kind that Paul is talking about." He looked at Elliott. "You want something that will convince everyone, right? Especially your academic peers."

Elliott smiled at Marcus' perception. "I suppose so."

"That might be unattainable. It depends on your criteria." He set his hand gently on Ethel's arm. "For example, I've made it clear that I am personally convinced that Ethel experiences reality in a way different from normal when she enters a trance state, and that she collects information that could not be gained by normal means while in that state." He smiled and looked at her as he continued. "She will tell you she gets her information from angels, or spirits of the dead, whatever. Disembodied entities. It's not my place to argue this with her, but neither can I find it in myself to accept her explanation without reservation. I obviously think it's a real possibility but I haven't personally had any such experiences. Maybe it's some kind of super-telepathy, or something different altogether." He squeezed Ethel's arm gently and removed his hand. "But I say this by way of saying I'm a sympathetic audience. Even before Ethel 'proved' herself to me I was willing to believe in a reality that was more plastic than what we usually allow for. And of course when she told me things about myself, bits of my personal history that she couldn't have had access to other than by my telling her, I was convinced that her abilities as a medium were genuine." He paused and raised his eyebrows questioningly. "Forgive me, I seem to be launching into one of my mini-lectures again. Do any of you mind?"

Deveraux laughed. "By all means, Marcus."

Elliott and Ethel both nodded.

"Alright then. So I've said I'm convinced that she has some extraordinary abilities. Now consider the history of parapsychological studies. You've had a number of eminent scientists studying the paranormal since at least the early 1800s. William Denton was a professor of geology in Boston. Buchanan, the guy who coined the term 'psychometry,' was a professor of medicine. The psychologist William James thoroughly investigated a medium named Leonore Piper and came away convinced. Even Alfred Russell Wallace, co-discoverer with Darwin of evolutionary theory, was a member of the British Society for Psychical Research and a firm believer in the reality of paranormal phenomenon. I could go on and on but the point I'm trying to get at is that the kind of 'proof' you're looking for is already out there for anyone to see. There are books, like Myers' *Human Personality and its Survival of Bodily Death*, that are like telephone directories for the subject – by which I mean they're massive compendiums of case studies thoroughly documenting the evidence for things one might call telepathy, clairvoyance, psychometry, life-after-death – you name it. Personally, I think that anyone who looks at this evidence with an open mind *must* come away convinced." He smiled and leaned forward. "The problem is getting people to look at it with an open mind.

"Parapsychology is a science. It's a big field with a long history. The bulk of modern scientists treat ESP, UFOs, near-death-experiences, and so on, as if they're the exclusive purview of tabloids and cheap paperbacks, thereby excusing themselves from having to consider them. That same approach would allow me to dismiss the entire field of microbiology as unbelievable because I can't see bacteria with the naked eye and I can't be bothered to look into a microscope.

"But of course microbiology and parapsychology are far more complex than that. You can't properly investigate the paranormal by reading the headlines of tabloids in the supermarket or watching superficial television shows about UFOs. Even most supposedly scientific attempts to refute the paranormal tend to be highly selective in the evidence they choose to attack. They'll either pick easy targets – maybe an obvious charlatan posing as a medium – or claim to have found methodological flaws in a particular study and ignore other studies without any such flaws. In a sense it's not a question of proof so much as what they're willing to believe.

"The best way to come to an understanding of a particular subject is to make a systematic study of it. This is what I feel I've done with the paranormal, and why I'm convinced of its reality."

Marcus sat back in his chair. "This might seem like a terribly long-winded way, Paul, of saying that your colleagues aren't likely to be sympathetic to any evidence you offer them. In fact, if you make too much of it you're likely to get fired."

Deveraux said, "Marcus is right."

Elliott looked down at the empty glass in front of him. The room was comfortably warm and he felt that he was among friends. "That became more apparent to me after talking with Bob Knight this morning." He suddenly felt the weight of impending decisions. He had come back to Seattle to enter the next stage of a promising professional career and he now found himself sitting across the table from a psychic. Comparing notes. He tapped the side of the glass absently with his fingernail as he thought. "Maybe you're right, Marcus, and I won't be able to convince the academic world of the reality of paranormal phenomenon, or even that the rock is sixty-five million years old. But I'm beginning to think I'll settle for something a little less."

Marcus said, "What's that?"

He allowed himself a faint smile. "Convincing myself."

29

They gathered where the hill sloped gently down to the west towards an enormous outdoor shopping mall. For some reason he did not find the gravestones out of place in such close proximity to the commercial development. The distant, steady stream of traffic noise accentuated the quiet of their immediate surroundings in the cemetery. Elliott noted with irony that this was the very same cemetery he had pictured in his mind last Saturday in Bill's office, when he had first realized that Bill was dying. He remembered the sprawl of the place, an open landscape dotted with fir trees and headstones, crosses and religious statues, such as the one depicting the Passion of Christ he had passed as he walked towards Bill's grave.

The small group consisted of Martha, her sister, three elderly couples whom Elliott did not know, and a minister. Elliott stood at the back of the group, feeling out of place but pleased that Martha had asked him to come. He had had no real experience with the death of anyone close to him. His father and grandparents had died when he was too young to understand what it meant, certainly too young to possess what he was feeling now: a smoldering sense of his own mortality. His eyes ranged over the field of gravestones. He had been surprised to see dates for people who had died only this year, then chastised himself for his reaction. People died all the time – but seeing dates so close to the present made it all seem more real.

As did standing before the small, open patch of earth

reserved for Bill's ashes.

Cold, gray sky. He shivered in his thin jacket, only partly concentrating on the service. He could not see Martha's expression. Earlier she had seemed calm and in possession of herself. His concern was tempered by an instinctive feeling that she could take care of herself. Further, with her sister and friends present, he saw himself as a kind of fifth wheel, uncertain as to how he fit into this private world of his mentor.

But he felt charged, vital, alive. Full of gratitude. There was a sense of immediacy, an intense awareness of the present moment. *Life is now.* As he thought about this he realized that what he was feeling was more than just a sense of the richness, the complexity and depth of life. It was a sense of possibilities and – just as important – of his ability to take hold of the world, to engage with it and bring to life the latent potential of the world and himself. This was not an unfamiliar feeling, but it was far more intense than usual. Ironically it generated a sudden flash of frustration: *So much wasted time.* He remembered with stark clarity a piece of his final conversation with Bill. He had spoken of his... conversion, for lack of a better word. Of his sense that he had been wrong about there being nothing more in the universe than the blind machinery he had spent his life researching. Of his regret that he would die before he could open himself up to a new way of understanding the universe. *If only I had a little more time. I could open that part of myself. You see, it's just a trick of the mind. Over the years I've trained myself to see only what I wanted to see, and now I understand there's far more out there. I just need time to break the habit.*

Elliott realized that the accelerated events of the past week had given him a chance to catch up. He had clung to certainties that he now saw were nothing of the sort. Whether Bill and Marcus and Deveraux were right about there being more to the universe than materialistic processes remained – strictly speaking – to be seen. But he would try to find out. He did not have to decide ahead of time, did not have to know right this second. The only certainty he could allow himself was that the universe was far more complex than he had ever imagined. He must resist the impulse – the need – to pretend that he understood it before he did.

I must not waste any more time.

The cold sent a shiver through him. With the help of the minister, Martha bent down and placed the urn with Bill's ashes into the grave. When she stood up it felt like a spell had broken. She faced the group, her expression wrinkled with a smile of warmth and happiness, her eyes and cheeks moist with tears.

Elliott stood back from the group as Martha chatted with individual couples. His gaze drifted over the fir trees dotting the landscape, swaying in the wind. The cold sank into him, a damp chill making him increasingly uncomfortable in his thin jacket. But he still felt a positive tension inside, a sense of purpose and determination that he did not want to let go of.

He felt a gentle squeeze on his arm and looked down to see Martha. He was surprised, because for an instant he saw past the age lines on her face, saw through them to the curve of a beautiful face, a willfulness behind the blue eyes, a sparkling intelligence untouched by defeat or cynicism. This vision was superimposed over her older features, but each image was distinct. He was aware of both at the same time. He had the feeling he was seeing her for the first time.

"Are you alright, dear?"

He smiled. "I'm fine. I should be asking that of you. But I guess you're okay?"

She nodded and took his arm. The group had broken up and people were walking up the hill to their cars. Elliott and Martha trailed behind them.

"Yes, I'm okay. I always felt like I got Bill for another year, one we weren't supposed to get together according to the doctors. And he was like a younger man for that last year, so excited about everything."

"Did he share his research with you?"

"Of course. I read his book." She paused and looked up at him. Her tone had an air of pragmatism as she said, "You don't have to publish the book, you know. I don't mean that I don't want it to see the light of day. Just that you don't have to be the one to put it out there." He opened his mouth to protest, but she continued, "I don't want you feeling obligated to do it for Bill. I know it could put you in a bind. He wouldn't want you to harm your career over it, and if you two had had more time together I'm sure he would have made that more plain."

He did not know how to respond. She patted his arm and said, "Don't decide now. Let's catch up with everyone." As they resumed walking she said, "Now, are you bringing this girl of yours to the party?"

He laughed in spite of himself. "You amaze me. Are you sure it'll be alright?"

"I said 'party,' and I meant 'party.' Nothing somber. You're leaving the day after tomorrow and I want to meet her before you go. Bring your reporter friend, too. He can write up something about Bill."

"I'm sure he will at that." He was impressed by the lightness of her tone and was uncertain if she was using it to stave off sadness. "I'll bring them both."

***

A half-hour later he and Deveraux picked up Rachel at her house. She knew they were running late and she opened the back door before Elliott could get out to greet her. Her first words as she got into the backseat were, "Are you sure this is okay?"

Deveraux said, "I asked him the same thing."

"And I asked Martha, too, and she practically insisted. So actually you're expected to come." He turned in his seat in time to see her shrug.

"Alright. I'm happy to meet her and spend a little more time with you before you go. I just hope it's not awkward."

Deveraux said, "If it is, you and I can sneak out and come back to pick up Paul later."

As they drove Elliott twisted around and reached into the back seat. Rachel took his hand in hers and said, "Ooh, cold!" She rubbed it between her hands and kissed it, then leaned forward to give him a quick kiss.

"Hi," she said.

"Hi. I don't feel like we've seen enough of each other."

"Me neither. I'm sorry I couldn't take much time off. If I hadn't just gotten back into town…"

"I know. I've been busy, too."

She laughed. "That's the understatement of the year."

Deveraux said, "If you guys are up for it, and we don't stay too late at Bill and Martha's, let's get together with Christine for dinner."

Rachel said, "I like her. Do you think she'll be my friend after Paul leaves me?"

"I think we should form a committee with the goal of

273

getting Paul to move back here."

Elliott laughed. "Would I have any say in the matter?"

Deveraux glanced back at Rachel. She shook her head. They both said, "No."

"Ahh… well it's nice to be loved at least. Your committee can work on finding me a job."

Deveraux said, "You're always sweating the small stuff, Paul."

The first drops of rain spattered against the windshield as they merged onto the highway. As the road rose up to give a view of downtown Seattle and the Space Needle they saw storm clouds approaching from the west, across the water, darkening the bay with heavy rain as they came. The view gave Elliott a feeling of nostalgia. He said, "Seriously, it's a shame to leave so soon."

Deveraux said, "I assume you really have to?"

"Someone has to finish teaching my classes this semester."

"When can you come back?"

"I don't know. Do you want to put me up over Christmas?"

"Absolutely."

Rachel said, "I certainly wouldn't mind that."

"I'm glad to hear you say so."

Deveraux said, "What will you do with the rock?"

"I had thought of bringing it back with me. Martha suggested it. But I worry about shipping it. If I'm coming back in December I might as well leave it here."

"What can you do with it? Or is there something I can do with it while it's sitting in my house?"

"I don't think so. You'd talked about figuring out how old it is. The problem is you can't date a rock just by looking at it. We'd need to figure out exactly where it was found, what level of strata and all that. Attenbaum's notebook isn't clear. I wouldn't mind figuring out if he wrote anything else about it. Or if he's got a field notebook detailing the find."

Deveraux braked as the stream of traffic slowed abruptly. In the space of a few seconds the light pattering of rain had turned into a downpour; there was a sea of red brake lights ahead of them.

Rachel said, "I hope there hasn't been an accident."

"It usually clogs up around here, even without the rain." The traffic came to a complete standstill and Deveraux took advantage of this to face Elliott. "Aren't there other ways to date the rock?"

"There's radiometric dating, I suppose."

"Which is what?"

"A method of measuring the ratio of radioactive atoms to the byproduct formed after some portion of them decays."

"Ahh, yes. Just what I thought." Deveraux turned to Rachel. "Can you explain that to me, my dear?"

"I could, but I think it's better if you figure it out on your own."

"The point is that the plaque is in a chunk of sedimentary rock, which is a composite of a whole bunch of different materials. So it's very difficult to date."

Rachel said, "What about the plaque itself?"

"That's a better candidate, especially if it's igneous rock – volcanic in origin. That's easier to date. But even then you'd be left with ambiguity. Say it turns out to be volcanic rock dating to sixty-five million years ago. That doesn't mean the carvings on it are that old. I could carve my initials into a hundred million year old piece of rock in the Geology Department but clearly that wouldn't make my carvings that old." He thought about this as the pace of traffic picked up again. The worst of the downpour was over. "There's one more thing, and that's the fossils on the outside of the rock encasing the plaque. If they really are index fossils – that is, if those pine needle impressions could really *only* date to sixty-five million years ago – then, it would basically prove that the plaque is that old. At least as far as I'm concerned. So two questions need to be answered: exactly where did Attenbaum find the rock, and are the pine needle impressions index fossils?"

Rachel said, "And how do you find that out?"

"I don't know. Unless I can get ahold of Attenbaum's field notebook, if it still exists, I can't figure out anything more about the actual excavation. But the question of index fossils could probably be solved by looking up another paleobotanist." He ran through a mental list of names of faculty at his college and said, "And I don't think there is one back home."

Deveraux said, "All the more reason to come back for Christmas."

★★★

They parked up the street from the house. Several other guests had obviously had to do the same because the rural road was lined with parked cars. At two guests per car, Elliott estimated there must be at least thirty people in the house. Then he remembered that they had driven past a row of cars on the other end of the street and revised his estimate upwards.

Rachel must have been thinking along the same lines. As they walked through the rain towards the house she said, "Well, at least I'll be able to blend in with the crowd."

Elliott took her hand. "Don't worry. I won't know most of these people myself. Besides, I know how you feel. The service this afternoon was smaller and I didn't know anyone except Martha and her sister."

Deveraux said, "Do you think Knight will be here?"

"I would be surprised if he wasn't."

"But he wasn't at the service today?"

"No."

They walked up the stone pathway to the house, brushing water from the leaves of the overgrown rhododendron as they squeezed past it. In the quiet of the evening they could hear muffled conversation through the walls of the house. Elliott opened the screen door and made to knock, but he noticed that the front door was already cracked open. When he pushed he encountered resistance. It swung open from inside; a silver-haired couple, both wearing long black overcoats, was leaving. Elliott backed up and held the screen door for them. As they passed Elliott caught the fragrance of a particular kind of pipe tobacco; he suddenly remembered the face of the professor who had just passed. He was tempted to call out, but he and his wife were already on the driveway and he was not sure he recalled his name correctly.

Deveraux said, "Shall we?"

The house was crowded. The overflow of jackets from the closet and coat rack were laid out on an oak chest by the front door. No one else appeared to be leaving. Instead, Elliott had the impression of entering a party in full swing. He was glad he was still wearing his jacket and tie – most people appeared to be dressed formally – then he remembered Rachel and Deveraux.

Rachel had already sussed out the crowd. She wore a

look of what he hoped was comic resignation as she said, "Under-dressed. Strike one."

He took her hand and pulled her closer, smiling as he kissed her cheek. "You look beautiful." And she did, he thought, as she took off her jacket and lay it on top of the others on the chest. She was wearing black slacks and a beige, angora sweater that looked soft and comfortable. Her dark hair, wet with rain, hung loose over her shoulders. Elliott turned to Deveraux and said, "You, on the other hand…"

"At least I'm not in jeans and a sweatshirt." This was true: he wore green khakis and a white dress shirt. It was the tousled hair that tipped the balance towards casual.

"Let's see if we can find Martha."

They walked past the closed door to Bill's study and into a large, open living room with a bay window looking out over Lake Washington. Elliott picked out a few familiar faces. He tried listening for Martha's voice in the crowd but the overall volume level was too great. Even the music from the stereo was buried beneath the tide of voices. He took Rachel's hand and wove through the crowd towards the kitchen. They passed through the dining room, the wall of which was dominated by a window overlooking the lake and the back deck; he caught a glimpse of Knight standing outside in conversation with a taller man who was smoking a cigarette. Beyond them another couple leaned with their backs against the deck railing, facing the house. The taller of the two appeared to be forming a circle in the air in front of him, its outline traced by the glow of his cigarette.

He heard Martha as they entered the kitchen. Standing on tiptoe he saw over the crowd to where she sat with a small group of people at a plain wooden table. He turned back to Rachel and Deveraux and said, "There she is." Then, still holding Rachel's hand, he made his way gingerly through the crowd and arrived at Martha's table. Her back was turned and she did not see him immediately. He waited for a pause in the conversation, but she saw him before one came. She smiled brightly, excused herself, and stood up with wine glass in hand, hugging him with her free arm and planting a kiss on his cheek.

"Paul, my dear. Thank you for coming." She smiled warmly as she took Rachel's hand. "You must be Rachel. I'm glad you could come."

"I'm sorry about your husband. He sounds like he was a wonderful man."

"He was. Thank you, my dear." She looked up to Deveraux and said, "And you must be Alex."

Deveraux nodded and shook her hand. "Elliott's told me a lot about Bill in the past few days, Martha. I wish I could've met him myself."

"I'm glad Paul has a friend like you out here to put him up and shuttle him around. You let me know if you end up writing something up about Bill and want to talk with me."

"That's very kind of you, Martha. I'd love to talk to you whenever you feel like it."

"Can I get you all some wine?"

Deveraux said, "I'll take care of that."

When he disappeared back into the crowd Martha smiled at Rachel and said, "Now, my dear, tell me all about yourself."

Elliott laughed. "I hope you're not screening her, Martha. I already know she's good enough for me."

Rachel said, "Just 'good enough'?"

By the time Deveraux returned with their wine – about ten minutes later – Martha had found it necessary to excuse herself to greet other newcomers. Rachel sipped her wine and said,

"Did I pass?"

"You knew I was joking, right? She wasn't screening you."

"I know. I like her. She seems very smart and sweet."

"Good. I'm glad you hit it off."

She made a show of scanning the room. "Well, let's see… That's one person that I know here, besides you."

Deveraux said, "Two my dear." He extended his arm, crooked at the elbow, and said, "Now what do you say we make our rounds together and leave Paul to talk to some of the people he already knows?"

Elliott opened his mouth to protest that he did not want to be left alone, but at that moment a female voice called his name. He acquiesced, turning to face a tall, slender woman with short brown hair. He recognized her immediately as someone who had been a graduate student at the same time as him, except that she had started several years after him.

"Jennifer! How are you?"

They hugged briefly. She stood back to look at him and he could not help but do the same with her: she was as pretty as he remembered, with her high cheekbones, small nose, and green eyes. Her glasses were fashionable but too angular for his taste. She wore a deep green dress that looked like it was made of soft wool.

She said, "I didn't know you were in town. I guess I should've seen you at the conference."

"I wasn't there as much as I could have been. How are you?"

"Almost done. I'll have to start looking for jobs soon."

"Well, apply to my college. One of the old guard's talking

about retiring next year."

"You can put in a good word for me?"

"Of course." He smiled as he thought: *If my word's worth anything by then.*

They talked until another mutual friend interrupted. It was clear that the two of them were dating: he greeted her with a kiss on the lips and said, "About ready to go?"

A few minutes later Elliott wandered into the dining room and helped himself to hors d'oeuvres, filling his plate with stuffed olives, cheese and crackers, thin slices of wheat bread and a dollop of smoked-salmon spread. As he entered the living room he saw Knight and Martha together in the same small group of people. The group as one laughed at something and the sound rose up to fill the room, a crest on the wave of conversation. Another familiar graduate student called his name and he joined a group that contained a former professor of his and several other faces he did not know. For the next hour he moved from group to group, occasionally reminiscing with people about Bill, more often talking shop and departmental politics. When he recognized one of the elderly couples from the funeral he introduced himself and the conversation ran its course without any reference to science, employment possibilities in anthropology, or whom people were dating at the moment.

When it ended he glanced towards the fireplace. Knight was leaning with his right hand on the mantle, a glass of wine in his left hand, his head bowed slightly as he listened to a younger man. When he nodded and looked up he caught Elliott's eye. He motioned to Elliott to wait, then said something to the person with whom he had been talking and crossed over to where Elliott stood by the bay window. They shook hands and Knight said,

"Good to see you again, Paul. How much longer are you in town?"

"I leave the day after tomorrow."

"Martha seems to be in a good spot at the moment. Handling it well."

"I'm sure it helps that she's got her sister here."

Knight nodded and in the pause in conversation Elliott watched him look around the room, taking in the crowd. From where they stood they could see the front door. Several couples were pulling on their jackets. Martha was embracing or shaking hands with guests as they left. But the house still felt quite full.

"Bill was well-loved, eh?"

Elliott said, "It certainly seems that way."

"Don't worry, Paul, I'm not going to try talking you out of getting involved in Bill's… later work." He smiled with a warmth that did not reach Elliott. "Not too much, anyway."

Elliott sipped his wine. "You're not going to tell me that these people will forget about Bill if I publish his last book?"

Knight arched his brows but then apparently chose to take the comment with good humor. He chuckled and said, "Not at all. Well, the thought had crossed my mind. But let's talk about you instead. Let's set aside Bill's book entirely for the moment."

Elliott felt ambivalent, but he made an effort at politeness and nodded. "You're thinking about what people will think of me if I publish the book?"

Knight shook his head. "Not necessarily. But it does seem you should concentrate on your own work at the moment."

"Meaning?"

"How many papers have you published?"

Elliott opted for a concession. "You're right. It wouldn't

hurt my tenure prospects to squeeze out another couple."

"I'm glad you recognize that. It's hard work getting tenure. Harder these days than it was in mine. The field's getting crowded." He fell silent. The general level of conversation and activity in the room allowed for a longer pause between them. Knight, still looking out over the room, said, "I saw you talking with some of our new grad students. I think we've got a good bunch this year."

Elliott did not know what to say. "They all seem bright. The ones I've talked to, anyway."

"You have good years and bad years with that sort of thing. Of course, you're likely to find that out on your own eventually." He sipped his wine and looked at Elliott again. "Bill was always good with grad students. With all students, for that matter. He really had a knack for getting people enthusiastic. He's probably single-handedly responsible for getting more undergraduates to major in anthropology than the rest of us combined."

The comment was an obvious hyperbole and it made Elliott wonder whether Knight was simply being polite or if he was attempting to ingratiate himself with Elliott. Looking at Knight, he suddenly felt impatient.

"Listen, Bob, why is it so important to you that I don't publish Bill's book? I mean, I can work on it between papers or –"

Knight was shaking his head before Elliott could finish talking. "There are only so many hours in the day, Paul. You can't go chasing ghosts and write respectable papers at the same time." He had attempted to make his tone light, but had spoken too abruptly and ended up sounding dismissive.

Elliott kept his expression impassive. "I don't have to make that decision now."

"No. But you will have to sooner or later.

"But, honestly, what's it to you whether I stand or fall? For that matter, if I drag Bill's reputation down with me by publishing his book? You won't be harmed. You could even write a rebuttal explaining exactly what you find so objectionable about the material. It could actually make you look good."

Knight rolled his eyes. "I don't need to look good, Paul. You should know that. If you think I'm motivated merely by ego then you've got less smarts up there than I thought."

"Then why, Bob?"

Knight shook his head and leaned forward, lowering his voice but speaking each word with emphasis. "Because Bill is wrong. And you're wrong, too, if you chose to follow him." He swallowed the last of his wine and looked away. His face scrunched with irritation. "Bill was a popular writer and a respected academic. That's a dynamite combination. People like that don't grow on trees. I know because I'm one of them. Maybe you will be, too. People like us have a responsibility. We're gatekeepers, educators of the public mind. We keep our world moving forward towards enlightenment. But even more importantly we keep it from slipping backwards into superstition.

"If you want to publish your own book, throw away your own career, go right ahead. Play around with your little rock – at least until you discover it's a fake or there's some other prosaic explanation for it. You're absolutely right – it won't hurt me, only you. But Bill's reputation is public domain. People know him. His name has authority and it bestows legitimacy. You'll most certainly ruin that if you publish his book. But even more, you'll undermine everything that Bill worked for his entire life, barring that single aberration in his last year. You will misinform. You'll open the door to people's superstition and ignorance by appearing to legitimize UFOs, Atlantis, and all that other… *shit.* Publishing Bill's book amounts to an act of betrayal: of Bill, of yourself, of all that we as scientists stand for."

"But, Bob, he wanted it published. He wouldn't have agreed with you."

Knight ignored him. "Look at the world, Paul. It's a mess. Give me that at least. It needs more reason, not less. Science offers this. Our work has brought light to the world. It's made sense out of chaos."

"But dammit, Bob, what if there's something we're missing? We don't have to abandon science! We can extend its reach." He felt like he was stepping off the edge of a precipice as he said, "What if, for example, psychic phenomena are real and could actually help us out of the chaos, help us to better understand our relationship to the universe at large? Isn't it a mistake to ignore that possibility? We can't be so arrogant to think that we can protect people from themselves if we don't really understand how things work. We can't be slaves to theory. We already dismiss huge swaths of human experience because we prefer the illusion of completeness, of comprehension, to the reality that we've got a long way to go."

Knight's face reddened with anger. "I'm less concerned about protecting people from themselves than protecting them from people like *you.*" He shook his head and looked away.

He kept the tension out of his voice as he said, "I'm sorry, Bob. I don't think we're going to get any further."

Knight's shrug reminded Elliott of a petulant child. "Please leave the rock here."

The comment took Elliott off guard. "Excuse me?"

"There may be a legal issue regarding ownership of the artifact that Professor Attenbaum found. Was it his to give to Bill in the first place or is it school property?" He spoke without looking at Elliott. "I'm sure you understand."

Elliott tried to shake off his surprise. "I'm not sure I do."

Knight faced him. "It's simple, Paul. Leave the rock here. If it's as old as you think it is, then it's inestimably valuable, right? We wouldn't want to risk transporting something like that through the US mail now, would we? We'll establish ownership eventually, and if it turns out that it really is Bill's property, we'll hand it over. But in the meantime, I think you'd better leave it in storage here."

Elliott had a hollow feeling in his gut. "But, Bob, that's absurd." Then it dawned on him. "You're controlling access to it." Knight shrugged. "You figure I'll need to study it more in order to publish Bill's book and you're buying yourself time."

"You can think whatever you want, Paul. I do have a responsibility to the department."

"And the public."

Knight gave a tight-lipped smile as he looked at his watch. "Well, as you say, Paul, I don't think we're going to get any further. Excuse me."

Elliott watched him walk towards the foyer and felt a sense of relief in spite of his tension. *Well, that's several more steps in the direction of throwing away my academic future.* He felt sick to his stomach. He drained his glass and headed towards the dining room. It had been at least an hour since he had seen Deveraux and Rachel, and now he felt like collecting them and heading back into town. Nonetheless, he paused in the dining room to pour himself another glass of red wine. As he did so he saw Rachel out on the back deck talking to the same man whom Elliott had earlier seen tracing a circle in the air with his cigarette. The sight of her so soon after leaving Knight brought about an incongruous feeling of pleasure and anxiety. He knew it was not entirely rational, but he thought: *If I give up my job will I lose her, too?*

No, you fool. You're more likely to lose her if you keep the job.

Outside the cold was refreshing. The rain had stopped and a few people were standing on the lawn below the deck; Deveraux was among them. Elliott approached Rachel as her companion again began gesticulating – this time transferring his cigarette to his left hand before tracing an arced line across the night sky and saying, "I painted it on top with heavier colors and let them bleed downwards, trying to get the sky to blend just right." He took a drag off his cigarette and added, "It failed miserably, left me with a soggy canvas, but it was worth a try."

Rachel smiled at Elliott and put her arm around his waist. "Hi. Paul, this is Terry. Terry, Paul."

They shook hands. Terry stood just shy of Elliott's five foot ten. His grip was firm, his smile broad and welcoming. He looked to be in his early sixties, with a full head of gray-hair, a well-lined face and solid build. His voice was gravelly and he cleared his throat before saying, "Pleased to meet you, Paul."

Rachel said, "Terry's a painter living on Bainbridge Island."

"It's good to meet you. How do you know Bill and Martha?"

"Through my parents, really. They were good friends.

Even after my mother died, Bill and my father spent a fair amount of time together. And Bill and Martha have always been good to me. I was very sad to find out he'd passed." He pulled on his cigarette again then stubbed it out in an ashtray on the deck railing. "What about you?"

"A former student of Bill's. He and Martha were always good to me, too. A kind of second family."

"So you must be a teacher here in town?"

Elliott shook his head. "It just so happened I was here for a conference this week. I leave the day after tomorrow."

Terry looked at Rachel and said, "So soon? I thought you told me you just met a few days ago."

She shrugged. "A whirlwind romance. But I'm working on getting him back for Christmas." She said to Elliott, "I told him I've got an art history degree and we got to talking about his work. He has a gallery on the island that we should go see sometime."

Elliott said, "I'd ask you what type of things you paint, but I'd probably betray my ignorance."

Terry smiled. "That's alright. Bill's got one of mine in his office, if you want to look at it later." He rubbed his hands together in the cold and let out a yawn. "Ahh… Excuse me. Have you got the time?"

Elliott looked at his watch. "It's about seven-thirty."

"I think I'd better make my rounds and say goodnight. I don't want to miss the eight-thirty ferry. My car's in the shop and I'm catching a lift home with a friend." He reached into the inner pocket of his jacket, pulled out his wallet and withdrew a business card. "It's the last one in here so you'll have to share, but feel free to stop by the gallery anytime."

Rachel took the card. Elliott shook hands with Terry.

"Paul…" Rachel tapped his shoulder and pointed at the

name on the card.

Elliott felt a shock of surprise. "Terrence Attenbaum? Gene Attenbaum was your father?"

"You knew him?"

Elliott shook his head and tried to quell his excitement. "No, but Bill told me about him. He spoke very well of him."

Terry smiled and leaned back on the railing. "Yep. They were good friends. I was glad they had each other."

Elliott said, "Forgive me for asking. I wouldn't normally be so abrupt, but do you have any of your father's research notebooks, anything that might have been cleared out of his office after he died?"

"A few boxes of stuff. I've been meaning to go through it for the past year, but you know how it goes. Why?"

"Well, he left his fossil collection in Bill's care." Terry nodded his head to indicate that he knew this. "And Bill in turn has left some stuff for me to go through. It'd be helpful to collect as much information as I can to catalogue the stuff."

"That makes sense. Now that I think of it, Bill asked me something about that a while ago, too, but he never followed up on it. You're welcome to take a look. But you're leaving so soon..."

"Well, I hate to ask, but would it be okay if we came over tomorrow for a quick look? I wouldn't normally impose, but–"

"Nonsense. It'll be good to have you both. My wife's been out of town for a week and I've been all by myself. We'll drink another glass of wine to Bill and my dad."

Elliott shook his hand again warmly. "I really appreciate it."

When he left, Elliott said to Rachel, "Well, I'm glad you

met him."

"Me, too. I finally found a use for my art history degree."

30

It was an unusually clear day. From their booth in the ferry they looked out over Puget Sound. To the west the snow-capped Olympics stood out sharply against the pale blue sky. The waters were bright with reflected sunlight and choppy in the wind.

He sat with his arm around Rachel. His free hand held a small cup of coffee which he sipped carefully as he waited for it to cool. He assumed she was as tired as he was; together with Deveraux and Christine they had stayed up well past midnight, first eating out at a different Thai restaurant, then talking and drinking at Deveraux's until sheer exhaustion sent them to bed. Elliott could not remember exactly when he had fallen asleep, but he was still tired; it could not have been too long ago. His head throbbed with dull pain. What had he had to drink? Not *too* much, but more than he was used to.

"Are you excited?" She continued looking straight ahead, out the front window towards the ferry's mid-deck. A few passengers braved the cold and wind outside for the thrill of seeing the bow of the boat slice through the water. *Probably tourists*, Elliott thought, but he briefly considered joining them for the experience. The warmth and comfort he felt were enough to overrule the whim.

"Filled with anticipation. I have no idea if we'll find anything useful. It could all turn out to be a waste of time."

"Well, not quite. It's a beautiful day, and we can always check out his paintings."

"That's right." He squeezed her shoulder. "It's good you didn't have to work."

"Actually, I did, but I got a friend to cover for me. I couldn't let your last day pass by with me at the bookstore." She yawned and sipped her own coffee. "Besides, I'm tired! How late did we stay up anyway?"

"Wake up, sleepyheads!" Deveraux dropped down opposite them in the booth, a splash of coffee escaping from the plastic lid covering his large cup. Elliott did a quick calculation: a pot at his house, emptied with surprising speed, a stop at a coffee shop in the ferry terminal, and now a third towering cup, all within about an hour. Deveraux did appear wide awake – too awake, in fact – but his blue eyes were grounded in dark circles and his face was paler than usual.

Rachel groaned and pushed herself up. Elliott freed his arm and sat up straight. He said, "So glad you could join us, Alex."

"All part of the story, Paul. I couldn't miss what might be the best part."

"We were just talking about that. We might not find anything."

"Ah. Well, that would just thicken the plot."

Elliott stared out the window and felt himself slowly waking up. It seemed strange that by early evening tomorrow he would be back in his house in Ohio. The place felt as remote as a distant memory. What felt real was the cold air sweeping into the room as someone returned from the mid-deck. Rachel's thigh pressed against his, the bright sun and the black water, Deveraux sitting across from him looking exhausted and wildly energized – these things felt real, vibrant, in motion. He had to ask himself again if this was a trick of the mind, and he decided that in a sense it was.

The simple fact was that he was having a good time, that he had allowed himself to relax, to drink, to laugh, to experience simple pleasures. There was no reason why such pleasures should not exist back home. But now he was paying more attention to them, to everything that was happening to him. It was as if his awareness had been notched up a degree. The events of the past week – the scare on the plane, his interactions with Bill and Rachel, the paranormal experiences – had automatically concentrated his attention, and now he was experiencing a dividend from the process. He was learning how to induce a state of attention that brought life to… well, *life*.

It was similar to what he might feel after drinking a glass or two of wine, when everything became slightly more interesting. Why did this happen? It relaxed his mind. Mental filters dropped and senses opened. It was the difference between catching a glimpse of a painting in a gallery as you walked past and pausing in front of it to absorb it, to enter into it. The only difference between such a state and what he was feeling now was one of degree.

Possibly this was a key to his paranormal perceptions, if they indeed reflected some objective – perhaps perceptually distorted – reality. Perhaps the trance state was a variation on the state of mind he was experiencing now, or the openness he felt after a few drinks. All levels of awareness existing on a continuum, degrees apart, but not fundamentally different. And what he was learning to do was to shift between them – or at the very least to stabilize them, to hold onto them and explore the different perceptions they made possible.

What would it be like, as a scientist, to explore reality this way? To recognize that there is not one but a number of ways, of perceptual frameworks through which one can explore reality?

If it would not mean the end of objectivity – the foundation upon which modern science rested – it would certainly necessitate a broadening of the definition, a recognition that studying "objective" reality was not as simple as directing the five senses outward. That method provided one view of one reality, but it seemed unlikely to him that it was the only legitimate one.

He thought to himself, *We've got a long way to go*, and was surprised when Deveraux said aloud,

"We're there. Did you fall asleep?"

He was about to respond when Rachel shook her head next to him and yawned. "I did." She pushed herself upright again and looked down at her lap. "I can't believe I didn't spill my coffee."

***

They drove off the ferry into the bright sun. Elliott sat in the front with Deveraux and read from the directions Rachel had taken from Attenbaum on the phone that morning. Elliott knew that if they turned left out of the ferry dock they would enter the main part of town. Instead they drove north, passing a few gas stations and a movie theater before entering a more rural area. They left the main highway and followed a series of winding backroads through forested hills. Occasionally the trees broke, allowing a view of the water. Twenty minutes after leaving the ferry dock they arrived at Attenbaum's house, which was nestled at the end of a long dirt driveway. As they drove up they were greeted by a pair of barking dogs that ran alongside Deveraux's side of the car. One was a Black Labrador and the other a Cocker Spaniel.

Deveraux slowed to a crawl as the animals paced the car, saying, "It wouldn't exactly endear us to him if I ran one over."

Attenbaum waited outside for them, standing in front of an open garage, wearing a navy blue wool sweater and black khaki pants. He called the dogs to him and they obliged, still barking. When they climbed out of the car the dogs ran back over, the Labrador standing on its hind legs to paw at Rachel – she made kissing noises at it – and the other wove excitedly around Elliott and Deveraux as they bent to pet it.

Elliott introduced Attenbaum and Deveraux and said, "Thanks again for letting us come on such short notice."

"Actually, I'm glad you did. I'm afraid I might have to impose on you. Or more specifically, Alex."

"Oh?"

"My wife called from the airport. Either I forgot or she gave me the wrong date, but she's going to be at the ferry dock in an hour. I am, at present, car-less. Mine's in the shop."

"I'd be happy to give you a lift."

Attenbaum smiled. "I was hoping you'd say that." He swept his arm towards the garage, indicating an open door that led into a kitchen. "Can I offer you some coffee?"

They followed him through the garage and were immediately greeted with the strong smell of espresso. Elliott declined but Rachel and Deveraux both took Attenbaum up on his offer. The kitchen opened into a large living room, the far wall of which was mostly window providing a view of a wooded hill descending gradually away from the house. In the distance, through the trees, the waters of Puget Sound were visible. The living room was spacious and decorated with a variety of artwork – several paintings hung on the walls and small, mostly wooden sculptures with Native American motifs dotted the room. The top half of a large bookshelf displayed delicate-looking china and pottery. They moved as a group into this room. Elliott and Rachel scanned the paintings on the walls. Deveraux wandered to the window and said,

"That's quite a view you've got."

"It's beautiful, isn't it?"

Rachel said, "Are any of these yours?"

"Yes."

Elliott said, "This one? The redwood? I recognize the style from the one that's hanging in Bill's study."

Attenbaum nodded, a pleased look on his face.

Rachel nudged him with her elbow. "And you say you don't know anything about art."

It was actually quite easy to pick out Attenbaum's style. Amidst the more abstract paintings of the four hanging on the wall, his stood out for its distinct visceral quality. Seeing it brought to mind the one he had seen in Bill's study of the water crashing against rocks underneath a turbulent sky. This one was of the bottom trunk of a redwood. The colors of the tree were on the darker side: deep green, browns and blacks, the trunk wrinkled with folds and creases like the lines of an ancient face. In the background there were hints of light illuminating the smaller trees and foliage, but the patches were so small as to appear distant and insignificant next to the redwood. Looking at it, Elliott almost had the feeling he could reach out and run his hand along the ragged bark. The work created an impression of imposing age and power

Rachel said, "It's beautiful."

"Thank you. I'll be happy to show you more later, but perhaps I should get Paul up to my study? I imagine you don't have all day."

They followed him up a set of unfinished stairs. "One of these days I'll stain these. So many projects…" The air smelled of wood and oil paint. They passed a bedroom on their left and a large studio on their right. Elliott glanced into the latter to see a half-filled canvas stretched out on an easel and rows of metal shelves holding paints and canvases. At the end of the hall they followed him into a small room with a window overlooking the same view as the living room. Attenbaum flicked on a light switch and said, "Here we are. I took them out of the closet this morning."

Elliott looked down at the five large boxes on the floor. Two were closed, and the other was filled with upright notebooks that extended past the lip of the box and kept it from closing. He crouched down and opened the other two boxes. The musty smell of old papers rose up. The contents were in disarray, a jumble of papers and notepads. He looked up and smiled. "Well, it might just take all day!"

Deveraux said, "I suppose if you can't look at them all today you've got more reason to come back in December?"

Elliott stood up. "Of course. All the same…" He was reluctant to allow for the possibility that he would not find what he was looking for today.

Attenbaum said, "Take as much time as you can. If you find anything you're looking for you're welcome to borrow it. Just let me know what you take." He stepped over the boxes and cracked open the window. "I know it's cold but you'll probably appreciate the fresh air."

Rachel said, "Can we help?"

He looked around the room. A small bookshelf sat against the left wall, facing a computer desk. A corner table stacked with magazines made it impossible to open the door all the way. The boxes themselves took up half of the remaining floor space. The room could only accommodate one person comfortably. He considered asking to move the boxes somewhere else in the house but realized he would probably work better by himself.

"That's alright. You might as well all go to the ferry. This will probably be a bit tedious anyway."

"Are you sure?"

He kissed her lightly. "Go ahead with them. If you get lunch, bring some back for me."

Attenbaum said, "That's a good idea. If you like, we can swing by the gallery before we pick up my wife. Paul, you know where the coffee is."

When they left he took a moment to look out the window. From this vantage he could see more of the water than from downstairs. From where the sun hung in the sky he guessed he was looking north. Deveraux was right: it was a beautiful view. He pulled out the desk chair and positioned the box with the large notebooks next to it, then sat down and swiveled the chair to face the window. From downstairs he heard first a flurry of barking from the dogs and then the rumble of Deveraux's car as it made its way down the driveway. A minute later the dogs stopped barking and the silence of the woods enveloped the house.

He opened the first notebook.

★★★

It took just a little more than an hour for him to find what he was looking for, but by then he had lost track of time. Gene Attenbaum was nothing if not meticulous, and it was clear from looking through his notebooks where his son had gotten his artistic talent. While many of the pages were filled with tables and ledgers listing data on species of plants that Elliott could not begin to recognize – all the scientific names were used, usually in shorthand – on other pages Attenbaum had taken pains to illustrate many of his finds in such detail and delicacy that they were a pleasure to look at. Elliott even came across an occasional landscape drawing that was probably as detailed as a photograph of the same scene would have been. The result was that rather than being tedious, the project quickly engaged him. He had begun it by flipping through pages feeling that the search was hopeless, but as he focused his attention on the details in the notebook his desperation dissipated. He was impressed by Attenbaum's technical work, but even more by his obvious love of it. He wished he had known him.

The notebooks were not in order in the box – whoever had packed things up in Attenbaum's campus office had apparently pulled things off of shelves at random. The two boxes full of papers did not at first appear to be in any particular order. But as Elliott sifted through them he realized that they were clumped in groups, as if there had been a stack of papers in the office that someone had packed a handful at a time. There were no page numbers, but many had dates written neatly in the upper right hand margin of the page. Rather than going through these page by page he decided first to attempt to put them in order. This was easier than anticipated. When he was done organizing the bulk of the material in one box he quickly ascertained that the year he was looking for – 1953, according to the catalogue Mathiesson had used – was not present. He gave a slight sigh as he looked at the next box but did not allow himself to feel dejected. It was, after all, a minor miracle to be sitting here with Gene Attenbaum's papers at all; if he did not find anything today he could make a more detailed search later. Perhaps there were even boxes from Attenbaum's office at Bill's house.

The thought distracted him. Why had Bill not already been here to look through these materials? He had had a full year. Presumably dating the rock would have been of prime importance to him. It had served as the impetus for his manuscript. More than that: it had launched him into uncharted territories beyond the accepted limits of his field. And Terrence Attenbaum had said that Bill knew the boxes were here. But instead of cutting to the chase and trying to solve the mystery of the rock, he let it lie, mysterious, in his basement while he went about studying the work of pseudoarchaeologists he had spent his life ignoring. This struck Elliott as a very backwards way of trying to solve the problem of the rock.

He continued organizing as the thoughts ran through his head, picking up another handful of papers and setting them on his lap. As he arranged them he glanced down at the stack still remaining in the box. There, at the top of it, was a finely detailed, almost photographic image of the plaque.

31

AFTER A WHILE HE SET aside the stack of notes and stood up, stretching. Outside the window the treetops caught the mid-afternoon light, leaving the forest floor looking dark and cool. The azure sky possessed a depth that seemed to go on forever. When he returned to his chair he set his focus on a patch of blue in the center of his vision, half-closing his eyes and concentrating on his breathing. He let the residual exhaustion of his late night wash over him, encouraging the comfortable heaviness with relaxed, deep breaths. The open window let in cool air and the distant rustling of an otherwise silent forest.

Slow down.

It was truly a process of letting go. Mind racing like a hyperactive child. So treat it like a child, gently. Soothe it, infuse it with calm. There was definitely something new in his ability to enter this state so readily, but at the same time it felt familiar, as if he had always been intermittently aware of it but had never pursued it. It was a human condition, one that he suspected everyone experienced often enough, but never paid much attention to, never followed through to see where it would lead. This was what had happened to him on the airplane, though: intense fear rebounded into such profound relief that he had no trouble collapsing himself into it, sinking deep within himself and allowing his usual protective filters to fall away. Perhaps his ability to continue doing this was a consequence of his brain learning the trick through repetition, as Ethel had intimated. In that sense, there was nothing mystical about it.

These thoughts came as insights, untethered by the step-by-step functioning of the intellect. But they were too tempting for his intellect to leave alone, so he let them slip away, along with his confusion and disappointment concerning the rock.

Time passed, but he gradually lost awareness of it, then…

…a faint pressure in his head, a gentle probing.

Contact.

In his trance it was far easier to cope with the stab of fear. A different part of him took control, relaxing with the mental equivalent of a deep breath. The probing was intelligent. And familiar. But he was still reluctant to let go, to open his mind and allow it access to his thoughts. Even in his trance state the concept seemed contrary to his essential nature: *My mind is my mind. If I let go I will lose control.*

Then he realized this was untrue. He was not in immediate danger. His reticence was an artifact left over from his everyday consciousness – reluctant as always to release the reins. There were layers of himself he had never consciously explored, so rich and active as to resemble other selves, and they understood his mental machinery as comprehensively as a mechanic understands an engine. He had only to trust, to acquiesce, and then let go.

And so he did, gently detaching himself from his concern, still distantly aware of the room he sat in but also of new images filtering into him, gradually displacing his external impressions. Again, the barren ocean, as if he was in contact with the rock and rewatching a recording that began again from the beginning. In the air, the glimmering entities effused buoyant delight. He felt a sudden pang of sympathy:

they were unaware of what was coming. He leaped forward to the age of the dinosaurs. The entities struggled in crude facsimiles of massive reptiles, grew desperate to halt their devolution into matter. Again the immense effort to break the bonds of matter, but this time he detected a sudden withdrawal of awareness, followed by catastrophic explosions on Earth.

How can I be seeing this without the plaque?

In response there flowed a peculiar mélange of images, ideas, impressions, words… all of which some part of him translated into:

We are in direct contact now. The plaque is merely a film, a physical record of what happened through the end of the Cretaceous. Left for us by us.

Elliott understood he had not been reading the plaque as he would have read a lump of clay or a fossilized dinosaur bone. By themselves these items would only reflect their own "experiences," not a sweeping vision of life's evolution.

Why?

As we grew more entrenched in matter, our minds degenerated like our physical forms. Amnesia. What are we? Where are we from?

This was even more horrifying than the loss of control over their physical forms. Their very identities were dissipating. Without knowing precisely what they had lost in their descent into matter they would never be able to recover it. All would be lost. The plaque was their reminder, "written" during increasingly rare moments of clarity, left like a time capsule to preserve the memory of their true nature. It was never intended to be read by humans; his ability to do so was mere fluke.

Not entirely true.

The familiar image of two sets of ripples in a pond, each moving towards the other. One side represented the vibrations of the entities. The other emanated not generally from all life – as was the case when the entities first arrived on Earth – but specifically from humankind. When they merged the resulting patterns were tighter, forming more readily into a single wave.

Mankind is closer in nature to us than other life forms.

Why?

Conifer forests, immense stretches of open plain, dog-like animals, shrews and rodents, hornless rhinoceri, miniature horses and gigantic sloths. The death of the dinosaurs opened doors for mammals. Images rushed past as he was pulled along. They served merely as background information necessary to answer his questions: what was the connection between humankind and the entities? Why was Elliott able to read the history they had impressed into the plaque?

But where were the entities? There was nothing resembling the semi-transparent forms that stumbled through the forests at the end of the Cretaceous, no whorls of energy in the air. Had they succeeded in breaking free of matter?

In response he received an image of a chain snapping, of individual links breaking apart, falling away.

For the first time we lost contact with one another.

The attempt to escape failed altogether, and with devastating consequences. A bond irrevocably broken. Previously the entities had existed like water molecules in the same ocean, discrete but connected, constantly aware of the whole. They played with matter. They played with thought. They were free and connected to one another, existing as one and as multiplicity: a condition of bliss and – for Elliott – inconceivable joy.

Now matter slowed them down. This "devolution" into matter was like a physical and mental degenerative disease – like a person rotting to pieces and losing his mind at the same time. Form and thought congealed, became less malleable, and the entities experienced the anguish of separation. Self entirely separate from the whole. As they lost their ability to play with matter, as they became trapped by it, they slipped gradually into a kind of insanity. More than just the amnesia that led to the creation of the plaques – Elliott had a sudden image of many more plaques scattered across the Earth, waiting to be found – their mental degeneration generated panic and fear for the first time. This was difficult for Elliott to conceive. The entities as a whole had never felt fear, separation, loss, or pain of any kind before. This was their first experience with anything going wrong at all. In this sense they were like children; they had no perspective and no immediate understanding of how to control what was happening to them. Consequently their fear and panic completely overwhelmed them, burning away their connections to each other. Understanding of their true nature grew fragmented, became broken strands of awareness punctuated by the acute pain of loss.

Alone.

The infinite vastness of the universe, with its limitless freedom and potential, was once its greatest appeal. Now – alone, disconnected, separate – this became the most terrifying thing about it.

Some of the entities surrendered, releasing individual awareness, dissipating into the flow of life-energy on Earth or merging with the background energy of the universe. But a few discrete packets of energy retained individual awareness.

By going to sleep.

This was difficult for Elliott to grasp. He experienced a rush of images and conceptual bursts again. The entity – or his own brain – was tossing out a variety of translations, trying to find one that stuck. Communication of this kind was far more complicated than mere translation of one human language into another. Elliott and the entity were like different species. No, more than that: they existed on different planes of existence.

Two things had happened to the entities, and they were somehow connected. If their free-fall into matter had continued unabated the result would have been total absorption – physical and mental.

So we split in two. We learned to voluntarily slow our physical vibrations but balance ourselves by keeping our thought vibrations as rapid as possible. We applied the brakes as we fell, slowing but not stopping the fall. We entered a controlled state of disequilibrium – with ourselves and with earthly life.

The image of ripples in a pond appeared again. When the ripples met in the middle and began to merge, an additional wave of energy rippled out from the entities' side and disturbed the harmony emerging in the center. The two sides continuously met, almost in synch, but never completely harmonizing as one.

This allowed us to decelerate the degenerative free-fall, maintain a spark of awareness, and indirectly influence the life-stream.

Physically, we became like rocks.

Mentally, we dreamed.

In this state of suspended animation, complete awareness was impossible. The remaining entities existed in a trance state similar to Elliott's at present. This was why they could communicate, but it was also why it was so difficult, why it relied on metaphor, sensations, fragmented impressions. Elliott and the entity were both dreaming.

Images of developing life flowed again, now focusing on the evolution of mankind. The first pictures were shrew-like animals clinging to tree trunks, round eyes and pronounced ears providing little hint of what they would become. Time skipped forward: visions of longer-limbed animals looking decisively more like primates: broader foreheads, pronounced noses, larger bodies. Then animals resembling orangutans and gibbons, apes and chimpanzees, and finally something looking altogether more human.

There was something unnatural about these later creatures. Human-like, but not quite human. A pack of them lingered at the edge of a forest. One of them balanced on its hind legs, resting a palm against a low-hanging branch, and stared out over the encroaching grassland. Its eyes took on a penetrating, searching quality, gleaming with an intelligence that set it apart from the panorama in which it existed. Seeing this in the animal's eyes was stranger than it might have been had the thing seemed more human. As it was, it created the disturbing impression of an intelligence that did not match the form in which it was encased.

The entities were still at work,

Elliott felt this clearly without knowing exactly what their new role was. But he understood that their influence was somehow muted.

Life no longer needed us.

When they first came to Earth the entities accelerated a

process that would have taken eons to advance. By now, however, a feedback mechanism inherent in nature – a kind of natural law – made them essentially superfluous to the evolutionary process.

Life evolved using its own momentum.

By way of explanation there erupted in his mind a burst of labyrinthine, interconnected images of complex and colorful patterns. Part of him struggled to grasp them, to translate their obvious, absurdly rich meaning. But he was overwhelmed. He had the impression that his brain was simply unable to break down the data into comprehensible pieces. It went beyond the lack of a language that could wrestle the vision into submission. It was more that his mind was structurally incapable of processing the meaning, as if it were a computer ten years older than the software he was trying to load it with. The main inaccuracy of this metaphor was that he understood some of the message, which was this: The reciprocal influences between earthly life and the entities also exist, like an impossibly complex spider web, between all life, all matter – even the inconceivably slow life of rocks. The result is the synergistic evolution of life and matter.

But the entities discovered a trick to exert a degree of conscious influence on the process.

Even as we dreamed some of us grew aware of one another again. We learned to reconnect, and in so doing we developed a way to focus a portion of our energy on increasing the evolutionary rate of primates.

Why?

We understood that the lower vibratory rates of life on Earth had plunged us so deeply into matter that we were unable to escape of our own volition. The obvious solution was to increase the vibratory rate of life until it resonated at the same speed as our own. A new, positive feedback loop would form. Instead of being dragged down, we would rise up. And we would take you – whatever you had become – with us. We focused on primates because their level of awareness resonated most sympathetically with our own. There was still an immeasurable gulf between us, but they were the best we had to work with.

Initially the entities sent pulses of vibrations broadly, attempting to influence all the various species of primates on Earth. This resulted in the accelerated development of early hominids like the one he had just seen gazing out over the grassland. For a time the jungles and forests sheltered vast communities of evolving hominids. It was an "age of hominids" like the age of the dinosaurs.

Gradually the entities honed their abilities, focusing on smaller populations of hominids in order to concentrate their awareness and increase its influence. Evolution was physical and mental. Concomitant with physical changes, primates became increasingly aware of self as distinct from the environment.

Life began to become aware of itself. This is one of the keys of evolution: the feedback loop created by ever-expanding awareness. Mental capacity is encouraged to increase when stimulated by challenges; this results in structural changes in the brain that permit comprehension of even greater degrees of complexity.

Small populations of hominids grew to resemble *Homo sapiens*. Elliott watched one of these "new" men running through tall grasses towards a forest, chased by a lioness. But the man's eyes betrayed no fear, only resolve and anticipation. Suddenly a group of men leapt up from the grasses, hurling spears as the lioness ran past. After a brief skirmish one leapt onto the beast's back and gashed its throat with a sharpened stone. Elliott sensed that the creature's skin would be removed and used for ritual. Another image appeared, this one showing a cluster of humans about a shallow hole in the earth. Inside was a carefully placed human corpse, beside which lay stone implements and pieces of red fruit.

Humans saw that matter can be manipulated by thought – magic – and conceived of an afterlife, an unseen world that they felt connected to.

Elliott experienced a thrill of exultation, along with the message:

This was a milestone. Our plan was working. Left to its own devices life might eventually have become self-aware, but we had no idea how long we could sustain ourselves without disintegrating altogether.

The satisfaction of this moment translated itself into a new determination. The entities now focused their attentions exclusively on a single population of this new race of humans. This group of perhaps a hundred individuals rapidly grew in number as the entities encouraged their development, shifting their own vibrations to resonate just slightly faster than those of the humans. As a result a race of child prodigies was born, a group of humans who saw possibilities in every aspect of their environment, including the realms just beyond the physical. They were even intuitively aware of the entities, interpreting their vague impressions of them as evidence of an intelligence existing in matter that could guide and direct them if they remained in harmony with it. They began to manipulate matter with such zeal and success that they soon created vast, colorful and populous cities. Images of these swept through Elliott's mind and caused a sensation of dissonance: their abrupt appearance seemed out of place in the unfolding timeline.

Outside these cities primitive man continued as hunter-gatherers developing in the "traditional" way. The advanced cities were rare, clustered on a single continent away from the more primitive societies. For a time these cities flourished. Their inhabitants' awareness of the subtler realms of existence gave them increased control over the world of matter in a way that Elliott could not grasp. He only sensed that their science and technology were informed by a more cohesive understanding of the relationships between matter, life and mind. In some way all three were connected. These early superhumans used what Elliott would call paranormal powers to manipulate massive stones into place in their buildings, to encourage the growth of crops, to in some way communicate with the underlying mechanisms of life that Elliott's science classified as arbitrary, mechanical laws. Theirs was a holistic vision of the interconnectedness of the universe and of their place in it.

But the civilization did not last. Images of rampant destruction, of broken buildings and bodies, flashed suddenly into Elliott's mind, accompanied by feelings of scathing frustration and anger. Something had gone horribly wrong with these supermen, and the result was the abrupt collapse of much of their civilization. His mind presented him with what seemed an absurd picture: a child striking a match. Eyes at first blue and innocent suddenly blurred with anger. The match caught fire and the child threw it into the air. When it struck the ground there arose a conflagration out of all proportion to what Elliott would have expected. The vision shifted back to the broken cities. He watched people fleeing in ships, fighting amongst themselves, their panic reflecting a lack of understanding at complete odds with the mindset that had enabled the creation of their civilization.

We failed.

An image of a balloon slowly filling with air came into his mind, loose skin growing tighter as it expanded, expanded, too far, then suddenly burst.

This was what happened to our prodigies. We interfered too much, forced their evolution beyond what their mental and physical structure could incorporate.

The effect was twofold. When earlier had Elliott experienced the confusing vision of an interconnected web of relationships, the message was too complex to understand, but his brain kept trying to process it. In response some part of him turned the vision down – filtered it so that it did not overwhelm him and he could continue to function.

Our prodigies could not do this yet. We increased our influence without realizing there was a threshold beyond which humankind, as it existed at the time, was incapable of crossing. In response, they short-circuited. The flood of influence from us gave them surges of power without the maturity or the physical capacity to control it.

This explained the image of the angry child with matches. The race of prodigies experienced a sudden, collective tantrum. Anger expressed itself in destructive urges; fear caused unthinking flight.

We panicked. We withdrew our presence, our awareness, decreasing our vibratory rate as much as possible without effectively committing suicide. Our experiment could not fail. If we withdrew, perhaps we could decelerate the development of our supermen and salvage our plan.

But we withdrew too far.

The ensuing scenes of cometary impact and large-scale devastation resembled those at the end of the Cretaceous. When the dust settled the civilization of the supermen was gone, burned and broken by volcanic eruptions and earthquakes, washed away by massive waves.

We were responsible. We had no way of knowing; or perhaps we once knew but had forgotten. We left the Earth vulnerable.

In response to Elliott's lack of understanding came an image of an elderly couple tending a small garden.

Order through awareness. The very act of awareness imposes a measure of order on the universe, keeps chaos at bay. Expanded awareness brings greater order.

Elliott did not fully comprehend what was being articulated, but he understood that the mass extinctions of the past were due to the sudden withdrawal by the entities from the Earth's vibratory "field." The ensuing destruction, whether dramatic – cometary impacts – or gradual – ice ages, global climate changes – represented a breakdown of a kind of protective order that originally resulted from the presence of active awareness.

Awareness is the constructive force of the universe. The goal of evolution is the transformation of inert matter into self-aware life. We are agents of this process. Even we do not know if this is by accident or design.

The failure of their experiment resulted in the further splintering of the entities. In the panic and chaos of their withdrawal, some disappeared altogether. Another group experienced what Elliott interpreted as a kind of psychotic break. The minute portions of individuality and self-awareness that survived degenerated further, retaining a hold on individual existence based only on an inconceivably painful awareness of loss – and a more obscure sense of blame directed towards the creatures responsible. Not just humankind, but all the material life that had, through its degenerate vibrations, dragged pure spirits into the sickly morass of matter. For this contingent of semi-aware entities, there existed a vague sense that only through the destruction of material existence would they be able to recapture their lost state of paradise. If all the entities could be said to exist in a dream-like state, then this group existed in a perpetual, violent nightmare, the reverberations of which even now infiltrated and negatively influenced living processes. This was the source of Elliott's own nightmare two days ago.

But one final group of entities managed to survive the group withdrawal relatively intact. Chastened, they ceased their directed influence on humankind.

Life could now, in large part, take care of itself. Feedback mechanisms in place. Resonant relationships. Life would evolve. All we could do was sit back, watch and wait.

Almost. We did not stop influencing you altogether. We simply became far more subtle.

The entities still had the goal of encouraging the development of life, of goading it to the point at which its vibrations would resonate in harmony with their own, and in turn allow them to regain what they had lost. But instead of forced evolution, the entities reduced their efforts to mere hints of their existence and the world existing just beyond the awareness of humankind: lights in the sky, synchronicities, premonitions, transcendent insights . . . nothing too abrupt, nothing too apart from what humankind's would eventually discover regardless. Nothing that would shatter the necessary sense of security and stability humankind needed to expand, to move forward on its own terms. A delicate balance. The entities took advantage of those moments when an individual's guard was down, when the mind was susceptible to their influence because it was resonating at a similar frequency to their own.

Then... a gentle "nudge" cracks open the door, allows you to see the wider universe. With repeated experiences – repeated prodding – your minds stretch past their boundaries to encompass more and more...

You evolve.

The survivors of the collapsed civilization diffused to different corners of the Earth; some to Egypt, others to Central and South America, still others to India and Mesopotamia. They transferred the technical knowledge used to build their once great cities to the indigenous peoples they encountered, who sometimes revered them as gods. This resulted in the rise of agriculture and civilization in these disparate places. But as time wore on the progeny of these first supermen lost the knowledge. All that remained of it was buried in and blended with the mystical traditions of these cultures, where it was carried down through the ages to the present, in most cases so jumbled and distorted as to be almost unrecognizable. Now the entities lay in their suspended state, dreaming, awaiting the time when humankind would itself awaken.

★★★

A gruff bark from one of the dogs initiated a cacophonous outburst from both. Elliott made out the sound of Deveraux's car coming up the driveway. He waited to stand up until he heard conversation, the slamming of car doors, praise and endearment directed at the dogs. It was difficult to take his gaze away from the window.

32

"BOB KNIGHT CALLED while we were gone." Deveraux had the phone to his ear as he spoke and raised his hand to motion Elliott and Rachel to silence until he finished listening to the voice message. "He wants to touch base with you before you leave." Deveraux pressed a button on the base of the phone and hung up, then said, "Oh. That was stupid of me. I should've let you hear it."

"That's okay. I know what he wants: to make sure I don't leave town with the rock."

"You weren't planning on it anyway."

"I didn't explain that to him at Martha's."

"What's he want with it?"

Elliott shrugged. "I don't know exactly. Probably to make sure I don't print up pictures of it claiming it's from a UFO." He stood over the kitchen table and removed the towel from the rock, then separated the two halves and sat down in front of the gleaming black plaque.

Rachel sat down across from him while Deveraux opened a bottle of wine. She said, "It's too bad you didn't find out anything more about it on the island."

He immediately felt guilty. He looked up at her and then at Deveraux. His guilt must have been transparent, because they both said, "What?"

Deveraux stopped unscrewing the cork and said, "You bastard! You did find something!"

Elliott could not help but laugh as he nodded. "I did."

After Deveraux, Rachel, and Attenbaum and his wife had

316

returned Elliott navigated an hour of polite conversation with them, feeling exhausted and disconnected. When he was alone again with Rachel and Deveraux he found himself telling them about his vision and holding off on the details of the rock. Now he said,

"Have you ever heard of a geologic feature called a 'syncline'?" Both Rachel and Deveraux shook their heads. Elliott raised his hands, palms down and flattened horizontally, the tips of his middle fingers touching. "Imagine this is level ground, and imagine that there are layers and layers of rock beneath the palms of my hands. Now imagine that on either side of my palms you've got immense pressure from some other kind of geologic force pushing the surface layers of rock downwards into something like a valley." He slowly bent his fingers down while keeping his palms in the same position so that his fingers formed an inverted triangle, his fingertips forming the point at the bottom. "Over the years – millions of years – this valley can get filled in with new layers of sediment so that from the surface you can't even tell that it's there. The opposite can happen too, only it's called an 'anticline'." He raised his fingertips up so that they pointed above the level of his palms and formed a steeple. "Anyway, in the case of a syncline, rocks that appear to be quite old based on how deep beneath the surface they are can actually be far younger. And in the case of an anticline, rocks that are close to the surface might actually be very old if they've been pushed upwards. In neither case can you know what's going on without a full picture of the stratigraphy of the area. Which is what Attenbaum didn't have when he found the rock."

Deveraux said, "So if you find a fossil at the bottom of a syncline…"

"You would think it's older than it really is, unless you understand exactly where you're working."

Rachel said, "So Gene Attenbaum found the rock at the bottom of a syncline?"

Elliott gave a tight smile. "That's the thing – he doesn't know. The area's been redated since he excavated there. A huge swath of the basin was painstakingly surveyed about twenty years ago to try to make sense of the rather turbulent geology of the place. There are synclines and anticlines, thrust faults, intrusive layers, all that sort of stuff. This wasn't all so thoroughly mapped out when Attenbaum dug up the rock. The survey documented formations that hadn't been noticed before. For example, some areas that had recently – say up till twenty-five, thirty years ago – had layers of topsoil and brush covering them had eroded away after several seasons of heavy rains and flooding. The result was that a new landscape of geological features was revealed: synclines, anticlines – as I say, all that stuff.

"What's more, I learned from his notes that Attenbaum didn't actually split his rock open and find the plaque until after the area had been redated. As far as he was concerned, there wasn't any mystery until about twenty years ago. And by then he must have realized that the area had been redated."

"So he just assumed he'd dug it out of a younger layer?"

"I'm not sure what he assumed, but if he had been confused by the plaque it certainly would have been easy enough to tell himself that he'd been mistaken about the dates of the rocks he'd found it in. It would've been awfully difficult to find exactly where he'd dug it up more than thirty years later, especially after the landscape had changed. He was meticulous, but I don't think he could've found the exact spot."

Deveraux shook his head. "But what about the fossils? You said Bill thought they were index fossils, that that species of conifer went extinct sixty-five million years ago."

"That's what Bill thought. And that's what Gene thought at first. But this is where guesswork comes into things. Even an expert in the field can find it difficult to positively ID a fossil when all he's got are fragments of it. When he entered the find in the catalogue Bill had, Attenbaum thought the fossils were of an extinct family of conifer called" – he found the word in the papers next to him and read it to them – "'Cheirolepids.' But he later decided they more likely belonged to the family known as Araucarians."

Rachel asked, "Which are how old?"

"Over two hundred million years. But they never went extinct. They're still around today."

Deveraux said, "Of course. I've made the same mistake myself dozens of times."

"When all you've got are fragments, you rely on best-guess estimates as much as the raw data. The point is, when Attenbaum found the plaque and realized the area had been redated, he naturally looked at his fossils again. To his mind, the presence of the plaque made it self-evident that he'd misidentified the species of conifer. So he reinterpreted the data and fit it into the accepted timeline."

Deveraux said, "He made it fit."

"That's right."

Rachel said, "That seems dishonest."

"I can see why you might think so. But I don't think he was dishonest. I think he originally dated some ambiguous fossils based on the assumption that he was working in a sixty-five-million-year-old layer of rock, then later assumed he'd made a mistaken identification when the new data came in."

Deveraux said "Or he felt obliged to assume it, to make sure the find fit in with accepted theories."

Elliott shrugged, "Probably. But he no doubt had the best intentions. And Bill made an honest mistake, too. When he looked in Attenbaum's catalog he saw 'Cheirolepids' and followed Attenbaum's lead back to sixty-five million years."

Deveraux shook his head, incredulous. "So how old is the rock?"

Elliott leaned forward. He hesitated before touching the surface of the plaque. When he did he felt the electrical tingle of excitement. Was it coming from him or from the plaque? He looked up and said,

"We don't know. I don't think we'll ever know. You're right about one thing, Alex. Attenbaum convinced himself that the rock was recent. The evidence goes both ways, but he chose to see it in a way that fits in with current scientific thought." He considered this, then said, "He chose to interpret it in a way that made him feel comfortable. From what I can gather he didn't attempt to figure out if his revised hypothesis was plausible – if, for example, the artifact could be attributed to a Native American culture that once inhabited the area. Or if there are synclines in the area that would even allow you to mistakenly assume a rock was so much older than it is. He just assumed his new interpretation had to be right. Knight will do the same. Anyone who puts their faith in the timelines of modern science will interpret the data the same way. But anyone who wants to believe that intelligent life existed sixty-five million years ago has enough wiggle room to see the plaque as potential evidence. It's a kind of ink-blot test."

Rachel said, "But what do *you* believe?"

"Ah. That's a bit more complicated."

Deveraux said, "But your vision explained how the rock could be that old. It showed that there was intelligent life that old. It gave you a reason for the plaque."

Elliott nodded. "That's right. My vision did that. But it came to me even without the rock. It's all in my head." The words sounded wrong as they came out, but before he could explain himself, Deveraux cut in:

"So you think it's all a fantasy?"

"No. I'll explain. But first, finish opening that bottle."

Deveraux looked down as if he had forgotten he was holding anything. The corkscrew protruded from the unopened bottle, and he began twisting it again, saying, "I'm sorry, I don't mean to sound so frustrated. It's just that I was hoping... I was hoping Marcus would be wrong, that we would find something to convince everyone."

"Me too." Elliott stood up and retrieved the wineglasses from the counter. He was about to set them on the kitchen table but thought better of this when he looked at the rock. "Let's go to the living room."

After they each sat down with a glass of red wine, Elliott said, "I don't think it's a fantasy. But I can't take my visions at face value either. When I was... Well, for the sake of convenience, let's say *communicating* with the entity in my vision today I was aware that my brain was working overtime as an interpreter. It was a creative, participatory process. This was especially clear when the focus was something abstract, like the idea of attention being key to evolution and order. My brain was receiving information from somewhere and it had to translate it into words and pictures that I could understand. I knew I wasn't getting the whole picture."

Rachel said, "I don't understand."

"Our language can't completely convey what I was being told. Not only that. It was beyond me conceptually, too. It's like this: I remember once a physicist trying to explain to me how string theory posited the existence of eleven-dimensional space instead of our usual three. I told him I didn't get it, and he said something like, 'Of course you don't.' Because our brains aren't wired to think in terms of eleven-dimensions of space. It's only the mathematics on paper that hint at dimensions beyond what we're used to."

Deveraux said, "But the way you explained your vision to us made it seem coherent."

Elliott nodded. "I know. But I think that's a consequence of my brain filling in the blanks, doing its best with the tools its got. Alex, you remember what Marcus told us about Blavatsky and Cayce, and other people who've had visions like mine."

"But not identical to yours."

"Right. Well, what makes my vision more valid than the one Marcus shared about aliens escaping to Earth and genetically modifying apes? I've been glancing through books all week that could've informed the wilder aspects of my visions, could've helped my brain fill in the gaps in my comprehension. What's more, your psychiatrist friend pointed out that of course I'd have visions about the evolutionary development of life on Earth: I'm here for a conference on that very subject.

"My point is it's hard to be satisfied with an incomplete picture. I think that's why some scientists – myself included – glom onto theories like neo-Darwinism even when a little thought makes it obvious that they can't explain everything.

It's more comfortable thinking you've got all the answers. And something in our brains wants to accommodate that desire."

Deveraux said, "I still don't get it: do you think your visions are real or not?"

"That's the thing. I keep trying to answer questions in an either/or kind of way: either the visions are real or they're imaginary. Either Knight's right or Bill is. Either God exists or we live in a meaningless universe. And I've needed to know the answers. The mistake I made was to hang not just my career on that need, but my sense of self-worth as well. And that's an absurd thing to do. Because then when some fact or perception I cling to turns out to be wrong, my self-esteem takes a hit, too. So out of fear I end up clinging to one idea or another even when the evidence is clearly stacked against it. Like I did with paranormal phenomenon. You told me the story of the lost girl. I saw Bill at the moment he died. The other day I knew Knight was calling me on your home phone before I picked up. Rachel, you told me about your precognitive dreams. Taken in isolation these kinds of anecdotes might not mean anything, but I'd be – and have been – willfully blind if I didn't consider them together. How stupid can I be? The universe is practically rubbing my nose in it."

"So why can't I shake the feeling that you're dismissing your visions?"

"I'm not dismissing them – I'm just not ready to accept them as literal truth. Are they spirit communications? Indications of our connection to a wider reality? Maybe, maybe not. Maybe they're metaphorical, or maybe," – he laughed – "maybe my higher self is trying to teach me something about cosmic evolution. That's the thing – maybe the impressions I received are like a carrot on a stick. I can't understand them now but maybe if I keep at it I'll reach a point where I make the leap."

Rachel said, "A paradigm shift."

He took her hand, delighted. "Exactly. I guess that's as far as I'm willing to go at the moment. If I had to wager I'd say there's some kind of inner process of vision that human beings possess that we don't yet understand, something we might be able to use to explore different realms of existence. An untapped potential. But I don't know that. I…" He felt himself start to fumble for words. He sipped his wine and stared out the window, then the insight came: "You know what it is? I'm not ready to trade one paradigm for another. I can't drop everything I've learned and uncritically accept a vision that no one but me has had."

Deveraux said, "Excuse my asking, but couldn't that just be because you're afraid to let go?"

Elliott shook his head. "Fair question, and until recently you would've been right. But I realize now that I simply don't know, and I can't be expected to."

Rachel said, "But don't you want to?"

Elliott laughed. "Of course! I'm more excited than I've ever been. I feel like I'm poised on the edge of an undiscovered country." He paused to look at them both before saying, "This will sound grandiose, and I wouldn't say it to anyone but you two at the moment, but I feel like my understanding of existence has broadened and grown deeper. I see reality as more complex, multilayered… Not just reality, but us, too.

Deveraux said, "So what do you do now?"

"The only thing I can do as a responsible scientist: keep looking. Stop shutting doors before I've gone through them and had a good look around. For example, it now seems to me more than just reasonable to hypothesize that in different modes of consciousness we perceive different realities, or different aspects of a much wider and stranger reality than the one we're used to. And as I said earlier, it follows that we are more complicated and multilayered than we're used to thinking of ourselves. I've just got to learn to live with uncertainty long enough to leap to a new level of understanding." He said this then drained his wineglass, leaned forward and added, "I feel like that's part of our raison d'être: to develop our minds so that they can encompass more of the complexities of reality. To become more aware. When this started happening and I tried to understand what was going on inside me, I felt incredibly frustrated. I thought, it's *my* mind, I should be able to explore its nooks and crannies and figure out exactly what's going on. But I see now that would be like trying to run a marathon without getting into shape first. Our minds are vast landscapes and we've got very little experience exploring them. The outside world is complicated and stressful and it takes up all our time. The inner world is – ironically – less obvious. One of our jobs is to understand it, to make better use of its potential. *Our* potential. At the moment, science is limited because *we* are limited. It couldn't possibly be any other way. We're under-developed. There are things we can't understand because we either don't have the right language or because our brains are the equivalent of calculators versus computers. We wouldn't expect a cat to understand the workings of a car engine. Maybe we're in the same relationship to the mechanics of our own minds, of reality. There are certain things we simply aren't wired to understand. Yet."

Deveraux's phone rang and startled all three of them.

Deveraux stood up and said, "That must be Christine."

They went back to the kitchen, Deveraux to get the phone and Elliott and Rachel for more wine. As Deveraux talked, Rachel pointed to the rock and said,

"What if Knight manages to take that away from you?"

Elliott thought about this again, then shrugged. "I guess he can have it."

"Just like that?"

"I'll fight him for it. But I'm not sure how important that one piece of evidence is, especially if I'm right that we'll never be able to date it conclusively."

Deveraux hung up the phone and said, "She'll be here in ten minutes. She's got a new restaurant she wants to try. I'll treat for your farewell dinner."

When he disappeared upstairs to change Rachel said, "Let me freshen up quick, alright?"

Alone with the rock, Elliott realized that he would have difficulty letting go of it – at the very least for sentimental reasons. The damn thing had probably extended Bill's life by a year. As much as it pained him to admit it, Knight had essentially been right about one thing: in the face of death, Bill had found his own beliefs stifling, and he had seized on the rock as an excuse to challenge them. But ultimately it wouldn't have mattered to him if the rock had turned out to be an outright fake – he only had to fool himself long enough to sneak past his own biases. This was why he hadn't followed up with Terrence Attenbaum, and his instinct had been sound. If Bill the orthodox scientist had found Gene Attenbaum's notes, his enthusiasm would have popped like a punctured balloon and he would have abandoned his quest before truly starting it. Instead, he had used the rock to wedge open the door to a new realm – and then squeezed through and found something well worth exploring. And then he had passed on the favor to Elliott.

Rachel hugged him from behind. He turned around and kissed her, relishing the taste of wine on her lips and the warm pressure of her body against his. She said,

"So what will you do? Publish the book?"

"Of course. And one of my own, too."

"And what will happen after that?"

He thought about this again, as he had been doing on and off ever since Bill handed him the manuscript. The question had always seemed fraught with import, heavy with his past, his future, all the idiosyncrasies of his personality and of life itself. It seemed impossible not to be concerned about the answer. But for the moment he was not.

"I don't know."

It felt good to say it.

Acknowledgments

To my many supportive early readers, critics, friends, my daughter, and the countless people who've touched my life: thank you.

About the Author

Chris Nelson is a writer, musician and book editor living in Seattle, Washingon.